Stéphanie Félicité comtesse de Genlis

Tales of the Castle; or, Stories of Instruction and Delight

Being Les veillées du château

Stéphanie Félicité comtesse de Genlis

Tales of the Castle; or, Stories of Instruction and Delight
Being Les veillées du château

ISBN/EAN: 9783744722469

Printed in Europe, USA, Canada, Australia, Japan

Cover: Foto ©Andreas Hilbeck / pixelio.de

More available books at **www.hansebooks.com**

TALES OF THE CASTLE:

OR,

STORIES

OF

INSTRUCTION AND DELIGHT.

BEING

LES VEILLEES DU CHATEAU,

WRITTEN IN FRENCH

By MADAME LA COMTESSE DE GENLIS,

AUTHOR OF THE THEATRE OF EDUCATION,
ADELA AND THEODORE, &c.

TRANSLATED INTO ENGLISH.
BY THOMAS HOLCROFT,

Comme raccende gusto il mutar' esca,
Così mi par, che la mia Istoria, quanto
Or quà, or là più variata sia,
Meno a chi l'udirà nojosa fia.   ARIOSTO.

As at the board, with plenteous viands grac'd,
Cate after Cate excites the sickening taste,
So, while my Muse pursues her varied strains,
Tale following Tale the ravished ear detains.   HOOLE.

The FOURTH EDITION.

VOL. II.

LONDON:
PRINTED FOR G. G. J. and J. ROBINSON,
No. 25, PATER-NOSTER-ROW, 1793.

THE

TALES OF THE CASTLE:

OR,

STORIES

OF

INSTRUCTION AND DELIGHT.

LEONTINE AND EUGENIA,

OR, THE

MASQUERADE HABIT.

MADAME de Palmena, yet young, though long a widow, dedicated her days to the education of an only daughter, the beloved object of all her tendernefs and all her attention. Her hufband dying left her deeply in debt, and Madame de Palmena had no other means of paying his debts, but by quitting Paris, and retiring to an eftate fhe poffeffed in Touraine, a fhort league from Loches *(a)*; her Château was vaſt and antique, it's draw-bridge, moat, and towers, re-called the memorable days of Dugueſclin and the Chevalier Bayard; thoſe days of Chivalry which ought to be regretted, if the valour and loyalty of good Knighthood could compenſate for the want of police and laws.

The inſide of the caſtle anſwered to the out; every thing there retraced the noble ſimplicity of our anceſtors; no gilding, no porcelain vaſes, no bawbles, ſuch as load our modern houſes; but beautiful tapeſtries, repreſenting ſome intereſting point of hiſtory, and long galleries, ornamented with family portraits, where the owner walked in the midſt of his anceſtors, and meditated on their paſt deeds; and whence he might diſcover through the windows a large foreſt, on the one ſide, and, on the other, the pleaſant banks of the Indre.

There it was that Eugenia, the daughter of Palmena, paſt her infancy, and the firſt years of her youth; there it was ſhe acquired her taſte for country amuſements, and a peaceable and retired life. During the fine days of ſpring-time and

(a) The town of Loches, ſituated upon the Indre, near a large foreſt, has a caſtle, in which Cardinal de la Balue was confined, and a collegiate church, in which is the tomb of Agnes Sorel. Loches is five leagues from Am-boiſe, another ſmall town, celebrated for it's manufactories, and a conſpiracy that bears that name. It is ſituated upon the Loire.

ſummer,

ſummer, ſhe took long walks with her mamma; and, when the heat of the meridian ſun made it neceſſary, ſought a cool ſhelter in the foreſt's ſhade.

Sometimes ſhe exerciſed herſelf with running, ſometimes gathered the freſh herbs, while her mamma inſtructed her in their names and properties; here ſhe often took her leſſons, here liſtened to intereſting tales; and, as the day declined, would quit the foreſt to courſe along the ſmiling banks of the brook.

When Eugenia had attained her eighth year, ſhe became more ſedate; a thouſand different occupations kept her more in the houſe; but ſhe would riſe with Aurora, and breakfaſt in the park or the meadows, and in the evening would ſtill walk a league or two with her mamma.

The companion of her ſports was the daughter of her Governante, her name was Valentina; ſhe was four years older than Eugenia, and was poſſeſſed of induſtry, a happy temper, and a good heart. She took care always to be preſent when Eugenia received a leſſon, by which ſhe profited ſo much that her young miſtreſs ever looked upon her, and with reaſon, as her friend.

When Eugenia was ſixteen years of age, her character was as ſtable as her heart was affectionate; the gaiety and ſimplicity of youth, a cultivated mind, and unalterable ſweetneſs, and

the

the moſt perfect equality of temper, were all, in her, united. Her love and gratitude to her mamma were unbounded; ever thinking of, and taking every opportunity to oblige her, there was no employment, no occupation in which ſhe did not find the means. Had ſhe verſes to learn by heart? She would ſay to herſelf, how happy my mamma will be to find me ſo perfect! How much ſhe will praiſe me for my memory and induſtry! Did ſhe ſtudy Engliſh or Italian? How ſatisfied my mamma will be, ſaid ſhe, when ſhe ſhall ſee that, inſtead of one page, I have tranſlated two! Writing, deſigning, playing the harp, the harpſichord, or the guittar, ſtill ſhe made the ſame reflections. This drawing will be placed in the cabinet of my mamma: every time ſhe looks at it, ſhe will think of her Eugenia. This ſonata, which I am juſt beginning, will delight my mamma when I can play it perfectly. Such ideas, which ſhe applied to every thing ſhe did, gave an inexpreſſible charm to ſtudy, ſmoothed each difficulty, and changed her duties to delights.

In order to finiſh the education of Eugenia, Madame de Palmena reſolved to let her paſs two years at Paris. She tore her from her agreeable ſolitude towards the end of September, and arrived in town, where ſhe hired a houſe, in which Eugenia often regretted the enchanting banks of the Indre and the Loire.

6

Madame

Madame de Palmena gladly renewed her acquaintance with several persons whom she had formerly known. Among them was one she distinguished above the rest, an old friend of her husband's, named the Count d'Amilly, worthy of that preference by his merit and his virtues. He had been several years a widower, and was possessed of an only son eighteen years of age, whom he had just parted from for two years. Leontine (so the youth was called) had set off for Italy, and was afterwards to make the tour of the north.

The Count d'Amilly came every night to sup with Madame de Palmena: at half past ten Eugenia went to bed. As soon as she was gone, the Count usually began to speak of her, and it was always in her praise. He admired her talents, her modesty, her reserve, and that certain air of mild gentleness, yet freedom, in her manners, which gave an inexpressible charm to her most trifling actions.

Madame de Palmena listened with transport to the praises of Eugenia; she heard not without emotion the name of Leontine so often pronounced, and, in this delightful converse, time was frequently forgotten; they frequently exclaimed with surprize, *Could you think it ! it's past three o'clock.*

The Count d'Amilly continued his assiduities, but without farther explanation: he only said, one

B 3   day,

day, my son will have a confiderable fortune, becaufe I am rich ; but, before I partake it with him,
I would teach him to enjoy wealth; he will be
twenty at his return; I will marry him, and give
him an amiable wife, whofe attractions and gen-
tlenefs will render all his duties pleafant, and
make him in love with virtue.

Madame de Palmena perfectly faw the portrait
of fuch a wife in Eugenia; but, reflecting on the
extreme difproportion between her fortune and
that of the Count d'Amilly, fhe fcarcely could
perfuade herfelf he had really any views upon her
daughter.

Madame de Palmena had now been twenty
months at Paris, and Eugenia approached her
eighteenth year, when one evening the Count
d'Amilly came, and begged permiffion to prefent
his fon, who was juft arrived, to the family.
Scarcely had he fpoken before a young man appeared, of a moft interefting perfon, and advanced
towards Madame de Palmena, with an air at once
eager yet timid, which added new grace to his
natural accomplifhments.

The Count and his fon ftayed fupper; Leontine
fpoke little, but he looked much ; his eyes were
continually turned to Eugenia, and every word he
did fay demonftrated an earneft defire of pleafing
Madame de Palmena.

The

The next day the Count and his fon returned, and Madame de Palmena, without circumlocution, declared fhe made it an irrevocable rule, never to admit young men of Leontine's age as vifitors. Nay! But, Madam, anfwered the Count, it is abfolutely neceffary you fhould fee him, in order that you may examine if he be fomething like what you could wifh.

Sir! What do you mean?

Do you not fee, Madame, that his happinefs and mine depend on your approbation? Take fome time to know him, and if he be happy enough to pleafe you, our wifhes, our vows will be crowned with fuccefs.

This was at laft fpeaking to be underftood, and Madame de Palmena teftified all the gratitude which the Count's declaration had infpired. She would not, however, enter into any pofitive engagement, till fhe had firft confulted Eugenia, and enquired more particularly into the temper and difpofition of Leontine. All fhe learnt only redoubled the defire fhe had to have him for a fon; and, the Count again preffing her to give him a decifive anfwer, fhe hefitated no longer. Every thing being agreed upon, the contract was figned, and next day Leontine received the hand of the lovely Eugenia with tranfport. The day after the marriage, the young couple went down to a delightful country-feat, belonging to the Count,

ten leagues diſtant from Paris, whence it was determined they ſhould not return till the end of
autumn.

Madame de Palmena paſſed three months with
them; after which ſhe was obliged, for a while,
to quit them. Determining to live hereafter at
Paris, ſhe was forced to take a journey into Touraine, for the arrangement of her affairs, and
though it was ſuppoſed ſhe would return before
winter, Eugenia had need of all her reaſon to
ſupport ſo cruel a ſeparation.

Her ſoft melancholy after the departure of her
mother, made her ſtill dearer to the heart of
Leontine: he found a ſecret kind of pleaſure in
contemplating her thus mildly, thus tenderly, dejected. What will one day be my power, ſaid
he, as the tears fell from her beautiful eyes, over
a heart ſo feeling and ſo grateful! Eugenia,
however, did not ſhew the whole of her grief
before Leontine; but compenſated for this con-
ſtraint with Valentina, the young woman I have
already mentioned, who had been the companion
of her infancy. The conſolation moſt effectual
to Eugenia was to ſpeak of her mother, and write
long letters to her every day, containing a full
and circumſtantial detail of her thoughts, employments, and pleaſures.

Two months had already glided away, ſince the
departure of Madame de Palmena, during which

time

time Eugenia had not made a single trip to Paris. In the company of her father-in-law and her husband, she wished for nothing but her mother. Leontine was her best support, and Leontine became every day more dear. Often would they ramble arm in arm through the woods and fields, the while Eugenia would question Leontine of all his travels, and listen with sweet delight to his narration. Often would they sit upon the banks of the brook, the while Eugenia sang sometimes sprightly airs, and sometimes pathetic ballads. Her sweet and melodious voice would often attract the shepherd and the reaper; the one left his work, the other his flock, and ran to listen; she, like a divinity, suspended labour,—and buried fatigue in forgetfulness.

One evening Eugenia observed, among her rustic auditors, an old man whom she had never seen before; his figure was venerable, his hairs were white, and his age upwards of seventy-five. Eugenia inquired his name, and was answered, Jerome; she learnt, likewise, that his sister was paralytic; and that he was grandfather to five young orphans, all of whom were maintained by his labour.

Eugenia had only a small allowance; for, though her father-in-law was rich, noble, and benevolent, wishing to give his children habits of order and œconomy, he had the prudence and the

fortitude

fortitude not to partake his fortune with them too soon.

When you shall have proved to me, said he, that you know how to make a worthy use of money, we will then have but one purse. If five years hence, for example, I am satisfied with your conduct, I will strip myself with pleasure to adorn a rational and domestic son; but I would never give up a fortune which I have acquired myself, and which I can justly dispose of as I please, to a silly head-strong prodigal.

Oh! my father, answered Leontine, you have given me Eugenia, and in her you have given me the riches of the earth.

Eugenia, on her part, did not wish a greater allowance than she possessed. Where reason and œconomy reside, the smallest fortune is always sufficient; and Eugenia was rich enough to be gene-rous and benevolent. Totally occupied by the re-membrance of the good old Jerome, she told Va-lentina, as she went to bed, that she should on the morrow carry him some assistance.

The next morning the Count d'Amilly came, as usual, to breakfast with his children. Here, my dear, said he to Eugenia, here is a masquerade ticket for you; there will be a very fine one in a fortnight at Paris, and you are invited. I beg you will do me the favour to go. You will want a dress; be so kind, my love, as to buy yourself one. So

saying,

faying, the Count toffed a purfe of fixty guineas into her lap.

As foon as Eugenia was alone, fhe called Valentina to her, and fhewed her the prefents fhe had juft received. I can buy a drefs quite good enough, faid fhe, for fifty guineas; I may very well, therefore, fpare ten out of this fum to poor Jerome; do you go Valentina then, and inquire in the village if all I have been told of this poor old man be true; and, if there be no exaggeration in what I have heard, I will carry him the money myfelf.

In the afternoon Valentina returned from the village, and told her young miftrefs that fhe had not only inquired of the vicar, and feveral of the inhabitants, but had likewife been in Jerome's cottage, where fhe had feen his paralytic fifter nurfed by the eldeft of his grand-children, a young girl of twelve years old; that the poor woman was in a chamber, kept very clean, while the beneficent old man lay in a kind of out-houfe upon ftraw; and that Jerome was the honefteft and moft unfortunate peafant in the village, as well as the beft brother, and the beft grandfather.

Come! faid Eugenia, come! I have the purfe, that my father-in-law has given me in my pocket, let us take him the ten guineas inftantly.

She waited not for an anfwer, but took Valentina by the arm, told Leontine, who had fat down

with

with a party to whift, he would find-her by and by at the walk of the willows, and away she went.

Eugenia came to the field where Jerome usually worked till the decline of day, looked round, and, not seeing him, asked where he was gone. They told her that, being overcome with heat and fatigue, he had lain down for a moment in the shade, and was fallen asleep by the side of the brook, near the great arbour of eglantines.

Thither Eugenia and Valentina turned their steps, and soon perceived the good old man sleeping, and surrounded by his little grandchildren; they approached with the greatest precaution for fear of disturbing him, and stopt at a little distance, to contemplate a picture the most interesting and the most affecting.

The poor old man was in a sound sleep; a sweet little girl, of eight or nine years old, lightly spread her apron over the wild rose branches that surrounded her grandfather's head, to keep the heat of the sun from his face; one of her brothers was helping her, while the other two, with branches in their hands, were occupied in chafing away the flies and wasps, whenever they approached. The careful little girl, as soon as she saw Eugenia, made a sign with her hand, not to make a noise and disturb her grandfather. Eugenia smiled, and advancing on tip-toe, kissed the dear little creature, and told her, in her ear, she wanted

to

to fpeak with her grandfather as foon as he awoke; therefore defired fhe would go and play with her brothers, ànd come back when fhe called her.

The young girl at firft was loath to go, and fo were her little brothers; who only gave their confent on condition that Eugenia would be fure to drive away the flies.

This bargain being made, Eugenia took their branches, and, fitting down with Valentina upon the bank befide their charge, the little family foon fell to their youthful gambols, and difappeared.

Eugenia then took her purfe, and put it in her lap to take out the ten guineas; but, fearing fhe fhould make too much noife in counting her money, fhe ftopped, and fixing her eyes upon the old man, the fweet tear of fenfibility began to trickle.

How peaceably he fleeps, faid fhe, good old man; how refpectable is his poverty; how venerable, how affecting his countenance! Seventy-five years old! Good God! During fo long a career, how many labours, how many cares, how many croffes, has he undergone! And now, when his ftrength has left him, when age enfeebles the body and the mind, virtue, benevolence, make him labour without ceafing!

The tears of gentle compaffion flowed, while Eugenia whifpered thus to Valentina.

Think,

Think, Madam, ſaid the latter, think of the eaſe, the joy, theſe ten guineas will give him.

This preſent, replied Eugenia, this ſmall ſum, cannot make him happy during the reſt of his life. Oh how tranſporting it would be to give peace and tranquillity to his age! To what raptures ſhould he awake! Ten guineas would only give him a momentary relief, but fifty would procure him entire eaſe. Fifty guineas! 'Tis the price of a dreſs! And what great pleaſure will that dreſs give me? It will ſcarcely be remarked. Shall I, in a robe decorated with ſpangles, and trimmed with lace, ſhall I, thinkeſt thou Valentina, be more lovely in the eyes of Leontine! How much this morning did he praiſe my ſhape! And yet I was only dreſſed in white muſlin, and a few blue-bells and cowſlips, which I myſelf had gathered in the fields. Ten guineas, Valentina, will buy me a dreſs; ſimple, I own, but more becoming, per-haps, than one more rich. Flowers are more ſuit-able to my age than gold. Doſt thou not think ſo, Valentina?

I confeſs, Madam, I ſhould be delighted to ſee you in a rich habit.

Look at that poor old man, Valentina, look at him, and I am ſure ſuch vain ideas will vaniſh from thy mind! Delighted to ſee me richly dreſt, ſayeſt thou? Think of the delight, think of the tranſports of my heart, when I ſhall have reſcued

ſuch

fuch a man, and fuch a family, from mifery. Oh, Valentina, with what raptures will he fup this evening, furrounded by his children! With what pure joy will he kifs them, and receive their innocent careffes; and what fhall I feel to-morrow, when I write an account of all this to my mamma! O how happy will fhe be; what pleafure, what tranfport will fhe feel, at reading fuch a letter!

But, Madam, you will be the only one at the ball fo fimply dreffed; may not this difpleafe your father-in-law; may not Leontine be angry? I own they are both very good, but——

True, Valentina; I muft at leaft confult Leontine: I muft do nothing without my hufband's confent. But come, let us remove hence; the very fight of this good old man is too powerful to be refifted. Come, let us look for Leontine, we will foon return; come, come——

So faying, Eugenia arofe; but, as fhe was rifing, fhe heard behind her a ruftling of leaves, which occafioned her to turn and look round; there fhe beheld Leontine, leaping the hedge, coming to kifs her, to adore her, to caft himfelf at her feet.

Leontine had left his card-party foon after Eugenia was gone, and come in fearch of her; knowing Eugenia's firft intentions refpecting Jerome, he had followed, and hid himfelf behind

the

the arbour, that he might liſten to her converſation with the good old man; he expected a pleaſure, and he received one, even beyond his expectations; for, being only ſeparated from her by
a light foliage, though Eugenia had ſpoken in a
whiſper, he had not loſt a ſentence of all ſhe had
ſaid.

Oh my dear, my charming Eugenia, cried he,
what have I heard; how great, how ſupreme is
my happineſs! Sentiments, feelings, benevolence
like your's, are ineſtimable! I knew you lovely,
and yet I ſcarce knew half your lovelineſs.

Leontine was ſpeaking thus when Jerome
awoke; Eugenia immediately diſengaged herſelf
from the arms of her huſband, and drew near to
the old man; he looked at her with aſtoniſhment,
and, out of reſpect, was going to riſe; Eugenia deſired him to ſit ſtill, but he excuſed himſelf by ſaying he muſt go to his labour. No, ſaid Eugenia,
reſt yourſelf to-day.

But my day's work, Madam—

I will pay it to you; here, accept this purſe, and
may the reception of it give you as much pleaſure
as the offering of it has given me!

So ſaying, Eugenia, with a tender and reſpectful
air, put the purſe, containing fifty guineas, into the
trembling hands of the old man, and turned her
head aſide to hide her tears. Leontine ſtood before
her, beholding her with rapture; never had ſhe

appeared

appeared fo lovely in his eyes; never had fhe made fo fweet, fo deep, fo powerful an impreffion upon his heart.

The old man, notwithftanding, looked at the purfe that lay open upon his lap with a kind of amazement; in his whole life he had never beheld fo great a fum; he rubbed his eyes, feared he was yet afleep, ftill dreaming, while Eugenia filently enjoyed the delicious excefs of his furprize. At laft Jerome clafped his hands in a kind of ecftacy, and fobbing, exclaimed, Oh God! what have I done; how have I merited fo vaft a gift! So faying, he raifed his head, and fixed his fwimming eyes on Eugenia, and added, may the God of mercies only grant, Madam, that you may have children like yourfelf.

He could fay no more; tears interrupted the power of fpeech. Juft at this moment his little family returned running, and Eugenia entreated the old man to put up his purfe and conceal the adventure, till fuch time as fhe permitted him to fpeak, to mention it. She then embraced the little Simonetta, bade adieu to the good old man, and arm in arm with Leontine and Valentina again returned to the Château.

Eugenia, from a very natural delicacy, did not wifh that her father-in-law fhould be informed of this affair before fhe had been at the mafquerade, left he fhould give her another habit. The day

at

at length arrived, the Count remained in the country, and confided Eugenia to the care of one of his relations, and of Leontine, who went with her to Paris.

At the ball every eye was fixed upon Eugenia, not only by the charms of her perfon, which were very fuperior, but alfo by the elegant fimplicity of her drefs, which diftinguifhed her from every other woman; neither gold, nor pearls, nor diamonds loaded her habit; nothing impeded her natural celerity, and fhe bore away the prize of dancing, as well as of beauty; the fweet remembrance of Jerome was often prefent to her imagination, and re-doubled her gaiety; often did fhe fay to herfelf, as fhe beheld the exceffive and mad magnificence of young women of her own age, how much do I pity them; alas! they know not peace, they know not pleafure.

At day-break, Leontine took Eugenia back to the country; he would have her appear before his father in her mafquerade habit, for he was enflamed with the defire of relating the hiftory of the old man. The Count heard the recital with feelings equal to his joy; a thoufand times did he clafp the amiable Eugenia in his arms, and from that inftant conceived all the affection of the moft tender father for her.

The next day Eugenia and Leontine went to fee the old man. Leontine informed him that he

fhould

should take charge of two of his children, the pretty little Simonetta, and her second brother. The girl was sent apprentice to a milliner, at Paris; the boy to a joiner in the country. The Count d'Amilly put the finishing hand to the happiness of good old Jerome, by giving him a cow, and an acre of land adjoining to his cottage. The happy mother of Eugenia, Madame de Palmena, returning from Touraine, received on the road a letter containing an account of all these events.

It is, my children, impossible, at your age, to conceive the impression which a letter like this must make on the heart of a tender mother; the affectionate, the feeling, the charming Eugenia, was shortly after in the arms of Madame de Palmena, who passed the rest of her days with a daughter so worthy of all her tenderness; yes, Eugenia was the delight of her husband, of her mother, of her father, of her family; she found in her own heart, and in the world's respect, a just recompense for her conduct and her virtues; and, to crown her felicity, heaven, attentive to the prayers of the good old Jerome, gave her *children, like herself,* in whom she found all the happiness she had occasioned to Madam de Palmena.

Here the Baronnefs ceased speaking, and Madame de Clémire, taking up the conversation, said,

Well

Well, my children, has not this story given you pleasure?

Oh yes, mamma, and I hope I shall one day resemble the amiable Eugenia.

And I too, because she made her mamma happy.

I, said Cæsar, will endeavour to imitate Leontine; but a-propos, mamma, permit me to ask you a question; Leontine hid himself behind the arbour to overhear Eugenia, you know; but pray was that right?

No; and I love to see this delicacy, Cæsar, because it is well founded. Leontine, it is true, was convinced Eugenia would only speak of Jerome; and that, besides, she had no secrets which she would conceal from him; but that does not excuse the action; whatever may be our motive, nothing should ever tempt us to become listeners. It is my wish, my children, to teach you to distinguish good from ill; and I am well assured, when you shall have acquired this precious knowledge, you will detest vice and love virtue, because nothing on earth is so lovely; therefore if you would be happy, if you would be respected, say to yourselves, I will never be guilty of the least unjustifiable action, whatever may be my situation, motive, or excuse.

Here Madame de Clémire arose, and after receiving and returning the embraces of her children,
each

each retired to reft. Madame de Clémire little fufpected, at lying down, the fhock fhe fhould receive at rifing. For two months paft, whenever fhe received news from Paris, or the army, it always fpoke of peace being proclaimed before the next campaign; but what was her grief the next morning at receiving letters, which informed her the two armies were met, and that a battle was inevitable.

When her children heard this cruel news, they partook of the chagrin and inquietude of their mother; play was fufpended, pleafure forgotten, and the hours of recreation were fpent in grief and tears. This continued a fortnight; at laft, on the eve of the firft of May, they were liftening with attention to the Abbé, who was reading aloud a chapter in the Teftament, when fuddenly they heard loud, yet broken accents and confufed cries; among others, they plainly diftinguifhed the voice of their mamma; trembling, terrified, they all ran at once to the door, and at the fame inftant found themfelves in the arms of their mother, who, with a fhriek of joy, cried, *The battle is fought! the battle is won! and your father is fafe!*

The children leapt into their mother's arms with tranfport, unable to exprefs their joy, unlefs by their fobs; Madame de Clémire, fupported by her tender mother, and clafping her children

to

to her bofom, difplayed to the family a moft affecting picture.

After a momentary filence, interrupted only
by the fweet tears which pleafure fhed, Madame
de Clémire, furrounded by her whole houfehold,
read aloud the letter fhe had juft received; every
circumftance added to the pure tranfports they
enjoyed, for it feemed certain that peace muft be
the confequence of victory.

Happinefs and tranquillity returned to the caftle,
and with them the fports and the pleafures. This
interefting day was precifely that on which they
were to plant the May, which was to be performed
in the caftle yard, and they waited with impatience
for the hour when this ruftic feaft was to com-
mence. Scarcely was dinner over ere they heard
the found of hautboys, bagpipes, and flutes; they
all flew to the court, which was already filled by
the minftrels, and all the young people of the village; the lads in white waiftcoats, decorated with
ribbands, furrounded the May-pole that lay extended on the ground, and held cords in their hands
to raife it at the appointed moment.

At a given fignal, a troop of laffes advanced,
carrying bafkets full of flowers, in which they
half buried the May-bufh; one bufied herfelf with
twining a wreath round the pole, another placed
a garland crown upon it's fummit, and in an inftant it was adorned with a thoufand feftoons of

4

white

white thorn and wild rofes, and a multitude of coronets, compofed of the violet, narciffus, and anemony.

Two elderly peafants then gravely approached, each with a bottle in his hand, and fprinkled wine round the pole; after this libation, they drank to the health of the Lord of the Manor. Cæfar, the reprefentative of his father, muft needs, according to cuftom, *do juftice* to the honeft peafants; he advanced boldly, made his falute, received a large glafs half full of wine, and drank to them with a good grace.

Then it was that they immediately reared the May-pole, and hand in hand the lads and laffes danced around it, finging a roundelay in praife of the pleafant merry month of May. Cæfar, Caroline, and Pulcheria, mingled in the dance, and repeated the chorus with all their might; the *fauteufes (a)* fucceeded the roundelay, and the feaft finifhed by a good game at prifon-bars in the gardens.

Cæfar was aftonifhingly agile and ftrong for his age, and diftinguifhed himfelf in this laft game; in which agility may be difcovered, quicknefs of foot, addrefs in putting the change on one's antagonift, fincerity, or delicacy, in condemning onefelf in doubtful cafes, and valour and gene-

(a) A village dance in Burgundy.

rofity

rofity in expofing one's liberty for the delivery of the prifoners of one's own party.

Nothing was wanting to complete this fine day, except a ftory in the evening, which Madame de Clémire promifed them on the morrow. At going to bed they agreed to rife at day-break, on purpofe that they might altogether take a long walk in the fields. Morning being come, the children were called, and in a quarter of an hour Madame de Clémire left the Caftle with them, followed only by the faithful Morel.

After about an hour's walk, the children began to find they had not breakfafted: they were two miles from the Caftle, and, being preffed by hunger, they determined to look for a cottage where they might get fome milk. Morel fhewed them one, and they followed eagerly the road he directed; they arrived in lefs than half an hour at the cottage, where they were furprized to hear a great noife, much laughing, and a numerous affembly of peafants, all in their Sunday clothes, except fuch as had nuptial habits.

The hufbandman, who owned the cottage, had married his daughter that very morning: they had returned from church, and were bufy preparing the wedding-feaft. Madame de Clémire went into the garden with her children, and fat down upon a green bank, where, a moment after, the Bride brought them fome excellent milk and

brown

brown bread. Caroline, authorized by a sign of
approbation from her mother, took off a large
golden crofs that fhe wore round her neck, and
paffed the ribband over the head of the young bride,
as the latter ftooped to her to prefent her with a
nice bowl of cream : the bride blufhed, and, looking at Madame de Clémire, refufed to accept the
prefent ; but the latter faid to her, Do not afflict
Caroline, Manette, by refufing fuch a trifle ; but
pray go and tell your father that I invite him, and
all his guefts, to come next Sunday and dine with
us at the Caftle.

Manette, delighted at this propofition, and
impatient to fhew the company her crofs of gold,
ran immediately, forgetting even to thank Caroline ; fhe foon returned with her father, and, after
many fimple, but fincere, thanks and apologies,
they both went back into the cottage.

I am like you, mamma, faid Caroline, I am
exceedingly fond of country people. How gen-
teel Manette is ! What fweetnefs, what fatisfaction in her countenance ! How charming when
fhe blufhes, and what excellent cream, and bread,
and milk, fhe has given us ! I am fure you have
made all thefe good people very happy, by inviting
them to come to dine at the Caftle ; they will
long talk of the chance that brought us to-day to
their cottage.

This little adventure, anſwered Madame de Clémire, calls to my mind an anecdote I have read in the Ruſſian Hiſtory.

Dear, dear mamma, do tell it us.

With all my heart. The Czar Iwan *(a)* ſometimes went about diſguiſed, in order that he might the better diſcover what the people thought of his government. One day, as he was walking alone in the country, near Moſcow, he came to a village, and, feigning to be ſpent with fatigue, aſked relief. His dreſs was ragged, his appearance miſerable, and what ought to have excited the compaſſion of the hearers, and inſured his reception, produced denial only.

Full of indignation at the hard-hearted inhabitants, he was about to quit the place, when he perceived one more houſe, at which he had not aſked aſſiſtance; it was the pooreſt cottage of the village. The Emperor approached, and ſoftly tapped at the door, when inſtantly a peaſant came, and aſked the ſtranger what he wanted. I am almoſt dying with wearineſs and hunger, anſwered the Czar, can you give me lodging for one night?

Alas, ſaid the peaſant, holding out his hand to him, you will have poor fare; you come at an ill

---

(a) About the year 1550. This anecdote has been taken from a work entitled *Faſtes de Pologne & de Ruſſie.* Tom. II. p. 40.

time,

time, my wife is in the pangs of labour, her cries will hinder you from fleeping; but come; come in, at leaft; you will be out of the cold, and fuch as we have you fhall be welcome to.

So faying, the peafant made the Czar enter a fmall place full of children; one cradle contained two fleeping foundly; a little girl of three years old was laid upon a rug, near her two little brothers, afleep. likewife; while the two eldeft fifters, the one fix and the other feven, were on their knees, crying and praying to God for the deliverance of their mother, who was in the adjoining room, and whofe plaints and groans were diftinctly heard.

Stay here, faid the peafant to the Emperor, I will go and get fomething for you to eat; fo faying, he went out, and foon returned with black bread, eggs, and honey. You fee all I can give you, faid he, partake of it with my children, I muft go and affift my wife.

Your charity, your hofpitality, faid the Czar, fhould bring happinefs on your houfe; I have no doubt but God will reward your virtues.

Pray for my wife, my good friend, replied the peafant, pray to the Almighty fhe may be happily delivered, that's all I wifh.

Would that make you happy?

Happy! Judge yourfelf; I have five fine children, a wife that I love, a father and mother

both

both in good health, and my labour is fufficient to maintain them all.

.And does your father and mother live with you?

Certainly! They are within, with my wife.

But your cabin is fo very fmall.

Oh! it's large enough, fince it holds us all.

So faying, the peafant went to his wife, who, an hour after, was happily delivered. The good peafant, tranfported with joy, brought his child to fhew the Czar. Look, faid he, look, this is the fixth fhe has brought me; may God prefereve him like my others! Look how ftrong and hearty he is.

The Czar took the child in his arms, and looked at him with a full heart. I know, by the phyfiognomy of this child, faid he, I am certain, he will be happy; I would lay my life he will arrive at great preferment.

The peafant fmiled.

At this moment the two little girls came to kifs their new-born brother, whom their grandmother was come to take back: the little ones followed her, and the peafant, laying himfelf down on his bed of ftraw, invited the ftranger to do the fame. In a moment the peafant was in a peaceful and found fleep, and the Czar, fitting up, looked round, and beheld, with tender emotion, the fleeping children and the fleeping father. The moft profound filence reigned in the cottage. What calm!

calm! what tranquillity! said the Emperor; virtuous, happy man; how peaceably he sleeps on
his straw; ambitious cares, suspicion, and remorse, trouble not his repose; how delicious is.
the sleep of innocence!

In such like reflections the Emperor passed the
night. The peasant awaked at the break of day,
and the Czar, taking leave of him, said, I must
return to Moscow, my friend, I am acquainted
there with a benevolent man to whom I will speak
concerning you; I am certain I can prevail on
him to stand godfather to your child; promise me,
therefore, that you will wait for me to come to
the baptism; I shall be back in three hours at the
farthest.

The peasant did not think much of this mighty
promise, but, naturally good-natured, he easily con-
sented to the stranger's intreaties; after which the
Czar immediately took his leave.

The three hours, however, were soon gone, and
nobody appeared; the peasant, therefore, followed
by his family, was preparing to carry his child to
church. As he was going out of his cottage, he
suddenly heard the neighing of horses, and the sound
of many coaches. The peasant looked out, and saw
a multitude of horsemen and superb carriages; he
knew the Emperor's guards, and invited all his family to come and see the Czar go by; they all ran
out in a hurry, and placed themselves before their
door.　　　　C 3　　　　The

The carriages and horfemen filed off orderly, in a circular line, and, at laft, the Czar's ftate-coach ftopt oppofite the cottage of the good peafant. The guards pufhed back the croud, which the hope of feeing their Sovereign had drawn together; the coach-door opened, and the Czar defcended, perceived his hoft, and advanced.

I promifed you a godfather, faid he, I am come to fulfil my promife; give me your child, and follow me to church.

The peafant ftood like a ftatue, looking at the Czar with amazement equal to his joy. In a kind of ftupefaction he examined his magnificent robes, the fparkling jewels with which they were adorned, the lordly train that furrounded him, and in the midft of all this pomp, could not difcover the poor ftranger who had lain all night with him upon ftraw. The Emperor, for a moment, enjoyed his perplexities and aftonifhment in filence, then fpoke to him thus:

Yefterday you performed the duties of hofpitality; to-day I am come to acquit myfelf of the moft delightful duty of a fovereign, that of recompenfing virtue. I fhall not remove you from a ftate to which you do fo much honour, and the innocence and tranquillity of which I regret; but I will give you fuch things as you want; you fhall have numerous flocks, rich paftures, and a houfe, in which you may with eafe perform the duties of
humanity;

humanity; the new-born infant fhall become my ward, for you muft remember, faid the Czar, fmiling, I predicted he would be fortunate.

The peafant anfwered not a word, but, with tears of gratitude in his eyes, ran for the child, brought him, and laid him down at the Emperor's feet.

The Czar was moved, took the child in his arms, and carried him himfelf to church; after which, not willing to deprive him of his mother's milk, he took him back to the cottage, ordering that the child fhould be fent to him as foon as it was weaned. The Czar faithfully kept his promife, had the boy educated in his palace, eftablifhed his fortune, and heaped benefactions on the good peafant and his family.

Ah! cried Cæfar, how feverely muft thofe villagers lament, who inhofpitably fhut their doors againft the difguifed Emperor; they were juftly punifhed for their hard-heartednefs; fhame and repentance are the natural confequences of ill actions.

But how is it, faid Pulcheria, that the wicked do not think of that?

A bad heart, my dear, ftifles the natural lights of reafon. The wicked are much to be pitied; it was therefore that a Perfian Sage made the following prayer: " Have mercy, Oh God, upon the " wicked. As for the good, when thou madeft them " good, thou madeft them happy."

So

So saying, Madame de Clémire quitted the cottage, and returned with her children to the Castle; they talked of nothing on their way but the Czar Iwan. Dear mamma, said Pulcheria, I wish you would relate something from history, every time that you are so good as to take us out a walking. Do mamma, said the rest; that is well thought of.

And so you would have me, regularly, every day, tell you a story in the morning, and a story in the evening! It seems you depend very much upon my memory.—

And upon your good nature, too, mamma.

Well, my dears, I will do my best to justify your good opinion of me.

At hearing this, each of the children ran again and again to kiss their mamma.

They were now almost at the Castle gates; as soon as they got home, Madame de Clémire gave her daughters their daily tasks, and Cæsar went to his studies with the Abbé. After dinner Madame de Clémire, having a letter to write, left her children in the hall with the Abbé, during the hour of recreation. In a quarter of an hour, Madame de Clémire, having finished her letter, returned; she perceived Caroline and Pulcheria sitting together reading in a corner.

What are you reading there, my dears, said Madame de Clémire?

It

It is a book, mamma, that Mademoiselle Julienne has lent us.

Mademoiselle Julienne, is she capable of direct-ing you in the choice of books! And, besides, ought you to borrow books without informing me?

That's what I told these young ladies, said the Abbé, who was playing at chess with the Curate at the other end of the room, but they would not believe me. Master Cæsar is more rational, he is overlooking our game, and reading the *Journal de Paris.*

Let me see what book it is, said Madame de Clémire.

It is *Le Prince Percinet, & La Princesse Gracieuse,* mamma.

A Fairy Tale! said the Baronness.

How can you be pleased with such a book?

I see, mamma, I have done wrong; but I con-fess I am fond of fairy tales; they are very amusing; they are so marvellous, so extraordinary, and have so many changes from cryftal palaces to golden caftles, that it's quite delighting to read.

But don't you know that all these miracles are false?

To be sure, mamma; they are fairy tales.

How does it happen that this idea does not dif-guft you, then?

C 5

We

We own, mamma, the ſtories you tell us are a thouſand times more intereſting. I could hear them for ever, and I ſhould ſoon be tired of fairy tales.

But, if you are ſo fond of the marvellous, you might far better ſatisfy that inclination by reading books which are inſtructive.

How ſo, mamma ?

It is your ignorance, only, that makes you ſuppoſe the marvellous exiſts no where but in fairy tales. Nature and art afford phænomena as ſurpriſing as the moſt remarkable incidents in *Prince Percinet.*

Is it poſſible, mamma ?

I will prove it is ; and, for that purpoſe, undertake to write a tale the moſt ſtriking and ſingular you ever heard ; the marvellous of which ſhall all be true.

Cæſar, who had overheard, in part, the converſation, left cheſs and the *Journal de Paris,* and, approaching Madame de Clémire, ſaid, are you in earneſt, mamma ?

You ſhall judge yourſelf : I muſt have imaginary perſons, and fabulous incidents ; but, obſerve *the marvellous ſhall all be true :* every thing that ſhall wear the face of prodigy or enchantment I will take from nature ; the events ſhall be ſuch as either have happened or do daily happen at preſent.

Well, that now appears incredible.

But

But I am sure of one thing, mamma, which is that you will have no cryftal palaces, with pillars of diamond, in your tale.

Yes, fince you defy me to it, I will have cryftal palaces, with pillars of diamond; and what's more, a city all of filver.

What, without the affiftance of magic, fairies, and necromancers!

Yes, without magic, fairies, or necromancers; with other events ftill more furprifing.

I fhall never recover from my amazement! Dear, dear, how impatient I am to hear your tale, mamma!

It will take me three weeks at leaft to write it, for I muft look over feveral voyages and works of natural hiftory.

What! can you find, in thofe inftructive books, things more marvellous than in Prince Percinet? How does it happen, then, that fairy tales are not out of fafhion?

Becaufe the kind of tales I fpeak of require previous knowledge, which is only to be gained by ftudy.

But how then, mamma, fhall we be able to un-derftand your tale?

I will employ no technical terms, and only re-late the effects without explaining their caufes; fo that, if you had not been told it fhould be all truth, you would have fuppofed it abfolutely a fairy tale;

but

but you muſt wait three weeks, during which time our evening and morning ſtories ſhall all be ſuſpended.

O dear, O dear, three weeks!

Do yourſelves juſtice, Caroline and Pulcheria; have I not forbad your ever looking in a book that was not given you either by me or your grand-mamma?

That is very true, and we deſerve a longer pe-nance.

To conſole themſelves as much as poſſible, the children paſſed their time in their garden every evening, and Madame de Clémire with them. Look, mamma, ſaid Pulcheria, at that bed of hyacinths; it is all mine, cried ſhe, with rapture; how happy, dear mamma, have you made your dear Pulcheria, by giving her that bit of ground: if I could but remember always to follow your in-ſtructions, and never diſobey you, nothing would be wanting to my happineſs. Ah! mamma, I am ſure you are as good as the Sage who prayed for the wicked; do pray that I may not be ſo for-getful, nor ſo inquiſitive, and that none of my hyacinths may die.

Then you are not tired of your garden?

Dear! no mamma; I am fonder and fonder of it every day.

That is not at all ſurprizing; ſimple and inno-cent pleaſures alone are durable; the palace and

the

the throne foon become tirefome; a garden, cultivated by our own hands, never. Dioclefian,
when folicited, by his former colleague Maximian,
again to take the imperial crown, which they had
both long abdicated, only wrote as follows in
anfwer: " Come, my friend, and fee the fine
" lettuces I have planted in my garden at Sa-
" lona." (a)

Ah! but what would he have faid if he had had
my hiacinths?

Take care, however, of being too fond of your
flowers; beware of excefs in every thing; beware
of an *exclufive preference*.

Why, mamma, can one's fondnefs for flowers
become a paffion?

Every thing may be abufed by thofe who do not
liften to reafon, and do not fubdue their whims:
would you think that there are people filly enough,
mad enough, to give two or three hundred guineas
for a flower-root?

Three hundred guineas!

I have feen feveral hyacinths, at Haerlem, in
Holland, which have coft fuch fums (1).

But what, mamma, could make a flower fo
dear?

(a) Hiftoire de Charlemagne, par M. Gaillard, Tom. I.
p. 287.

The

The minute delicacy of amateurs; they, for example, feek for uncommon tints, and require a hyacinth fhould have certain properties, on which they fet an imaginary value, and into which they enquire with the moft fcrupulous exactitude.

Lord! mamma, amateurs are greater children than I am; their flowers of three hundred guineas do not fmell better than mine, nor look better, in my opinion; and fo I would as lief have my little bed of hyacinths as any bed at Haerlem.

You are very right, my dear, to be fatisfied with your own.

As they were thus converfing, a fervant came to inform Madame de Clémire of the arrival of a coach. It was a vifitor's carriage, and contained M. and Madame de Luzanne, with their only daughter, Sidonia, a young lady of fifteen. Madame de Clémire had never yet feen them, becaufe, though neighbours, they had paffed the winter at Autun; and, fuppofing them come back, fhe had been to pay them a vifit in the beginning of April, which they were now come to return.

M. de Luzánne was about forty, and rather handfome, of which, and having in his youth been two or three times at Paris, he was very vain. He had a profound contempt for every body bred in the country, and treated his wife

with

with difdain, and his daughter with indifference, fuppofing himfelf utterly fuperior to all fuch petty people; and confoling himfelf for the misfortune of living with none but his inferiors by imagin-ing that his fuperiority was too evident not to be generally felt.

Having never lived in the fafhionable world, he confequently was ignorant of its cuftoms; he yet had the ridiculous vanity of pretending to know it well, and piqued himfelf on his gallantry, which he exprefled by phrafes collected from tales and novels; the authors of which, by endeavouring to paint the manners of the great, had reprefented thofe only of their vulgar and humble imitators; this kind of erudition gave M. de Luzanne a tone of familiarity, a ftrange jargon, and manners as difagreeable as impertinent.

Madame de Luzanne had none of thofe fopperies: her behaviour was fimple and amiable; though contemned by her hufband, fhe loved him to ex-cefs; and, unable to overlook the fingularity of his character, the blindnefs of her too tender af-fection made her fuppofe his filly antics fo many graces.

Their daughter Sidonia was mild, modeft, in-genuous, and fenfible; fpoke little, anfwered with timidity, and blufhed often; but there was no-thing aukward in her embarraffment, nothing au-ftere in her referve, and there was no company in
which

which her behaviour, her perſon, and her diſcourſe, would have appeared miſplaced.

Madame de Clémire, followed by her three children, entered the hall, where ſhe found M. and Madame de Luzanne with their daughter. M. de Luzanne, ambitious of pleaſing a lady from Paris, never diſcovered ſo much folly and extravagance. After the firſt compliments, uſual on ſuch occaſions, madam, ſaid he, addreſſing himſelf to Madame de Clémire, I dare not imagine that we can, may, or ought, to flatter ourſelves with the hope of having you in our neighbourhood, next winter.

I am in expectation, ſir, of not returning to town before the autumn after next.

You are in expectation, madam! What a polite phraſe!

I am delighted with the country.

I hope, however, you will allow, madam, that when one has once lived in the capital, the country is no longer ſupportable. " Life is at Paris! Vegetation only is here." But a-propos, madam, how does Verglan do?

Do you mean my brother, ſir?

Yes, madam, he was once one of my intimates; many a delightful evening have we ſpent together; a little elevated I own ſometimes; his adventure with Bleinville made a noiſe; he is married ſince, and marriage is an excellent cooler for the brain.

He

He has an amiable wife, fir, and is very happy.

Yes, I know——fhe is very rich; I have heard that one of her old uncles died lately, and has left her ten thoufand crowns a year (1250l.) That uncle was once a man of great gallantry; the country produces few fo polite.

My fifter, fir, was greatly afflicted at the lofs of her uncle; a worthy relation is a precious and a certain friend.

To be'fure, madam; but a groaning old uncle, you will own, is no great lofs; each muft have their turn to live, and the young would have great right to complain if the old were immortal. But do, madam, oblige me fo far as to inform me if Blandford be ftill as fond of Champaigne as formerly.

You mean my uncle, fir, I prefume?

The very fame, madam.

Upon my word I don't know.

He had a moft delightful country-houfe, it was a paradife. You, madam, are too young to re-member the Countefs de Blane in her prime. When I was at Paris fhe was *the rage, the ton,* the toaft of the time! I remember fhe had a box at the Opera.

Madame de Clémire endeavouring to make the converfation general, addreffed herfelf to Madame de Luzanne; but M. de Luzanne perceiving

Caroline

Caroline and Pulcheria, exclaimed, in pretended raptures,——There is beauty indeed! There are features! There are ſhapes! There are eyes! No, no, thoſe eyes were aſſuredly not made to remain in the country! It would be a public robbery, high-treaſon in the Court of Cupid, to keep them from the capital.

What age is your daughter, pray ſir, ſaid Madame de Clémire?

She knows that, anſwered, careleſsly, M. de Luzanne; meaning his wife; for my part, I always forget.

Madame de Clémire ſeized the opportunity of aſking Madame de Luzanne the like queſtion, and, at the ſame time, of ſpeaking highly in praiſe of Sidonia; to which her mother liſtened with evident ſatisfaction, while M. de Luzanne, with a cold and abſent air, tumbled over ſome pamphlets that lay upon the chimney-piece; then, turning ſuddenly to Madame de Clémire, ſaid, what think you, madam, of our old La Paliniére? Could it be believed that he had paſt his youth at Paris? Such is the effect of the country air, it eats into and deſtroys that ſmooth varniſh, thoſe elegant graces, which can only be *conſerved* at the court, or in the capital; and I don't doubt, madam, but you find *us* a little ruſty.

Theſe words, pronounced in a ſelf-ſufficient tone, aſked for a compliment which they did not obtain:

obtain: Madame de Clémire contented herself
with rendering juſtice to the underſtanding and
merit of M. de la Paliniére; after which ſhe ſpoke
on indifferent ſubjeċts, and, in about a quarter of
an hour, M. de Luzanne made a ſign to his wife,
which put an end to the viſit.

Returning home, Madame de Luzanne and her
daughter ſaid, they thought Madame de Clémire
exceedingly amiable; but M. de Luzanne, with
a dry and diſcontented air, ſilenced them by an-
ſwering, Madame de Clémire was abſolutely deficient in wit, judgment, and good breeding.

What an odd man, ſaid Cæſar to his mamma,
M. de Luzanne is.

Which way, Cæſar?

I cannot deſcribe which way, mamma, but he
is ſo droll; his walk, his ſmile, his geſtures have
ſomething in them ſo odd; and then he ſpeaks in
ſuch an affeċted manner, that—that—

But what do you mean by an affeċted manner?

Something unlike every body elſe, mamma;
ſomething at which one is every moment ready to
laugh, and yet can give no reaſon why; juſt as
one does, you know, mamma, at the antics of an
ape.

Your ſimile is a little hardy, Cæſar, but very
juſt.

And

And then, he fays, *conferved*, inftead of *pre-ferved*; and the *capital*, inftead of Paris, or the town.

Very true, though your criticifm is rather minute; thefe expreffions are all, in their own nature, equally proper, but cuftom determines which is to be preferred; and it is, in reality, thefe nice diftinctions, which give one perfon's language a fuperiority over another's. He likewife fays, the *rage*, and the *ton*, which are ridiculous and affected words, and, like many other, that are at moments fafhionable, fhould be carefully avoided by people who wifh to fpeak with that eafy elegance, fo pleafing to the ear, and fo honourable to the underftanding.

And did not you obferve, mamma, when M. de Luzanne enquired after my uncle, he called him plain Verglan?

Yes; fo in fpeaking of M. de la Paliniére, he faid La Paliniére: and this is an affectation of eafe; a thing in its own nature exceedingly eftimable in fociety, but exceedingly difficult to obtain, without degenerating into rudenefs, as M. de Luzanne did in the above inftances. And I am forry to obferve, that, at prefent, M. de Luzanne is far from being the only perfon who miftakes rudenefs for eafe, though no two qualities can poffibly be more oppofite. But let us, at prefent, fpeak of

Madame

Madame de Luzanne, and her daughter Sidonia: what do you think of them?

O, mamma, I think Madame de Luzanne exceedingly amiable; and her daughter appears to me quite charming.

You are very right; her behaviour is obliging, modeſt, and natural, and thoſe are qualities which will pleaſe every perſon, and all nations.

I talked ſoftly with Mademoiſelle Luzanne, and ſhe anſwered me with ſo much gentleneſs and complaiſance that, to be ſure, thought I, ſhe would have been a miracle, had ſhe had a good education.

But pray tell me what you underſtand by a good education.

Why, mamma——ours——

I am much obliged to you for the compliment, my dear; but it is not an eulogium, but a definition, I demand.

A good education——a good education is—— is——is to have——is to have a great many accompliſhments. Mademoiſelle de Luzanne told me herſelf ſhe neither underſtood muſic, drawing, nor dancing.

Don't you remember to have heard ſpeak, at Paris, of an Opera ſinger, called Mademoiſelle Flora?

Yes, mamma, the perſon that my aunt would not have at the entertainment ſhe gave you.

The

The fame; and that air, which you remember was fo ill fang, would have been fung delightfully had Mademoifelle Flora come.

Yes, mamma; but you know Mademoifelle Flora is not a woman of character.

Very true; and yet Mademoifelle Flora fings delightfully, dances well, plays on feveral inftruments, and has *a great many accomplifhments*; thus, according to your definition, fhe has received a good education.

No, mamma, I perceive fhe has not.

I am glad you do; I would have you underftand, that a brilliant is not a good education. I have a thoufand times repeated to you that you ought not to place too high a value on things which, in their own nature, are of no importance.

A well accomplifhed perfon is poffeffed of a thoufand attractions, a thoufand graces, a thoufand refources of pleafure, both to themfelves and others. But can graces and attractions make us happy without virtue?

Certainly not, faid Cæfar; for, to be happy, we muft be loved and efteemed.

Dancing, drawing, and mufic, cannot render us either eftimable or beloved.

And are they nothing, then, mamma, but trifling accomplifhments?

Even fo; though infinitely lefs trifling than beauty or perfonal charms; becaufe, befides the
inexhauftible

inexhauſtible amuſement they afford us, it coſts great pains to acquire them; and it is with great reaſon ſuppoſed that a young perſon, ſo accompliſhed, is tractable, induſtrious, and perſevering; therefore, in this point of view, theſe talents, undoubtedly, merit a certain degree of eſtimation.

And what muſt we think of inſtructive ſtudies, mamma?

Whatever may inform the mind, extend it's powers, and give perfection to our reaſon, muſt neceſſarily make us better: an extenſive reading, a knowledge of various languages, of geography, geometry, and other ſciences, enlarge the faculties, conſequently erudition cannot be called trifling.

Certainly not, ſince it contributes to render us more eſtimable; it is, therefore, far above things which we call accompliſhments.

That cannot be diſputed; nor, indeed, is there any thing ſuperior to erudition, except the qualities of the heart. And now tell me, ſuppoſe you were to meet a young woman totally unaccompliſhed, ignorant of every language but her own, without the elements of any one art, yet a lover of work and reading, never idle, always modeſt, of an equal obliging diſpoſition, fearful of doing wrong, deſirous of inſtruction; in fine,

4   joining

joining franknefs to prudence, anfwer me, I fay, Pulcheria, would not you allow fuch a perfon had received a good education ?

I fee, mamma, I was wrong. If Mademoifelle Luzanne is, as I believe her to be, all that you defcribe, I affure you I now think her education has been excellent.

Yes, fince the true end of every teacher, her principal objeft, ought to be to weed out the defefts, and encourage the virtuous propenfities of her pupil; if at laft fhe renders her a worthy and good woman, fhe has well fulfilled the noble duty of the difficult-tafk fhe has undertaken.

I feel the truth of all this, mamma; but yet, if to fuch virtues the pupil could likewife add knowledge and accomplifhments, education would then become perfeft: and this feems very poffible.

It affuredly is fo: and I flatter myfelf with the agreeable hope that you fhall one day be a proof of its poffibility. I could cite feveral young perfons in whom, not only the good qualities of the heart, but, thofe of the mind and body are, likewife, all united, without reckoning Delphine, Eglantine and the amiable Eugenia.

Well, mamma, I hope I fhall never forget this converfation. I hope I fhall always remember that we ought not to place a great value on any but effential things, and that I fhall never

ver again confound brilliant with good educa-.
tions; that is to fay, with thofe which render us
virtuous.

All this goes to prove, that a tender mother,
though buried in the country, without fortune,
and without the affiftance of any mafter, may,
aided by vigilance and reafon, give her daughter
an excellent education; affection, patience, and a
few well chofen books will be fufficient.

The fame evening that this converfation happened, Cæfar and his fifters, at fupper, allowed
themfelves to take fome liberties with the foibles
of M. de Luzanne. Madame de Clémire repri-
manded them very feverely on that account.
What, faid fhe, I imagined I had received a great
proof of your confidence in me; I am forry now
to find it was nothing but the effect of your ma-
lignity.

O dear, mamma!

It is natural, and neceffary, you fhould confult
me, tell me your opinions, and acquaint me with
the impreffions you receive, in order that I may
know if you judge well or ill. I, therefore, think
it very proper you fhould tell me, with franknefs
and fincerity, what you think of fuch perfons as
vifit here, provided your obfervations do not turn
upon frivolous points. Thus, if in converfation,
fomething fhould be faid which you think contrary to good manners or good fenfe, I authorize

you to acquaint me with your remarks; this liberty is nothing more than a proof your confidence in me; but the fame liberties taken in the prefence of others, are malicious, or, at leaft, very indifcreet.

Dear mamma, we have done very wrong.

You have, indeed. Malice is an odious vice, and is, in youth, efpecially, as ridiculous as it is hateful and difgufting. Are you, at your age, or will you be at the age of eighteen or twenty, capable of judging and deciding on things that are to be condemned? Your reputation will not then be eftablifhed, and how will you obtain the general efteem, if you fhew yourfelves fickle, indifcreet, and malicious? Without experience yourfelves, will you not ftand in need of the indulgence of others? And who will be indulgent to youth, when malicious? In giving way to the emotions of malice, you would lofe all the graces of fuch an age, and prove yourfelves equally deficient in difcernment, underftanding, and principles.

This leffon made fo much the more impreffion upon Cæfar and his fifters, for that Madame de Clémire terminated it, by declaring their conduct had retarded the recommencement of the evening tales.

For how long, mamma? cried they, mournfully.

At

At prefent, anfwered Madame de Clémire, I am writing the marvellous tale that I promifed you.

And, when it is finifhed, fhall not we begin again ?

No; not till a fortnight after.

Dear, that will be very long.

It is occafioned by your own error, for which you ought to be forry; murmuring, you know, would only prolong the penance.

Murmur, mamma! Could we be fo ungrateful? No; we know your juftice, and it is that which afflicts us fo much.

A few tears were here fhed, which were wiped off by maternal tendernefs, while the gentle careffes of fo good a mother comforted them for fo fevere a punifhment.

Madame de Clémire, however, continued bufily to employ herfelf in writing the tale fhe had promifed them; and, the fifteenth of June, fhe informed them it was finifhed and copied. Their joy would have been very great had they not fighed to remember they muft yet wait another fortnight, before they fhould hear it read. The fweet and varied pleafures of the moft delightful of all the feafons rendered this privation, however, much lefs painful than it would have been during the long evenings of winter: the cherries began to redden, and the woods already produced wild

ftrawberries:

ftrawberries: Cæfar had learnt from Auguftin how to climb trees, and had feveral times brought home, in triumph, nefts of goldfinches or chaffinches, with half fledged young. Happy was the fifter to whom fuch precious gifts were deftined: what joy! what gratitude did they excite! And yet, in receiving them, they remembered with pity the poor mother, deprived of her young; but they treafured up the nefts, and bought cages for the birds.

They bufied themfelves in making ofier bafkets, and coronets of rufhes. Thefe amufements did not make them neglect the cultivation of their garden: the jonquils and pinks had replaced the hyacinths; the lilies were no longer in flower: but who could regret them when the rofe was half blown?

One morning, when Madame de Clémire was walking with the Abbé and her little family near the children's garden, Pulcheria afked permiffion to pay a vifit to her rofe-trees. Leave given, away fhe ran, entered the garden, and there, unexpectedly, found a fine full blown rofe; defirous of gathering it for an offering to her mamma, and the ftalk being thick and thorny, and fhe without either knife or fciffars, patience or ftrength, fhe thought fhe might wrap her hand in her apron, and, without danger, thus defended, feize and pluck it. No fooner had fhe laid hold on it but
fhe

she shrieked, drew back suddenly her bleeding
fingers, and gave so violent a shake to the tree,
that the beautiful rose shed above half its leaves.
Pulcheria could not retain her tears at this sight;
the loss of the rose was even more painful than
were the wounds in her fingers; she was sorry that
the blood, which had dropped from her hand, had
tarnished the flower; she drew it away, and found
some relief by weeping over the remains of her rose.

Madame de Clémire, pale and trembling, ran
precipitately into the garden; the Abbé, and her
brother and sister followed; she heard the cry of
her child, and hastened with fear to her assistance.
Pulcheria, at the sight of her mamma, was ashamed
of having cried so loud for such a trifle, and ran
into her arms. After she had related her adventure,
she added, it was the finest of all the roses, mamma,
and I intended to give it you.

Well, but the loss of your rose could not be
the ridiculous occasion of a cry which terrified me
so greatly?

Dear mamma, I did not think I had cried so very
loud.

It seems to me that I never-heard a shriek so
piercing.

That was because you knew the sound of the
voice. Dear mamma, you can hardly stand, you
tremble so; pray sit down.

D 3

Well,

Well, well, I am very glad you wept only at the lofs of your rofe, and becaufe you meant to give it me; the motive is fo amiable.

Mamma!

What's the matter with you, my dear? Why do you feem fo much embarraffed?

Becaufe——becaufe, mamma I——I weep a little at the pain of the thorns too.

That frank confeffion, procured the tendereft careffes and praifes to Pulcheria. Always preferve the fame candour, the fame generofity, my dear little girl, faid Madame de Clémire, always tell the truth, and never accept of falfe praife. There is a meannefs as well as injuftice, in accepting praife we do not merit: a noble mind is happy becaufe it has done good, and not becaufe it is applauded.

It is certain, faid the Abbé, that Mademoifelle Pulcheria has a natural franknefs, which cannot be too much admired; but it is much to be wifhed fhe could acquire as much fortitude as fincerity.

Happily for me, anfwered Pulcheria, fortitude is a quality not neceffary to a woman.

It is true, replied the Abbé, that a woman, not having the ftrength of a man, cannot have his valour; fhe is not intended to wield the fword, nor command armies; therefore may, without difhonour, be deficient in fortitude: if, however,

fhe

she is abfolutely deftitute of that quality, she is much to be pitied, and, indeed, cannot be perfectly efteemed: it is not required she should be a heroine, but abfolute pufillanimity is unpardonable.

Befides, added Madame de Clémire, if you weep at the wound of a thorn, what would you do at the drawing of a tooth? How will you fuppoit numerous other ills, infeparable from humanity; fuch as a violent head-ache, cholic, or nervous attack?

I wish, mamma, I was more courageous.

It depends entirely on yourfelf, my dear—

On me, mamma! How?

Imitate your brother, and learn to fuffer without complaining: that is the whole fecret.

But that is very difficult, mamma.

Not in the leaft; a little command over yourfelf, and a few reflections, will foon shew you it is very attainable. Complaints aggravate and augment our fufferings, while our endeavours not to complain divert the mind from dwelling on them. The other day, for example, during your walk, you were thirfty: what were you the better for repeating a hundred times, as you did, "How thirfty I " am! O dear, O dear, how thirfty I am! I shall " die with drowth!" You were very importunate, made every body uneafy, took no part in the con-

D 4

verfation;

verſation; and yet all your complainings did not procure you a ſingle drop of water.

'Tis very true, mamma; it is a bad habit I have got; and what vexes me moſt with myſelf is, that I wearied you, my dear mamma.

No, Pulcheria, it is not wearineſs, it is not that kind of ſenſation I feel; when you complain, I partake in all your ſufferings, whether real or imaginary; I am your mother, I am therefore afflicted when you are unhappy; but if you were not a child, I ſhould have more contempt than pity for you; for, generally ſpeaking, we have no compaſſion for trifling pains, except when they are borne with patience.

I will endeavour to correct myſelf, mamma; I promiſe you I will.

A few days after this, the penance being ended, Madame de Clémire promiſed, in the evening, to read them the tale ſhe had written. After ſupper they ran directly into the hall, and Madame de Clémire, ſitting by the ſide of a table, took her manuſcript from her pocket.

Before I begin, ſaid ſhe, you ought to recollect, that I have undertaken chiefly to relate extraordinary, yet poſſible events; incidents which to you ſhall appear incredible, but which, however, have, or might have, all happened: in a word, phænomena, the exiſtence of which, paſt or

preſent,

prefent, is well proved. I have only invented the plot of the ftory, that is to fay the fole part which to you fhall appear credible ; while all that you will think marvellous, all that will recall to your minds your fairy tales, is precifely true and natural.

O, that will be charming !

You will think my *incredible truths* a thoufand times better than your common well confirmed *every day truths.*

But what ! mamma, muft we continually believe what we cannot comprehend ?

Do not think yourfelf humbled by that, Cæfar ; that is a deftiny common to manhood, as well as to infancy ; our capacities are too confined to com- prehend all the truths which are demonftrable; and it would be abfurd to affirm a thing does not exift, becaufe it is beyond the limits of our underftand- ings. Let us not adopt errors, but let us not give way to that vain and ridiculous prefumption which rejeats, with difdain, and without examination, every thing that reafon cannot conceive.

Well, mamma, you have told us that every thing in your tale is well authenticated ; therefore we may blindly believe, and take the facts for granted, and that is as much as I defire.

I wifh to underftand what I hear, mamma; and therefore fhall be glad of your explanations.

I will willingly explain whatever I can; but that will not be much. I am not learned : befides, as

D 5 I have

I have said, there is an infinity of phænomena in existence of which the most learned men cannot explain the causes.

And will you interrupt your tale, mamma, at each marvellous circumstance, to give us an explanation ?

O, no : for, as you may well think, such interruptions would spoil my story. I have written notes, which we will read with attention, another time. At present, if you will listen, I will begin.

Ay, that we will, willingly, dear mamma. So saying, they drew their chairs nearer to Madame de Clémire, who opened her manuscript, and read aloud the following tale :

ALPHONSO

ALPHONSO and DALINDA;

OR, THE

MAGIC of ART and NATURE.

A Moral Tale.

Ce n'est point en se promenant dans nos campagnes cultivées, ni même en parcourant toutes les terres du domaine de l'homme, que l'on peut connoître les grands effets des variétés de la nature: c'est en se transportant des sables brulans de la Torride aux glacières des Poles, &c. (a) M. DE BUFFON.

ALPHONSO, the hero of my history, was born in Portugal. His father, Don Ramirez, enjoyed riches and preferment, because he was a favorite. Born of an obscure family, but with a subtle, intriguing, and ambitious character, he introduced himself at court, found pro‑

(a) It is not by walking in our cultivated fields, it is not in riding post through any habitable country, that the great varieties and effects of nature may be known, but in transporting oneself from the burning sands of the torrid zone, to the icy mountains of the Poles. M. DE BUFFON.

tectors,

tectors, formed partizans, and became, at laft, the idol of his fovereign. The young Alphonfo was educated at Lifbon, in the fumptuous palace of his father: an only fon to the richeft and moft powerful man in the kingdom, adulation kneeled at his cradle, accompanied and corrupted his youth.

Don Ramirez, occupied by great projects and little cabals, could not be at the fame time an affiduous courtier and a vigilant father; he was, therefore, obliged to commit the care of his fon's education to ftrangers. Alphonfo had teachers of languages, hiftory, geography, mathematics, mufic, and drawing, all of whom wondered, or pretended to wonder, at his prodigious capacity and ftrength of genius. Notwithftanding which, Alphonfo learnt little, except to draw flowers, and play a few airs on the guittar.

This was fufficient to charm all the ladies of the Court, efpecially when he gave them to underftand he was, alfo, a profound mathematician, an excellent naturalift, and a great chymift. Neither did he tell them any thing he did not himfelf believe; for his governor, his teachers, his valets, and the croud of complaifant people that paid their court to his father, all declared he was a miracle, fo repeatedly, he could not doubt of its being a certain fact.

He

He not only fuppofed himfelf the moft diftinguifhed young man at Court, by his talents,
beauty, and knowledge, but he likewife believed
his birth to be as illuftrious as his fortune. Don
Ramirez, during his leifure moments, had invented
a lift of his forefathers, as far back as the fabulous
times of Lufus (a); which genealogy, every body
but his fon laughed at; the world is not apt to
credit old titles, never heard of till the pretended
owner is become rich. Alphonfo, however, too
vain not to be credulous, on fuch a fubject, faw
no one fuperior to his father, except his fovereign,
and the branches of the royal family; and yet
Alphonfo, inebriated with pride, full of ignorance,
folly and prefumption, fpoilt by pomp, flattery,
and fortune's favours, Alphonfo, I fay, was yet not
loft paft retrieving; he was poffeffed of courage,
a feeling heart, and a good underftanding; and the
inconftancy of fortune was preparing a leffon, that
would teach him to know himfelf.

As Don Ramirez owed his elevation only to
intrigue, fo a new intrigue unexpectedly changed
his deftiny; he was difgraced and ftript of all his
employments, juft as Alphonfo was feventeen.
This unforefeen revolution not only deprived Don

(a) The Portugueze were anciently called Lufitanians,
from Lufus or Lyfas, one of their kings, who, according to
the fable, was either the fon or companion of Bacchus.

Ramirez

Ramirez of titles that flattered his pride, but alſo of a great part of his wealth ; and he was one of thoſe little ambitious people who equally regret titles and riches : beſides, he was in debt, and his diſgrace made his creditors as preſſing and importunate as they had been formerly moderate and forbearing ; in fine, Don Ramirez ſaved nothing of all his fortune, except his magnificent palace at Liſbon.

It is true, that this palace contained immenſe riches, in furniture, plate, paintings, and eſpecially in diamonds ; all which Don Ramirez only waited for a favourable opportunity to ſell, when a dreadful adventure happened, which gave the finiſhing ſtroke to his misfortunes. He had not yet ventured to tell his ſon, that the ſtate of his affairs forced him to ſell his palace, and return in the country. At laſt, he determined to declare his real ſituation, and, accordingly, ſent for him, one morning, to open his heart to him on that ſubject.

As ſoon as they were alone, tell me, Alphonſo, ſaid Don Ramirez, what effect has my diſgrace, and the loſs of my fortune had upon you? I have always thought, my father, ſaid Alphonſo, from having always heard, during your proſperity, that never miniſtry was ſo glorious as your's, nor ever miniſter ſo loved and reſpected by a nation :

the

the love of the people, therefore, and the glory you have acquired, ought to confole you for your unjuft difgrace. Befides, you have many friends, who, no doubt, will all return as ufual, the moment you fhall wifh them fo to do. Don Nugnez, Don Alvarez, and many others, whom I have met, have all protefted as much to me; feveral of them have even told me, that they have only feemed to abfent themfelves, the better to ferve you in fecret: add to which, you ftill have an immenfe fortune, and an illuftrious birth; and, in fpite of the fnares of envy, will ever remain the firft peer of the realm.

You are deceived, Alphonfo, interrupted Don Ramirez; what! are you ignorant, that the name of my father was abfolutely unknown?

I know it was, replied Alphonfo; but I alfo know that the old titles which you have retraced in our family make it equal to any in the kingdom. You yourfelf, my father, have deigned to read thofe precious proofs of honour, which are contained in the cafket that is locked up in your cabinet.

Don Ramirez liftened, and fighed; he had had the ridiculous vanity to purchafe a genealogy, and never fufficiently felt, till his difgrace, how fuperfluous, unworthy, and contemptible is fuch deceit. At laft he faw what flattery till then had hidden, which was, that, except his fon, every body knew

his

his birth, and laughed at his filly pretenfions. He wifhed to undeceive Alphonfo, but could not refolve to confefs a falfity which muft make him appear fo mean.

He was in this mournful perplexity and filence when he was fuddenly ftaggered, and faw Alphonfo reel; the colour forfook his cheeks, and he rofe; fave yourfelf, my father, cried Alphonfo, fupport yourfelf on my arm, follow——come——

So faying, he impetuoufly hurried his father away; at the fame inftant, a thoufand confufed cries were heard; they ran towards the ftair-cafe, and, as they ran, the floor opened beneath the feet of Alphonfo, who, that he might not drag his father down to deftruction, quitted the arm of Don Ramirez, inftantly funk, and feemed buried in the ruins.

Alphonfo had the good fortune, however, to be only flightly wounded; he rofe, and found himfelf in his father's cabinet: amongft the rubbifh which furrounded him, were two cafkets, one containing the jewels of his father, the other, the fo much vaunted genealogy. Alphonfo did not hefitate: willing to fave, amidft this dreadful difafter, that which appeared to him moft precious, he feized the box of titles, and fled into the garden; but, recollecting the danger of his father, was determined, at the hazard of his life, again to enter

the

the houfe, when he heard Don Ramirez calling him at the other end of the garden.

It was not without difficulty they rejoined each other; the earth on which they trod, like the fea, agitated by a violent tempeft, rofe in mountains, or funk in dreadful vallies, beneath Alphonfo's feet. His ear was ftruck by a fubterranean found, like the roaring of waves, furioufly breaking upon the rocks; he ftaggered, fell, got up, and fell again, and unable to keep upon his feet, crept on all fours, with great difficulty, towards his father. He faw the earth open on all fides, and forming gulphs, whence iffued fire and flame, which rofe and vaniſhed in the air; the heavens became dark, the pale and livid lightning pierced through the black clouds that covered them, the deep thunders rolled, and Alphonfo beheld the bolts of heaven ready to fall on his head, and hell opening beneath his feet.

Often when he imagined himfelf within a ftep of his father, a new ſhock threw them at a diftance; the fweat ran down his face, his clothes and hair were covered with fand and duft: yet, amidft the fcene of horrors, he never abandoned his dear caſket; he imagined Don Ramirez would receive it with tranfport: that idea fuftained his courage and his ftrength. At laft, he rejoined his father, who received him with open arms, though

with

with an aching heart. Oh my father! cried Alphonso, look, I have saved the casket.

The jewels! haftily interrupted Don Ramirez.

No, no, replied Alphonso, I knew better how to chufe; it is your genealogy.

Don Ramirez, in dreadful conſternation, raiſed his eyes to heaven: I am juſtly puniſhed, ſaid he, for my ridiculous vanity. He could ſay no more, his tears interrupted his ſpeech. Alphonſo, too much prepoſſeſſed and agitated to comprehend the meaning of theſe words, continued in his former error, and thought only of ſaving his father. A moment's calm left them time to conſider the mournful objects that ſurrounded them.

They ſat down oppoſite their palace, now half deſtroyed: that magnificent palace built within the laſt ten years; that palace ſo new, ſo rich, ſo admired, is now only a heap of ruins. He who had beheld the bare walls, the mouldered columns, the glaſsleſs windows, muſt have believed that time alone could have produced ſo terrible a revolution! Ages ſeemed neceſſary to deſtroy a monument built with ſo much ſolidity, and yet the fearful deſtruction is the work of a few minutes!

The garden too, that maſter-piece of art and nature, is now an unmeaning chaos of duſt, mud, and mouldered leaves. In the morning there was ſeen a ſuperb caſcade, where is it now? In the

very

very fpot where an artificial mount was raifed, at a prodigious expence, gapes a dreadful gulph. What are become of the citron groves, the marble ftatues, the vafes of alabafter and of porphyry? A few veftiges ftill remain, a few broken fragments; the reft is fwallowed up and loft!

Don Ramirez looked at the furrounding diffolution; he was fitting near a little wood that had rifen beneath his own eyes; the trees are all torn up by the roots, fcattered here and there, buried or extended in the mire: thofe trees, deftined to furvive the hand that planted them, are torn from the bofom of the earth, with as much eafe and rapidity, as the verdure and yielding flowers that grew beneath their fhade.

Oh! day of horrors! cried Don Ramirez, aloud, loft labours, treafures interred in this place of terrors; why did not I make a better ufe of the money this building and this garden have coft? But the earthquake is abated (2), let us endeavour to regain the ruins, let us fave my diamonds, if poffible.

So faying, he arofe, and, at the fame inftant, a new and dreadful fhock extended him again upon the ground: the remaining walls tumbled, the rubbifh was ingulfed, and the palace difappeared; a whirlwind, and cloud of fmoke and duft, rofe as it were at his feet; yet, amidft this fcene of defolation, Don Ramirez perceived, a moment after, a band a band of hardened wretches, bearing lighted torches, and creeping towards the ruins of the palace, with an intent, before the laſt ſhock, to pillage (3).

Alphonſo wiſhed to puniſh ſuch unbridled villainy, and would have ruſhed upon them, had not his father caught and retained him in his arms. Oh! my ſon, ſaid Don Ramirez, bathing him with a deluge of tears, let us fly from this ſcene of horrid deſtruction; we are near the banks of the Tagus, let us ſeek ſhelter and ſafety on board the ſhips.

Alphonſo gave one arm to his father, held the caſket in the other, left the garden, and entered one of the public ſquares; the houſes were all in ruins, overthrown, or conſumed, by the flames of a general conflagration. After a thouſand fearful riſks, Don Ramirez and the young Alphonſo, at laſt, found protection on board a veſſel, commanded by the brave and generous Fernandes. The ſame Fernandes, who, formerly, had ſo much cauſe to complain of Don Ramirez, but who, in this time of public calamity, ſaw, only, in an ancient enemy, an unhappy man, to whom his aſſiſtance was become neceſſary. He ran to Don Ramirez, embraced and conſoled him; for, compaſſion in great minds is ſo forcible, and ſo delicate, that it can ſoften woes the moſt cruel. In the mean time, as Fernandes did not once bewail his

own

own situation, Don Ramirez questioned him concerning it. You had, said he, a great fortune, is
it not all lost in this dreadful day?

My ho se at Lisbon is consumed.

The loss is, no doubt, considerable.

No; the building was small and simple.

Your jewels and diamonds; are they saved?

I had none.

You had a garden.

Yes; but far removed from Lisbon, where I
passed the greatest part of my time; it is in Alen-
tejo (a).

I have heard of it, and hope to God the earthquake has not ravaged that province. Is your
country-house a fine one?

No; but it is convenient.

Have not you formed some advantageous establishments there?

Some satisfactory ones; a manufactory, and a
hospital. (Don Ramirez sighed.)

Is your manufactory profitable?

Yes; it gives subsistence to a number of work-
men, and defrays in part the expences at the hospital.

I see you make a worthy use of your wealth;
heaven preserve it to you. It is, indeed, horrible,

(a) A province of Portugal, between the Tagus and the
Guadiana. Evora is the metropolis.

to be ruined with a benevolent heart, and to be obliged to relinquish such honourable, such glorious establishments.

. One should then find confolation in the remembrance of the good one had formerly done.

Don Ramirez again heaved a profound figh, and bitterly regretted the ufe he had made of his fortune; his eyes at laft were opened; but too late, alas! either for his glory or repofe.

Thus totally ruined, Don Ramirez received from his fovereign, thanks to the folicitations of the noble Fernandes, a fmall penfion, though fufficient to afford the means of fubfiftence. With this he determined to retire to the province of Beira, whither he departed with his fon, and fettled in an obfcure but pleafant retreat, on the agreeable banks of the Mondego; but, followed by deep regret, and inceffant recollection, he found not the tranquillity he fought.

. Alphonfo, devoted to ambition, and nothing abated in prefumption and pride, confoled himfelf for the lofs of fortune, by the hope, that, in time, he fhould eftablifh a more brilliant, and far more folid one than what his father's had been. He formed a thoufand extravagant and chimerical projects, the abfurdity of which his ignorance and vanity did not fuffer him to perceive: incapable of reflecting and employing his time in a ufeful and rational manner, he paffed a great

part

part of it in reading romances; thefe frivolous and dangerous books heated his imagination, and gave him falfe ideas of men and things.

Not far from the retreat he inhabited was the famous Fountain of Love; a name it owed to two unfortunate lovers, who, in ancient times, often met on its brinks, drawn thither by an imprudent paffion. There it was that Don Pedro and the beautiful, the tender Ines, a thoufand times difcourfed of their fecret loves *(a)*. Two antique palm-trees overfhaded the Fountain, united to each other by a flexible garland of vine branches and ivy. The water rifes impetuoufly from a majeftic rock, returns in a cafcade, and forms, upon a bed of fhells, a large rivulet, which flowly winds, and gently murmurs, among eternal verdures, fhrubs of myrtle, of citron, and the laurel rofe.

Thither Alphonfo often went to read and ruminate. One morning, happening to go later than ordinary, he heard, as he drew near the Fountain, two perfons fpeaking in an unknown tongue: in one of their voices Alphonfo found an inexpreffible fweetnefs, which wonderfully excited his

(a) Such is the tradition. This fountain ftill exifts in Portugal, near the Mondego, and is called the Fountain of Love. Camoens, in his beautiful poem of the Lufiad, gives birth to this fountain, from the tears which the nymphs of the Mondego fhed at the death of Ines.

curiofity;

curiofity; he hid himfelf, with emotion, behind a myrtle bufh, through the branches of which he difcovered an object moft worthy of fixing his attention: a young nymph, for fo fhe feemed, fcarce fifteen, of the moft perfect beauty, was fitting on the banks of the Fountain, befide a man, who appeared to be her father; to him fhe was liftening with the utmoft attention, and, by her looks, it was evident he was reciting fome interefting event.

As he proceeded, he often pointed to the palm-trees and the fountain, whence Alphonfo fuppofed he was relating the hiftory of the unhappy Ines. The angelic liftener had fixed her eyes upon the unknown relater, and kept a profound filence; but, from the expreffion of her countenance, her thoughts might eafily be divined; curiofity, fear, and pity, were fucceffively painted in her eyes; and with fo much energy, that Alphonfo imagined himfelf was hearing a tale that fhe was telling; he faw her tears, and wept with her the death of Ines. Prefently her eyes became fuddenly dry, her cheeks pale, and terror and indignation fucceeded to pity. Alphonfo fhuddered in fympathy, detefting the excefs to which paffion, and a defire of vengeance, had carried the unfortunate Don Pedro.

The hiftory of Ines is ended, and yet the ftranger continues fpeaking; no doubt he is making pru-

dent

dent reflections on the danger of the paffions, and on the criminal and fatal imprudénce of a young woman, who, without the confent of her parents, dared to chufe for and difpofe of herfelf.

The beauteous hearer ran to the arms of the ftranger, with all the expreffion of the ftrongeft fenfibility: then, turning her gliftening eyes towards that Fountain, which had formerly been a witnefs of the indifcreet vows of love, fhe fighed, fell on her knees, raifed her clafped and eager hands to heaven, and feémed to promife the author·of her days an eternal obediénce; her beauty, in that attitude, had fomething celeftial and angelic.

Alphonfo could not contain his ecftatic tranfports; an exclamation efcaped aloud, and, fearing to be difcovered, he haftily fled from his hidingplace, full of the idea of what he had feen. He followed the firft path he found, but, prefently, awaking from his dream, again returned towards the Fountain. The beauteous ftranger was gone, and Alphonfo contemplated with grief the place where fhe had fat, and thought he ftill faw her on her knees before her father. The next moment he remembers her abfence, his heart is oppreffed, his eyes filled with tears, he is plunged into a profound and melancholy meditation, when fuddenly he hears a cry of terror, which pierces him to the very heart.

He runs, he flies; but what does he behold!
It is the ftranger, alone, pale, difhevelled, and
flying from a mad bull that purfues her. Alphonfo
darts towards her, feizes her in his arms, and bears
her off, at the very moment, when, overcome by
the excefs of fear, fhe was fallen, not ten paces
from the furious animal.

Alphonfo, charged with a burthen fo precious,
rapidly turns afide behind the palm-trees of the
Fountain, and bears her fenfelefs in his arms in
fafety upon a high rock.

Here he perceived the father of the ftranger,
running wild, and, as foon as he faw his daughter
in fafety, blefling God and her deliverer. At the
fame inftant the bull returned, and bent his courfe
towards the father, who had not time to avoid
him, or mount the rock. In vain did Alphonfo
ftill hold his fenfelefs prize in one arm, and extend
the other towards her father; the latter cried aloud
to him in Portuguefe, not to abandon his daughter
on that dangerous fummit, and ran himfelf immediately behind one of the largeft of the palm-trees
of the fountain.

The bull endeavoured to pafs between them;
the paffage was narrow, he was in full fpeed, his
body became fixed between the tree, and his head
and horns entangled in feftoons of the ivy and the
vine. The ftranger feized the advantage of the
moment, drew an etwee cafe from his pocket,
                                        opened

opened it, took out a pin, and ran it in the back
of the bull; but how great was the furprize of
Alphonfo, when he heard the bull bellow dreadfully, faw him drop, ftruggle to rife, again fall
down, and, after a few vain efforts expire!

Nay now, but fure, cried all the children at
once, that is not poffible.

Pardon me, faid Madam de Clémire, but it is.

What, mamma! cried Caroline; a bull killed
by the prick of a pin!

Yes, my dear; it is very true.

Then I hope you will not fay, faid Pulcheria, I
was fo very wrong to cry, when the rofe-thorns
pricked my fingers.

That thorn was not quite fo dangerous as the
pin of the ftranger.

Was it very long, mamma?

Much fhorter than the pins with which I pin on
my hat.

This feems incredible. Shall we find the explanation of this prodigy in your notes?

Affuredly.

That will be very curious.

Oh, I have many other things, far more aftonifh-
ing to tell you yet.

It is a delightful ftory: do, dear mamma, have
the goodnefs to go on; we will not interrupt you
any more.

E 2   Alphonfo,

Alphonſo, continued Madame de' Clémire, was not leſs ſurpriſed than you are, at the ſudden death of the bull; amazement rendered him motionleſs, while the ſtranger aſcended the rock, and took his daughter in his arms, juſt as ſhe began to recover the uſe of her ſenſes and look around. Alphonſo was not an unfeeling witneſs of the pure joy teſtified by the father and daughter; the latter did not underſtand Portugueſe, therefore could not thank Alphonſo; but ſhe related to her father, in a few words, the dreadful danger from which ſhe had been delivered.

The ſtranger teſtified a lively ſenſe of gratitude towards the generous protector of his dear Dalinda, for that was the name of his lovely daughter; and, while he ſpoke, Dalinda caſt a tender glance at Alphonſo, ſtill more expreſſive than the thanks of her father. Alphonſo, penetrated and enraptured, endeavoured to prolong a converſation ſo ſweet, by queſtioning the ſtranger, concerning the manner in which he had been ſeparated from his daughter; he replied that he had been culling ſimples; that Dalinda, occupied after the ſame manner, was at ſome diſtance from him, but not out of ſight; that, lifting up his head, he had ſeen her running with incredible ſwiftneſs; that ſhe had already got above ſix hundred yards from him, and that at the ſame moment he perceived the bull purſuing her; that he ran after her with all his

power,

power, but had ftumbled over the ftump of an old
tree and fallen.

Having finifhed this recital, Alphonfo afked if
he intended to ftay long in Portugal? No, anfwered
the ftranger, we fet off immediately for Spain, being defirous of feeing as much of that kingdom as
poffible. This intelligence threw Alphonfo into
the utmoft confternation! He hung down his head,
and was mournfully filent; the ftranger, after again
repeating his thanks and gratitude in the moft affectionate terms, rofe, took his leave, and difappeared with Dalinda.

Alphonfo remained, fome time, petrified, and
fcarcely feeming to breathe; at laft, coming to
himfelf, he ftarted impetuoufly from the Fountain,
and flew to find the ftranger once again, to afk
him a thoufand queftions, and, efpecially, to enquire what was his name, and what his country.
He wondered how it was poffible he could have
let him depart without firft gaining fuch interefting information. He ran here and there,
like a madman, but all his fearchés were in
vain.

Overcome with fatigue and defpair, he returned
once more to the Fountain. As he drew near,
he faw fomething fhining in the path, and, approaching, found it was a large blue ribbon embroidered with gold; his heart beat, he knew it
to be the fafh of Dalinda. It was in that very

place

place that Dalinda, overcome with terror, had fallen fenfelefs; and there it was that Alphonfo, raifing her in his arms, had untied the ribbon that girded her waift.

Alphonfo, affected, ftooped, with tranfport and refpect, to take up a ribbon fo precious; the fafh of Dalinda was the ceftus of innocence, and the girdle of the graces. He fighed, and vowed for ever to preferve a pledge fo dear to his heart, which he had thus acquired by chance. In the mean time, the hours glided away, Alphonfo could not tear himfelf from the Fountain; and night and darknefs had furprifed him, ftill plunged in his reverie, if Don Ramirez had not come to fearch for him himfelf.

Don Ramirez had never taken any part in his fon's education; had never afked, nor ever poffeffed his confidence. Alphonfo did not mention his adventure to him; but, on the contrary, carefully concealed the thoughts and emotions of his foul. Devoted to the romantic ideas which feduced his imagination, he had only one pleafure, that of paffing his hours at the Fountain, where he firft beheld Dalinda; there every thing recalled the object, which reafon ought to have erafed from his memory; here Dalinda, at the knees of her father, was retraced in his fancy; here, in his fixed thoughts, fhe ftill lived in all her bloom of beauty, adorned with every charm of innocence and virtue; near

this

this ſhrubbery, Dalinda owed to him her life; upon
that rock ſhe opened her eyes, and caſt a look of
ſweet thankfulneſs upon Alphonſo; beneath theſe
palm-trees did ſhe ſit, and that clear water once re-
flected her ſeraphic form.

Thus did Alphonſo conſume his days, in vain
regret, upon the dangerous brink of this fatal
ſpring. Such does fable paint the wretched Nar-
ciſſus, a feeble victim of infenſate love; and ſo did
Alphonſo, pale, dejected, without force, without
courage, fix his eyes, drowned in his tears, upon
the Fountain of Love. The echoes of this ſolitary
place, which anciently ſo often reſounded with the
name of Ines, repeat at preſent only that of Dalinda. Dalinda is carved upon every tree, even on
the very palm-trees, on which formerly Ines alone
was read. Alphonſo ſung to his guittar the verſes
he had written on Dalinda, and engraved upon
the rocks the rhymes that love and melancholy
dictated.

Theſe romantic follies totally occupied him for
ſome time: but, as the pleaſures which reaſon diſ-
approves are never durable, his imagination cooled
by degrees, and weariſome diſguſt ſucceeded en-
thuſiaſm; his ſongs and complaints began to ceaſe,
the echoes of the Fountain became mute, and the
trees, the ſtreams, and verdure, no longer could
inſpire him with poetry and profound reveries.

Don

Don Ramirez obſerved the alteration of body and mind which had happened to his ſon; he queſtioned him, and Alphonſo confeſſed himſelf diſſatisfied and conſumed with *ennui*. He had not forgotten, that the ſtranger told him he ſhould remain ſome time in Spain; and Alphonſo added, he ardently deſired to travel through, and become acquainted with, that country. Don Ramirez, who, for his own part, had none of thoſe reſources in himſelf, which make men fond of ſolitude, gladly ſeized this propoſition, and two days after they departed for Spain. After traverſing the province of Tralos Montes, they entered Spain by Galicia; they then travelled through the northern part of Spain, the Aſturias, Biſcaye, Navarre, Arragon, and arrived at laſt in Catalonia (4).

Alphonſo's paſſion for Dalinda was rekindled by this voyage; the hope and the deſire of once more finding her acquired new force from thoughts which an enthuſiaſtic imagination had at firſt produced. He was impatient to arrive at Madrid, thinking he could not fail to meet her in this metropolis, but Don Ramirez would abſolutely remain ſome time in Catalonia, in order to viſit the famous Mont-Serrat; this mountain, compoſed of ſteep rocks, is ſo high that, when arrived on it's ſummit, the neighbouring mountains that ſurround it ſeem ſo diminiſhed as to

lo:k

look little more than mole-hills; and the views
from thence are the moſt majeſtic and extenſive
poſſible *(a)*.

At the foot of one of theſe ſolitary rocks is an
antique monaſtery *(b)*. "But the moſt intereſt-
"ing part of the mountain is the deſert, in which
"are ſeveral hermitages, affecting aſylums in the
"eyes of true philoſophy; each of theſe retreats
"contain a chapel, a cell, a ſmall garden, and a
"well, dug in the rock. The Hermits, who in-
"habit them, are moſt of them gentlemen, who,
"diſguſted with the world, come to this place of
"tranquillity and reſt, and give themſelves up en-
"tirely to meditation *(c)*."

At break of day, Don Ramirez and his ſon began to aſcend Mont-Serrat; the aſpect of the
mountain, might well have made them renounce
their deſign; it's prodigious elevation, and the
enormous and craggy rocks, which projected on
every ſide, promiſed no agreeable walk; but, in
traverſing theſe menacing ſteeps, delicious vallies,

(a) It is ſaid you may ſee the iſlands of Majorca and Mi-
norca from this place, which are more than ſixty leagues diſtant. See *Nouveau Voyage en Eſpagne*, Tom. I.

(b) Saint Ignatius there devoted himſelf to penance,
and, there, formed the deſign of founding the Society of
Jeſuits.

(c) See the work laſt cited, Tom. I.

E 5　　　　　　meadows,

meadows, enamelled with a thoufand flowers, thickets formed by the fimple hand of nature, and cafcades, which throw themfelves from the white and ftony ridges with animating tumult, give a thoufand varieties, and embellifh this folitude, which is become the fortunate refuge of peace and virtue (5).

Don Ramirez, on entering the defert, met one of thefe Hermits, reading as he walked. He was ftruck by his noble and venerable figure; he paffed near them, and, as Don Ramirez was fpeaking with his fon, the Hermit, hearing the Portuguefe tongue, took his eyes from his book, and approached the ftrangers. He told Don Ramirez how happy he was, once more, to meet a countryman, and invited them both to reft, a while, in his hermitage. The propofition was gratefully accepted, and the venerable Reclufe brought them vegetables and fruit.

After the repaft, Alphonfo, defirous of continuing his walk, left them, telling his father he would wait for him in the defert. The old man led Don Ramirez to his garden, and, there they fat themfelves down, befide a gentle water-fall, upon a rock, over-grown with mofs.

Don Ramirez, then addreffing himfelf to the Herm't, faid, what revolution, what cruel reverfe of fortune, my father, can have torn you from our native country, and fixed you in this defert? It is

eafy

eafy to fee, by your manners, you were not born
to end your days in a wildernefs like this.

No, replied the Hermit, it has been my misfortune to know the world, and the Court.

Thefe words infpired Don Ramirez with the
moft ardent curiofity, which the Hermit confented
to fatisfy.

It imports you but little, faid he, to know my
name: I have been twelve years an inhabitant of
this mountain. By this time they believe in Portugal that I am dead. I have devoted myfelf to
oblivion, therefore, I will not fpeak of my family,
but, in as few words as poffible, relate my deplorable
ftory.

Madame de Clémire was continuing to read,
but the Baronnefs gave the fignal of retreat; in
vain were feveral voices, at once, heard, entreating
for one quarter of an hour more; the rule was
abfolute.

The following evening, Madame de Clémire
again opened her manufcript, and faid, we left off
yefterday where the Hermit was going to recount
his hiftory. Don Ramirez liftened; the Hermit
fighed, and thus he faid:

" My family is one of the moft ancient in all
" Portugal. I received a good education, in-
" herited a tolerable fortune, and, by my fuccefs
" in war, obtained the efteem and benefactions of
" my Sovereign, married a woman whom I

" loved,

" loved, became a father, and, of courfe, became
" happy.

" Such was my fituation when the late King
" died. This event deprived me of a beloved
" mafter, a protector, and a father; for, to a
" faithful fubject, a good King is all thefe. I re-
" tired from Court, to an eftate in the country,
" and dedicated my time folely to the education
" of my fon. This fon, the object of a moft
" tender affection, was fuperior even to my
" hopes.

" As foon as he was of an age proper to ap-
" pear at Court, I entrufted him to the care of a
" relation, fent him to Lifbon, and remained in
" my country folitude. I was now, for the firft
" time, feparated from my fon, and, yet, never was
" happier. I imagined his future fuccefs, and
" indulged the fondeft hopes of his rifing fame.
" ——Hope, though the moft uncertain, the
" moft deceitful, is, yet, perhaps, the greateft of
" bleffings, and which the heart of a father, only,
" can properly eftimate. When our own in-
" tereft produces the flattering illufion, it is mo-
" derated, enfeebled, or, perhaps, difpelled by
" fear; but what father ever yet prefcribed
" bounds to the hopes he conceived of his fon?
" Alas! I thought to have beheld fome of mine
" realized!

" My

" My fon fet out with the moft brilliant fuccefs.
" His name, his family, my fervices, which his
" prefence brought again to remembrance, but,
" efpecially, his underftanding, good temper, and
" accomplifhments, obtained that refpect at Court,
" which the jealoufy of courtiers looked upon as
" the beginning of favour.

" He faw a young lady of Lifbon, who, in
" addition to perfonal attraction, talents, and
" virtue, was of a noble family and large fortune.
" My fon afpired to her hand, I approved his
" choice, and this attachment, authorized by my
" approbation, fixed the fhort deftiny of his life.
" Her parents confented to an union, by which his
" happinefs would be enfured, but, on condition,
" that he obtained a place at Court. My fon afked
" a place, and he was promifed one in three months;
" it was only required he fhould keep his fuccefs a
" fecret, for reafons affigned, till the moment of
" actual poffeffion; with permiffion, however, to
" inform the parents of his miftrefs of the event,
" which he inftantly did.

" He was, accordingly, prefented to the young
" lady as her future hufband, and fhe, at this inter-
" view, thus authorifed, confeffed an affection for
" him which crowned his felicity.

" As the marriage was, of courfe, deferred till
" the period when he fhould be in actual enjoy-
" ment of his promifed place, he tore himfelf
" from

" from Lisbon, and came to tell me all his hap-
" piness.   I had then the pleasure to hold in my
" arms, and press to my bosom, the child whom
" I so dearly loved, and whom I considered as at
" the summit of all his wishes.   Alas! while I
" supposed myself the most fortunate of fathers,
" a Barbarian, a Monster, was forming the black
" plot, which at once deprived me of wife and
" son.

. " My son's natural candour prevented him
" from suspecting the probity of a traitor who
" only wished his confidence that he might ruin
" him with greater certainty.   This wretch, who
" had been dragged from obscurity by the caprice
" of his Sovereign, imagined he beheld in him a
" dangerous rival; but, dissembling his jealousy,
" he sought, and soon obtained, the friendship of
" the unsuspecting youth."

Don Ramirez was greatly disturbed at this part
of the Hermit's recital, but the old man perceived
not his emotion, and continued his story.

" When my son solicited the place of which
" he was desirous he trusted the secret to that
" abominable man; who, not having, just at that
" instant, the power to injure him, pretended to
" second his request, and participate his joy; but
" the absence of my son gave him an opportunity
" to exercise his fiend-like malignancy.   He knew
" his own ascendancy over the King; he calum-

5   " niated

" niated my fon, and infpired a young and in-
" experienced Prince with falfe fears; the gift
" was revoked, the place given to a creature of
" this unworthy favourite, and my fon exiled the
" Court. By his Majefty's order, I was firft in-
" formed of this terrible calamity, which forbad
" my fon to quit his country-feat; and my fon,
" at the fame time, received a letter from the
" young lady he loved, which contained thefe few
" words:

" You have moft unworthily deceived us; we
" know, from the beft authority, the place now
" difpofed of, was never promifed you; forget,
" therefore, the name of one, who will never for-
" give herfelf for having once efteemed you.

" After having read this fatal billet, my fon
" exclaimed, Thus, then, I have loft the woman I
" loved, and am difhonoured! In faying this, his
" knees knocked violently together, the blood for-
" fook his face, and he dropped into my arms.
" He was taken to bed, whence he never rofe; a
" violent fever for ever deprived me of him, in lefs
" than a week. Oh horrible remembrance! Oh
" moft unfortunate father!

" His unhappy mother, a witnefs of the vio-
" lent emotions of her fon, feemed equally ftruck;
" her reafon became difordered, in a few hours
" fhe loft the ufe of it, yet appeared fenfible of her
" afflictions,

" afflictions, and, at laft, a victim to maternal love,
" funk into the fame grave with her fon.

" Condemned to live, I fupported life only by
" the hope of vengeance. Oh thou! cried I, So-
" vereign Arbiter of the fate of miferable mor-
" tals! Being Supreme! whofe heavy hand has
" fallen upon me! deign, at leaft, from the bot-
" tom of that abyfs in which thy wrath has plunged
" me, deign to hear the cries of my defpair!
" The voice of the oppreffed can reach thee, and
" never haft thou rejected his prayer. I afpire not
" to happinefs, that is for ever loft; 'tis ven-
" geance I afk, 'tis juftice I implore. May the
" perfidious wretch, whofe infernal arts have rob-
" bed me of my wife and fon, lofe, at once, fortune
" and favour. He is a father; let him weep bit-
" ternefs, like me, and may he, above all, be un-
" happy in his fon!"

The Hermit ftopped, he faw Don Ramirez
look wildly round, and rife from his feat. You
tremble, faid he; my excefs of hatred, and defire
of revenge, has made you afraid of hearing the remainder of my ftory; but fear not, I have nothing
farther of tragic to tell. Heaven converted my
heart; I foon abhorred the revenge which religion
condemns.

Don Ramirez again moved, without anfwer-
ing; and, after a few minutes, aftonifhment and

terror

terror made him motionless; then, suddenly starting—Where am I! cried he; in what asylum!

What is the meaning, sir, said the Hermit, of that fearful agitation in which I see you? What imprudence have I been guilty of? Is my persecutor known to you? Is he your friend?

This Persecutor! this Barbarian! this Monster! was Ramirez!

It was, sir, I confess it; he was the author of all my misery.

This Ramirez! this——

Repeat not that dreadful name, sir; I shudder when I hear it.

Unhappy Alvarez! Learn, at least, heaven has punished your enemy.

What say you? Does he no longer govern Portugal?

Ruined, stripped, without relations, without friends, he has little left but vain regret, and never ending remorse.

Does he suffer! I am sorry!

Sorry! Is it possible?

Doubt it not. But wherefore do you weep, sir? What ray of light breaks upon my mind? Oh God! Can it be?

Yes!—I am that wretch, cried Don Ramirez, casting himself at the Hermit's feet, who, penetrated with involuntary horror, drew back. Oh! reverend father, continued Don Ramirez,

falling

falling on his knees, and feizing his veft, Stop, hear me, holy man! I own I have merited thy hatred; no words can exprefs the horror with which my prefence ought to infpire thee, but remember I now am unfortunate. And yet I have a fon, who might confole, might——Oh! ceafe, holy father! to curfe me! Ceafe to pray my fon may make me more miferable!

Oh God! cried the Hermit; Don Ramirez! in this place! beneath this poor roof! a fuppliant at my feet, and giving me the facred title of father! a title, formerly, my greateft glory and my blifs! a title which he robbed me of!——Yet——fear nothing, faid he, cafting a look of compaffion on Don Ramirez; I again repeat it, hatred has long been banifhed this bofom. Thou calleft thyfelf unhappy; complaineft of fortune! Art thou perfecuted? Art thou profcribed? Speak——This grotto fhall become thy place of refuge; in partaking it with thee, I fhall obferve the holy rites of hofpitality. Fear no unworthy reproaches; if my fuccour be neceffary to thee, thou fhalt find in me only the father and the friend.

Oh! greatnefs of foul, which confounds me! exclaimed Don Ramirez. Can man, then, elevate his foul to fo fublime a degree of virtue?

No, Ramirez, anfwered the Hermit; feek not for that generofity, in the heart of man, which is not in nature; admire not the feeble Alvarez;

but

but acknowledge, and adore, the high hand of heaven.

Thus saying, he held out his arms, and advanced to embrace Don Ramirez, whose tears bedewed the bosom of the virtuous man; that bosom, which formerly he had so cruelly torn.

A quarter of an hour after this reconciliation, Alphonso returned to the Hermitage. Don Ramirez took his leave of the Hermit, and quitted the mountain, bearing with him remorse the most grievous, and apprehensions the most fearful; he could not remove from his mind the malediction so solemnly pronounced against him by Alvarez; he saw its effect already in the loss of his fortune; and, notwithstanding the generous pardon he had received, he felt himself too guilty not to dread the wrath of heaven, and it's justice towards the injured Alvarez. Alas! cried Ramirez, in his height of anguish, he remitted vengeance to the arm of God! Such vengeance must be terrible! Oh, my son! thou art to become the instrument of my punishment; Alphonso must chastise his father; he is the avenger of Alvarez!

Full of these melancholy thoughts, Don Ramirez became absent, silent, and gloomy; often as he looked at his son would the tears rush to his eyes: a vague dread would come over him, and an inexplicable terror seize his heart. He no longer felt the happiness of being a father.

They

They left Catalonia, after having vifited Tarragona and Tortofa (6), and went to Madrid, where Alphonfo vainly hoped, once more, to meet Dalinda. He learnt, however, from the defcription he gave of her, fhe had been there; that her father was a Swede, his name Thelifmar; that he intended to remain fome time in Spain, and that he had then taken the route to Grenada.

This intelligence, which he had been careful to procure, unknown to his father, gave him an ardent defire to go to Grenada; and Don Ramirez, who every where carried his inquietude with him, readily confented to leave Madrid fooner than he had intended.

They went firft to Toledo, where they faw the Alcazar, or ancient Moorifh Palace *(a)*; the architecture of which is a mixture of the Roman, Gothic, and Morifcan. What they moft admired, in this palace, was a hofpital, for the poor of the city and it's environs, eftablifhed by the Archbifhop of Toledo. This hofpital contains manufactories, and drawing-fchools. They educate about two hundred children, to whom they give a habit of labour, and a love of virtue. Old men and women, likewife, find an afylum in this ancient palace, thus confecrated by religion to fuffering humanity. (7).

(a) There is alfo an Alcazar, or Morifcan Palace, at Seville, but not fo beautiful as that of Toledo.

After

After a fhort ftay at Toledo, our travellers went to Cordova, in their route to which they croffed the Sierra-Morena (a), a wild and uncultivated tract of land, which the active and beneficent genius of an individual (8), has fince metamorphofed into an habitable and agreeable country.

Cordova is built upon the borders of the Guadalquivir, and is overlooked by a chain of mountains, continually covered with verdure, which are a part of the Sierra-Morena. This city, formerly fo famous, retains little of it's ancient grandeur, except a large extent of ruins, and a fuperb Mofque, built by Abderama (9).

Don Ramirez ftaid three days at Cordova, and continued his journey. Alphonfo faw not the walls of Grenada without emotion (10); he flattered himfelf he fhould find Dalinda in that city, but he did not long preferve that hope. Notwithftanding the cares of love, he was forcibly ftruck with the delightful fituation of Grenada, the beauty of it's buildings (11), and the antique and curious monuments, the remains of which, at every ftep, recall the remembrance of Moorifh magnificence. Alphonfo vifited, with rapture, the Alhambra, and Generalif, and amufed himfelf in places full of

(a) A long chain of mountains, fo called, for that, being covered over with rofemary, holly, and other ever-greens, it appears black at a diftance.

infcriptions

inscriptions and verses, which retraced to his memory the ancient gallantry of Grenada's Kings, the misfortunes of the Abencerages, the persecutions and triumphs of a virtuous Queen (12), and all the marvellous adventures with which history and romance abound.

Alphonso, however, more and more uneasy about Dalinda and her father, soon learnt they had left Grenada, almost a fortnight, and were gone to Cadiz; and that they talked of staying there six weeks, and, afterwards, of embarking for the coast of Africa. This news afflicted him much; he endeavoured not to persuade his father to go thither, for Don Ramirez had declared Grenada should be the last place he would wander to, and that he would afterwards return to Portugal.

The desire of travelling, of finding Dalinda, the hope of making a great fortune, ambition, love, and, especially, pride, idleness, and curiosity, inspired the culpable Alphonso with the imprudent and cruel resolution of secretly flying to Cadiz, and abandoning his father. He felt great uneasiness in coming to this determination, but he suppressed such salutary remorse, which he could not help feeling, and employed all his powers to find specious reasons that might excuse, and even dignify this criminal act.

My father, said he, has lost his fortune; he has only a small pension, not sufficient for both of us;

in

in taking half his expence away, I ſhall double his income. I feel I am a charge to him; I even perceive my company is not ſo agreeable to him as formerly; he is become penſive and ſilent, my converſation fatigues, and my preſence lays him under reſtraint. Beſides, in ſeeking to diſtinguiſh myſelf, and emerge from obſcurity, is it not for him I labour? If I can procure wealth, to him ſhall it be dedicated. My abſence may give him ſome uneaſineſs, for a time, but my return will enſure his felicity.

Such were the reflections of Alphonſo, who ſighed, while thus he reaſoned, and his cheeks were bedewed with tears. Had he conſulted his heart, duty, honour, and reaſon would ſoon have reſumed their functions; but he endeavoured to deceive himſelf, and he ſucceeded; without the power, however, of totally ſtifling the voice of conſcience.

He had taken care to ſeduce one of the ſervants into his deſign, and had conſulted with him on the means of flight. It was agreed, that Alphonſo ſhould go off in the evening; that the ſervant ſhould wait for him, at the city gate, with two horſes, on which they ſhould ride, without ſtopping, as far as Loxe, to which place the ſervant knew the road.

Alphonſo had no money. Certain jewels, which he happened to have about him on the day

of

of the earthquake, had been faved, all of which his father fold, except two diamond rings, which he had given his fon. One of thefe Alphonfo privately fold for four hundred piaftres (about feventy guineas) which he thought a fum fufficient to make the tour of the world, if he pleafed.

On the day fixed for his flight, he pretended a violent head-ache, in order to conceal his own anxiety, and induce Don Ramirez to go betimes to bed. Accordingly, about eight o'clock, his father retired. Alphonfo's heart was ready to burft, when he bade him good night, and he ran, and fhut himfelf in his chamber, whither he was purfued by his remorfe.

Bathed in tears, he wrote to his father, to inform him of the motive of his flight, without mentioning what route he fhould take, or his paffion for Dalinda. He fealed the letter, and left it on the table, that his father might find it on the morrow; then, wrapping himfelf in a countryman's cloak, he put on thick-foled clouted fhoes, took a ftaff in his hand, with his purfe, and a pocket-book that contained his other ring, and Dalinda's fafh, properly concealed, opened a window, leaped into a court-yard, and went out of a private door, of which he had procured the key. He paffed haftily along the ftreets, got through the

4

the city gate by means of his country difguife, found his fervant waiting, a little way out of town, mounted his horfe, followed his guide, and proceeded towards Cadiz.

The darknefs of the night would not permit him to travel as faft as he wifhed, while the fear of being purfued, the grief of leaving his father, his inquietude, remorfe, and repentance, all ftung him to the heart, and infpired him with a certain infurmountable terror, which was doubly increafed by the blacknefs of the night.

He had quitted Grenada about two hours, when he was awakened from his gloomy reverie by a moft furprifing phænomenon : furrounded as it were by the thick, the profound obfcurity of night, darknefs in an inftant difappeared, and light, the moft radiant, dazzled the aftonifhed eyes of Alphonfo. He raifed his head amazed, and beheld a globe of bright and fhining fire in the heavens, precipitating itfelf fomewhat horizontally towards earth, and augmenting as it fell. It exhibited a thoufand dazzling colours, and left a long train of light that marked its path in the atmofphere. Having traverfed a part of the horizon, it began to rife again by degrees, and fhot forth on all fides fparks, and blazing fheaves, that feemed like vaft artificial fire-works. At length, the enormous ball opened, and fent forth two

kind

kind of volcanos, which formed themselves into two prodigious rainbows, the one of which vanished in the north, the other in the south; the fiery globe became extinct, and the most impenetrable darkness instantly succeeded to gleaming light the most fervent (13).

Alphonso was forcibly and irresistibly alarmed by this prodigy. All uncommon accidents are ill omens to a troubled conscience. This was highly so to him; his grief and doubts were doubled, he increased his pace to get rid of his fears, and galloped the rest of the night without stopping.

At day-break his Valet perceived they had lost their way, and had struck into a cross road. Alphonso looked round, and saw a barren mountainous country covered with rocks. Unable to discover any beaten track, he alighted, tied his horse to a tree, and, followed by his Valet, went towards one of the highest and nearest rocks, hoping to discover from it's summit the town of Loxe, from which he imagined they could not be far distant.

Observe, his country shoes were clouted with hob-nails all over; and his staff, being a peasant's, had a thick iron ferrule at the end.

Scarcely had Alphonso proceeded twenty paces upon the rock he meant to ascend, when he felt his

feet

feet fixed to the ftone! He could not lift! he could not ftir them! And his ftaff, too heavy to move, ftood upright, and feemed to take root on this fatal rock! (14)

Oh, my father! cried he, heaven has undertaken to punifh my ingratitude by a new, an unheard of miracle.

He could fay no more. Remorfe, aftonifhment, terror overwhelmed him, took away what little ftrength he had left, made him immoveable and mute, caufed his hair to ftand erect, and fpread a death-like palenefs upon his cheeks.

Oh dear mamma! cried Pulcheria, is he changed to a ftatue?

Not entirely, anfwered Madame de Clémire, fmiling; though he himfelf dreaded he was, for that idea ftruck him as well as you.

And well it might, mamma. That invincible power that fixed him to the rock might make him expect worfe.

However, my dear, that invincible power was not fupernatural. You remember I told you, the feemingly marvellous in my ftory fhould all be true.

And yet the globe of fire and the fatal rock appear fo extraordinary! But tell us, dear mamma, what became of poor Alphonfo.

While he remained, petrified with terror, in the

F 2   fitua-

situation I have defcribed, the fky became covered with clouds, the winds howled in the air, and
the rain began to fhower. But how was the terror, how was the horror of Alphonfo increafed,
when he beheld that dreadful rain! When he faw,
what he thought millions of huge round drops of
blood, inftantly, cover the white rocks that furrounded him; felt them run in ftreams from his
face, hands, and all parts of his body, and viewed
rivulets of blood defcend on all fides to the green
vallies! (15)

Uncommon terror gave uncommon ftrength.
Alphonfo quitted his ftaff, which remained erect,
planted on the rock, and with violent efforts
wrenched his feet from the adhefive ftone, and fell
almoft fenfelefs on the fand.

His Valet foon after, fhocked with the miraculous fhower, came, running, and affifted his mafter.
He had been feeking a track which he had difcovered, and, as foon as they could fufficiently
recover their ftrength and recollection, they once
more mounted their horfes, and left this fcene of
horrors.

Arrived at Loxe, he ftaid two or three hours to
recover, then ordered mules and a guide, and purfued his journey. He croffed Mount Orefpeda
(16), paffed the ancient city of Antequerra, and
did not ftop till he came to Malaga. He arrived
                                        without

without any remarkable accident at Cadiz *(a)* and put up at the firſt inn he came to.

As he was going up ſtairs he heard a female ſinging, and accompanied by the harp. Alphonſo trembled, and, guided by the ſound, approached the door of the apartment whence it iſſued. It was ſure an Angel ſinging, and the harmony was heavenly! He could not miſtake the voice, it went to his heart. Delighted, raviſhed, aſtoniſhed, he haſtily deſcended the ſtairs, enquired for the maſter of the houſe, queſtioned him, and learnt his heart had not deceived him. Dalinda and Theliſmar inhabited the houſe whither he had been conducted by chance.

Tranſported with the diſcovery, he went into the court-yard, was ſhewn which were the windows of his Love, and then went and locked himſelf in his own room, that he might enjoy his unexpected felicity without reſtraint.

In the afternoon he ſent for a guittar, and, in the evening, after ſupper, planted himſelf under Dalinda's window; with a trembling hand he ventured to ſtrike a few arpeggios. The window opened, and, fearing to be overheard by Theliſmar, who underſtood Portugueze, Alphonſo durſt not ſing the verſes he had written on Dalinda at the

(a) In going to Càdiz, it is neceſſary to take a boat at Port-Sancta-Maria, a pretty town, two leagues from Cadiz. The paſſage is dangerous, and the boats are frequently loſt.

Fountain

Fountain of Love; but, in timid accents, and an irrefolute voice, he fang the Torments of Abfence.

In about a quarter of an hour the window was fhut, and on the morrow Alphonfo again began to fing, but in vain; it opened no more: and this rigour afflicted him as deeply as though it had deftroyed hopes that had had fome foundation.

Alphonfo formed a thoufand projects relative to his paffion, and executed none of them. He ardently longed once more to fee Dalinda, but never could determine to prefent himfelf as an adventurer. His intention, when he left his father, was to offer himfelf as a companion to Thelifmar during his travels, not doubting but bis knowledge and talents would make this propofition very acceptable; and fuppofing likewife that gratitude, for having faved the life of Dalinda, would put his reception out of doubt.

When paffion forms projects, it is blind to all obftacles, will hear no objections; but, fearing all reafons which may deter it from what it is previoufly determined to do, it never difcovers it's own folly and imprudence till they are paft remedy.

Full of fear, incertitude, and hefitation, Alphonfo could refolve upon nothing. He had carefully concealed himfelf from Dalinda and her father, when one night he was informed that Thelifmar had prepared every thing for his departure,
and

and that he was to go on board the Intrepid at break of day, which veffel was to carry him to Ceuta (a).

This intelligence determined the irrefolute Alphonfo; he fold his remaining ring, went to the captain of the fhip, obtained his paffage, got on board before day-break, and took poffeffion of his little cabin. He had not been there a quarter of an hour before he heard the voice of Thelifmar, and, prefently afterwards, the anchor was weighed, and the veffel fet fail.

Before dinner-time, when the paffengers muft meet at the Captain's table, Alphonfo collected force enough to defire a moment's audience of Thelifmar, which was immediately granted; and, with an anxiety and agitation impoffible to paint, he entered the cabin. Thelifmar was alone, and turning his head at the creaking of the door, he beheld Alphonfo. He could not forget the deliverer of his daughter; he inftantly arofe, ran to Alphonfo, and embraced him with all the warmth of the moft tender friendfhip.

Tranfported with joy, Alphonfo felt hope fpring in his heart! He anfwered the queftions of Thelifmar, however, with more embarraffment than

(a) A town in Africa, oppofite Gibraltar. John, King of Portugal took it from the Moors; after which it belonged to the Spaniards, to whom it was ceded by the treaty of Lifbon, in 1668.

truth.

truth. Afraid to confefs his faults, my father, faid he, had formerly an immenfe fortune; but now, with barely what is neceffary, he lives, retired on the peaceful banks of the Mondego. He approves my defire to travel, and hopes, with the education he has beftowed on me, I may become known and acquire fame, and———

What is your age? And what are your projects in quitting your country and your father?

I knew, fir, you were in Spain, heard you intended to go to Africa, and flattered myfelf you would permit me to follow you as a companion in your travels.

You were not deceived in me; I mean to traverfe a great part of the known world; if you will be the affociate of my labours, I joyfully confent.

Here Alphonfo, at the height of his hopes, embraced Thelifmar with tranfport, and fwore never to forfake him.

But, continued Thelifmar, my travels will not end in lefs than three or four years at fooneft, how do you know your father will confent to this long abfence?

Oh I am very certain———

Well, if you love ftudy, and, as I have no doubt, poffefs noble and virtuous fentiments, you fhall find in me a faithful friend, and a fecond father, happy, too happy, if by my cares and affection I

may

may fhew a part of my gratitude. Dalinda owes her life to you, and your empire over me is abfolute.

Alphonfo blufhed at the name of Dalinda, and, too much affected to reply, was filent.

I have need, added Thelifmar, of confolation, and hope to find it in your friendfhip.

Of confolation! Are you then unhappy?

I am feparated, and for four years, from objects the deareft to my heart! from my wife and daughter!

From Dalinda!

Yes. I durft not expofe her to the fatigues and dangers I fhall undergo. We travelled through a great part of Europe together, I parted from her at Cadiz, and while we are riding towards the African coaft, fhe is returning with her mother into Sweden.

Oh heaven! cried Alphonfo in anguifh; Africa and Sweden! What immenfe! what dreadful diftance between her and——you! How I pity you!——

Alphonfo could no longer reftrain his tears, and the converfation being interrupted by the entrance of the Captain, Alphonfo went into his cabin to hide and affuage the agitation of his heart. In defpair to think he muft be four years abfent from Dalinda, he yet was in fome meafure confoled by the friendfhip of her father, and determined

F 5   to

to neglect nothing by which it might be confirmed and increafed.

Thelifmar put feveral queftions to him, in the evening, and afked if he underftood the elements of any of the fciences?

Oh yes, anfwered Alphonfo, with great felf-fufficiency. There is nothing I have not been taught.

Do you know any thing of geometry?

I had a mathematical mafter ten years.

Have you any acquaintance with natural hiftory and philofophy?

Every thing of that kind is familiar to me: be-fides, I am paffionately fond of the arts, under-ftand mufic, and delight in drawing. I draw *flowers* charmingly.

Flowers! Do you love reading?

Very much.

Your language is not rich in good authors; but you know the Latin?

Oh perfectly! as you inay imagine, for my teachers faid I conftrued Virgil and Horace well. at ten years old; fo that I left the ftudy of the claffics at twelve, and have not looked at them fince, having had other employment.

And I warrant you left mathematics alfo foon after?

I did. I then read generally, and foon began to write verfes.

And

And from a fcholar became a wit. The meta-morphofis is not always fuccefsful.

My poetry was highly applauded.

By your friends, I fuppofe.

Oh univerfally.

How do you know?

Every body who vifited my father told me fo.

Alphonfo's anfwer made Thelifmar fmile, and he changed the converfation. Prefently afterwards the youth retired, perfuaded he had given Thelif-mar a high opinion of his knowledge and genius. The next day Alphonfo recollected the adventure of the mad bull, killed by the prick of a pin at the Fountain of Love, and afked Thelifmar the meaning of fo extraordinary a death.

Thelifmar replied, he had that very day received, from an old friend, juft returned from America, a poifon, fo powerful and fubtle, as to produce the effect of which he had been a witnefs; that this friend had given him a cafe, which enclofed the fatal pin that had been dipped in the poifon, and, defigning to make an experiment of its power, he happened to have it in his pocket (17).

But what furprizes me, faid Alphonfo, is, that I have never heard fpeak of this poifon.

I do not think that fo very furprifing, replied Thelifmar; for, if I am not miftaken, there are many other extraordinary things of which you have never heard.

I will

- I will not fay there are none, anfwered Alphonfo, but I dare prefume their number is very limited; for I have had teachers of all forts, and am not ignorant; add to which, I have read much, and feen and remarked more.

What prompted Alphonfo to brag with greater confidence was, he fuppofed he might do fo with-out danger of detection; he looked upon Thelif-mar as a plain man, who had only one purfuit, that of Botany, and imagined him to be exceed-ingly ignorant of every thing elfe; in which he was frequently confirmed, by the natural referve and modefty of Thelifmar.

Here Madame de Clémire flopped, put up her manufcript, and ended that evening's entertain-ment.

The next night, at the ufual hour, after having begged her children not to interrupt her any more by their queftions, Madame de Clémire thus con-tinue her narration.

At length they landed at Ceuta, and Thelifmar hired a lodging for himfelf and Alphonfo, at one of the beft houfes they could find.

Alphonfo's firft care, on his arrival, was to write to his father a long letter, very contrite and fubmiffive. In this he made a faithful confeffion of all his proceedings, implored his pardon, and permiffion to follow Thelifmar in all his travels; and, as the latter intended to flay at Ceuta long enough

enough for Alphonſo to receive an anſwer, he conjured Don Ramirez to ſend his orders inſtantly, promiſing they ſhould be obeyed, be they what they might. Not doubting his father had returned to Beira, his letter was directed accordingly.

Something eaſier, after thus in part relieving his conſcience, Alphonſo fell into his cuſtomary habits, ſung, played on his guittar, and drew various flowers, which he thought maſter-pieces, and which he conſtantly carried to Theliſmar, who he continued to believe was highly delighted with his talents.

Theliſmar ſent for him one morning, and ſaid, as I know you are exceedingly fond of muſic and drawing, I thought I might do you a favour, by bringing you to ſee two very extraordinary children. One is a little boy who draws aſtoniſhingly, in your ſtyle ; and the other a girl, who plays charmingly on the harpſichord ; come and ſee them.

So ſaying, he conducted Alphonſo into another room, but deſired him to ſtop at the door ; for, ſaid he, youth you know is timid ; and, as you are a connoiſſeur, you might diſturb them were you too near.

Very true, anſwered Alphonſo ; the girl bluſhed as we entered.

And

And can you then obferve her emotion? added Thelifmar.

Oh very plainly; fhe can hardly breathe, tho' her bofom heaves.

All this paffed at the far end of the room from the young artifts, and Alphonfo, happy in the fuppofition of his own repute, encouraged the muficcian as fhe played, calling out *brava! brava!* with as much pedantry and pride as any other demi-connoiffeur, who fuppofes a word like that from him confers fame and fatisfaction.

When fhe had finifhed her fonata, the little mufician made a low courtefy; Alphonfo applauded, and Thelifmar advanced.

Come, faid he, now let us fee the boy draw ——ftand there, behind him, and then you will overlook his work with more eafe. Alphonfo followed his directions, and remarked, it was odd enough the child fhould keep his gloves on, and furprifing enough that he fhould defign from his own invention, without any drawing to copy from.

And yet, faid Thelifmar, fee how that flower grows as it were, and is embellifhed beneath his fingers.

Wonderful! cried Alphonfo; aftonifhingly correct! Courage, my little fellow! There, fhade that outline a little; that's it! The little angel! I declare I could not do better myfelf.

All

All thefe praifes gave no difturbance to the child, who continued his work without remiffion, except removing it, to obferve it at a diftance occafionally, and blowing away the light duft of the crayon.

When the flower was finifhed, Alphonfo ran directly to kifs the child, and as fuddenly ftarted back with an interjection of aftonifhment.

Gently, faid Thelifmar, laughing, take care left you fhould demolifh the young artift.

Good heaven! It's a doll! a figure!

It is an automaton *(a)*.

And the mufician, what is fhe?

Own fifter to the defigner.

But did I not fee her breathe?

You thought fo; and you really faw her play with her fingers upon the harpfichord. Hence you may learn, Alphonfo, that it is unreafonable to place too high a value upon accomplifhments which automatons may poffefs.

I will break my guittar directly, and burn my drawings.

That would be wrorg, anfwered Thelifmar. We fhould be aftonifhed to fee a man pafs his life

---

(a) Every body at Paris, in 1783, faw the Automatons, of which this is a defcription. Another has fince been fhewn ftill more remarkable, for it plays at chefs with any perfon.

in

in playing on the guittar, and defigning flowers;
but no one will blame you, when you ufe fuch
things only as recreations, by way of agreeably
faving time, which would otherwife be loft, and
without being proud of fuch trifling accomplifhments.

This leffon made fome impreffion upon Alphonfo; but it was neceffary he fhould receive
many more, before a thorough reformation could
be effected.

Thelifmar was ready to depart from Ceuta, yet
Alphonfo had received no letters from his father:
imagining, therefore, that Don Ramirez approved
his projects, by his not being in any hafte to recall him home, he determined to proceed with
Thelifmar.

Some days previous to their departure for the
Azore Iflands, Alphonfo had obferved work-
men bufy about raifing a kind of machine in the
garden, the ufe of which he did not comprehend,
and learnt that it was done by the order, and under
the direction, of Thelifmar, of whom he therefore
enquired its ufe. The proprietor of this houfe
has told me, faid Thelifmar, that the lightning has,
twice, within thefe twenty years, fallen upon and
damaged the building, and I have promifed him it
fhall do fo no more.

And which way can you prevent it?

5

By means of the thing you have feen.

I confefs I do not comprehend how.

That I can readily believe; and yet it is not the lefs true that the lightning will now fall at the other end of the garden.

Four or five days after, there was a violent thunder-ftorm; Thelifmar went to the window, and pointing with his cane towards a black cloud, which was feen over the houfe, look, faid he, to Alphonfo, at that cloud; it is going foon to remove from us, and follow the path which I fhall direct: I intend that it fhall open, and be difperfed at the end of that walk; fo faying, Thelifmar raifed his cane towards the fky, while the cloud feemed obedient to his will, and durft not depart from the path which he prefcribed in the air; at that inftant he had the appearance of an enchanter, who, by the power of his magic wand, commanded the elements.

Good God! cried Alphonfo, what do I behold! You direct the clouds and they obey, they go to the fpot that you ordain.

You fee them affembled, faid Thelifmar, and now they fhall defcend, and the lightning fhall fall not thirty feet from yonder fpot. Scarcely had he fpoken before the thunder began to roar, and its bolts were difcharged exactly as Thelifmar prefcribed (18); who then fhut his window and

went

went out of his room, leaving Alphonſo petrified with aſtoniſhment.

The next day Theliſmar, in preſence of Alphonſo, read aloud a letter he had received from Dalinda. Alphonſo had by this time learnt the Swediſh language, to the ſtudy of which he had applied with great aſſiduity, ever ſince he had firſt been told Dalinda was a Swede; and, ſince he had travelled with Theliſmar, his progreſs in that language had been aſtoniſhing. He was enchanted at the letter of Dalinda, and could not repreſs his feelings while he heard it read; he found an inconceivable delight in underſtanding words traced by the hand of Dalinda; he heard the ingenuous detail of her thoughts and ſentiments, and imagined he heard her ſpeaking; he obtained a knowledge of the goodneſs of her heart and underſtanding, and that knowledge fixed for ever in the boſom of Alphonſo the moſt inconſtant of all the paſſions.

Alphonſo was very deſirous of having the letter in his own poſſeſſion, and ſeeing Dalinda's writing; but Theliſmar, after having read, put it in the drawer of his bureau. Alphonſo, with his eyes fixed upon this drawer, heard no longer the diſcourſe of Theliſmar, but fell into a profound muſing; Theliſmar therefore took up a book, and Alphonſo, recollecting himſelf, left the room.

In

In the evening Alphonſo returned to the ſame chamber, and Theliſmar, riſing as he ſaw him enter, ſaid, As you know we ſhall embark to-morrow morning for the Azores (a), I have various orders to give; if you will ſtay here, I ſhall be back in half an hour. So ſaying, he left Alphonſo ſitting oppoſite the bureau.

This bureau encloſed the letter of Dalinda, and the key was not taken out of the drawer: Alphonſo felt a temptation which at firſt he did not give way to; he paſſionately deſired to open the drawer, and once more read the letter. He felt how much ſuch an action was to be condemned, and yet, ſaid he, this is not to pry into the ſecrets of Theliſmar; he has read me the letter, I ſhall learn nothing new; I only wiſh to ſee, to contemplate, the writing.

At laſt, after various ſtruggles, Alphonſo ſtifled his ſcruples, approached the bureau, and tremblingly took hold of the key; but ſcarcely had he touched it before he received a ſtroke ſo violent

(a) The Azore Iſlands are ſituated between Africa and America, about two hundred leagues from Liſbon. Gonzallo Vello firſt diſcovered them about the middle of the fifteenth century, and called them Azores, or Hawks, from the number of thoſe birds he ſaw there. - They are nine in number; the town of Angra, in the Iſland of Tercera, is the capital.

that

that he thought his arm was broken. Alphonſo, terrified, ſtarted back, and fell into an arm chair. Juſt heaven! cried he, what inviſible hand is it that ſtrikes? (19)

The door opened, and Theliſmar appeared. What have you done, Alphonſo? ſaid he, with a ſevere tone of voice.

Oh, ſir, replied Alphonſo, you, whoſe ſupernatural art produces ſo many prodigies, you ſurely have the power to penetrate my moſt ſecret thoughts, and read my very heart.

I can read nothing there, anſwered Theliſmar, that can excuſe an act like this. Remember Alphonſo, to betray a truſt is unpardonable, and that a ſecond fault of this kind would for ever deprive you of my eſteem. As for the myſterious key, cried Theliſmar, it is only hoſtile to indiſcretion; it ſtrikes none but thoſe who would turn it without my leave. I now give you my permiſſion to open the drawer, which you may do without danger.

Alphonſo advanced, as he was deſired, towards the bureau, opened the drawer, and cried, yes Theliſmar, I ſee that nothing is impoſſible to you; your diſcourſe is full of wiſdom, and your actions of aſtoniſhment: deign, ſir, ever to be my guide, my tutelar genius! My ſubmiſſion, affection, and gratitude, will, I hope, render me worthy of your cares.

cares. So saying, Alphonfo, with a tender and
refpectful air, drew near to Thelifmar, who only
anfwered him by holding out his arms, and em-
bracing him with affection.

The next day, after this adventure, Thelifmar
and his young travelling companion embarked for
the Azores. After a happy voyage they landed
at the ifland of St. George (a) where they refted
for fome days.

Thelifmar lodged in a fmall houfe, the afpect
of which pleafed him; the owner was a Swede,
who had been fix years in the ifland. As they
had only one agreeable apartment, Thelifmar partook his bed-chamber with Alphonfo, and had a
bed made up for him befide his own. One night,
as Alphonfo and Thelifmar were in a found fleep,
they both awakened, and leaped up at the fame
moment; they imagined they felt the violent fhock
of an earthquake, and fled into a fmall garden,
whither the mafter of the houfe, and feveral fervants, who had likewife experienced the fame fenfation, ran for refuge; the latter brought flam-
beaux, for the darknefs of the night was extreme;
and, in expectation of a difafter like that of
Lifbon, they remained there in great anxiety for
the fpace of three hours; not having, however,
felt any more fhocks during this whole time, they

(a) Twelve leagues from Angra.

determined

determined then to return again to the houfe. Thelifmar and Alphonfo did not go to bed, but converfed till day-break.

Alphonfo, who now no longer hid the name of his father from Thelifmar, and who had often related to him the circumftances of the earthquake at Lifbon, did not let this occafion flip; but again gave a pompous defcription of the magnificent palace of Don Ramirez, and an emphatic enumeration of the jewels and diamonds he poffeffed before that cataftrophe.

When day began to appear, Thelifmar and Alphonfo went to the window, whence they had an extenfive and moft unufual profpect; how great was their aftonifhment, to fee the houfe they lived in, and the garden, totally feparated from the land, and forming a fmall ifland in the midft of the fea; they fhuddered at the danger they had been in, and could not conceive by what means the houfe, which had been thrown feveral fathoms from the main land, could fuftain fo violent a fhock without being deftroyed. It is no doubt, faid Thelifmar, the humble dwelling of a virtuous man, preferved in fo miraculous a manner by the juftice of a divine Providence.

As Thelifmar was fpeaking, his chamber-door opened, and the mafter of the houfe entered. This venerable old man, as he approached Thelifmar, fetched a deep figh, and faid, I come to

implore

implore your protection, fir—— not for myfelf,
but for my fon. Though fix years an exile from
my native land, I have not forgotten thofe men who
are an honour to it; your name, fir, is not unknown to me. Our Monarch is the protector of
genius and fcience; he honours you with a particular efteem, and I come to beg you will give me
letters of recommendation for my fon.

You intend to return into your own country
then?

Yes, Sir.

What accident firft brought you out of it?

I was boin in an humble condition; but, notwithftanding the fmallnefs of my income, I found
the means to give my fon a good education, much
fuperior to my rank of life. This fon anfwered
my expectations and cares fo well that he obtained, by his merit, at five and twenty, an honourable and lucrative employment. Some time
after he fell in love with an amiable, rich, young
lady, and was upon the point of marrying her,
when a dreadful accident obliged me to quit my
country. There was a rich merchant who
lodged in my houfe; this unhappy man was found
one morning murdered in his bed, and his coffers
broken open and robbed; all his fervants were
taken into cuftody; and I, immediately, delivered myfelf into the hands of juftice. The
                                        wretch

wretch who had committed the crime became my accuser; I had enemies, and the affair took an ill turn. Thanks, however, to the cares and protectors of my son, as they had not sufficient proof, I obtained my liberty; but could not recover my character, nor could endure to live with ignominy, in a land where I had been generally beloved, therefore determined to become a voluntary exile. I endeavoured to conceal my intentions from my son; but he guessed them too certainly from my preparations. I sold the little I possessed, and secretly departed by night; I regretted only the loss of my son. I left him, however, in possession of a good post; and knew that, notwithstanding our misfortunes, the young woman whom he loved still preserved her first affection. Consoled by such ideas, I endeavoured to support the excess of my misfortunes. I travelled in a postchaise, and at day-break perceived myself escorted, as it were, by a stranger galloping on horseback at some distance from my carriage; I looked out ——but what was my surprize at the sight of my son; it is impossible to express what I felt; I stopt, jumped out of my carriage, and was instantly in my son's arms. What hast thou done, cried I?

My duty, answered he.

But what is thy design, said I? bathing him with my tears.

To

To follow you, to confecrate the life you gave to your fervice.

But thy poft, thy future fortune.

I have left them, abandoned all for your fake; all, even the woman I love: you fee me weep, yet do not fuppofe, my father, but that I gladly facrifice every thing to you.

Since thou faweft my fatal refolution, wherefore didft thou not oppofe it; knoweft thou not the afcendant thou haft over me?

Appearances condemn you; and, though you are dearer than ever to me by your misfortunes, yet, having loft your honour, your prefent flight is neceffary; be comforted, you are ftill innocent and virtuous.

And doft thou not complain of thy own fate?

My own fate! Can it be happier! Have not I now an opportunity to prove my gratitude and filial affection? To comfort my father in his diftrefs? Shall not my hand dry his tears? Shall not my zeal and tendernefs deftroy their fource? Oh, yes, my father; fuffer the love and reverence of a fon to drive from your memory an unjuft country, ungrateful relations, and faithlefs friends. Heaven has deftined me to fulfil the facred duties of nature in all their extent; and fhould I, fhould you, complain of my fate? No; you my father, who are a model for parents, you fhould enjoy the folid glory, the fweet happinefs of having formed, by your own inftructions and your own example, a fon worthy of yourfelf.

You, fir, are a father, continued the old man, therefore can eafily imagine how readily I refigned myfelf, thus fupported, to my deftiny. We travelled for fome time before we fixed our abode here. My fon undertook fome branches of commerce, in partnerfhip, and bought this houfe, where we have lived in a contented mediocrity.

It was my intention here to have ended my days; but the intelligence which I received, about two months fince, has made me change this refolution. My innocence, at length, is fully acknowledged; the monfter who had been guilty of the murder, having committed new crimes, was apprehended and condemned. Before his death, he publicly acquitted me, by confeffing himfelf to be the murderer. We learnt, at the fame time, the young lady my fon loved was ftill unmarried. This has made me wifh once more to return to my native land. We intended to have departed in half a year; but the difafter of laft night, and the lofs of my houfe, which, though not deftroyed, is no longer habitable, muft haften my departure. It is therefore I come to afk recommendatory letters of you, fir.

I will

I will give them you with pleafure, anfwered Thelifmar, with emotion, and fuch as I would give a dear friend or brother. · Oh, yes; doubt not but our juft and beneficent fovereign will worthily reward the virtue of your fon.

Oh, fir! cried the old man, with tears of joy in his eyes, permit me to bring him hither, that he may thank you himfelf.

So faying, he went out, without waiting for an anfwer; and Thelifmar, turning towards Alphonfo, faw him mournfully leaning over a chair, and covering his face 'with his hands. Thelifmar perceived he was weeping; wherefore, faid he, would you hide your tears from me? Let them flow freely, they are an honour to your heart.

Thelifmar was miftaken: he attributed thofe tears to compaffion, which repentence and bitter remorfe made flow. How criminal did Alphonfo feel, when he compared his own conduct with that of the young man's whofe hiftory he had juft heard. This touching recital had torn his very heart, and made painful and afflictive the fweeteft of all fenfations, the admiration of virtue.

The old man returned, leading his fon by the hand; Thelifmar clafped the young man to his breaft, renewed the promifes he had made his father, and difmiffed them, penetrated with gratitude and joy.

G 2

Several

Several inhabitants of the island soon arrived, in light boats, to inquire the fate of those who inhabited the small house, which they had seen so suddenly thrown as it were into the sea; they told Thelismar, that all the neighbouring houses had been destroyed, while that belonging to Zulaski (for that was the name of the virtuous young man) had been thus miraculously preserved.

Thelismar and Alphonso went on board the boats, and desired to be conducted towards that part of the island which had suffered least from the earthquake. Scarce had they made a quarter of a league before they were petrified with astonishment, at beholding eighteen islands newly risen from the bottom of the ocean (20).

Ye new creations of a just and beneficent God! cried Thelismar; ye new-born isles, how does your aspect move my heart! Human industry will soon make you fertile. Oh, may you never be inhabited but by the virtuous!

After having coasted along some of the islands, Thelismar landed, and was received in a house, where Zulaski came to rejoin him the same evening. As Zulaski embarked on board a vessel bound for Lisbon, in his return to Sweden, Alphonso committed two letters to his care; the one for his father, in which was set down their route, and the places they meant to stop at, earnestly conjuring him to write, and inform Alphonso of his

will

will and pleasure; the other for a young man, who lived in the province of Beira, whom Alphonso entreated to write him news of his father, and to whom Alphonso likewise sent an exact itinerary of his travels.

Zulaski, after receiving these letters and those of Thelismar, departed without delay; and, a few days after, Thelismar and Alphonso embarked for the Canary Islands (a). Thelismar made a long stay at Teneriff; his first object was to go and admire the delightful district that lies between Rotava (b) and Rialejo: Nature seems there to have assembled all she has of pleasant, useful, and majestic. Mountains covered with verdure; rocks which cast forth pure water; fertile meadows,

(a) The number of these islands is seven; *Teneriff, Great Canary, Gomera, Palma, Ferro, Lancerrotta, and Fuerta-Ventura.* Their first discovery was strongly contested by both the Spaniards and Portugueze, each of which nations claimed the exclusive honour. It is, however, certain, the Spaniards, assisted by the English, first subdued them. Beside these seven, there are six smaller ones which surround Lancerrotta : the Canaries were not unknown to the ancients; they called them the Fortunate Islands.

(b) Two towns of Teneriff. Laguna is the capital of the island, and stands near a lake so named. At the time of the conquest, about 1417, the Spaniards called the natives Guanches; and the town of Guimar, in the island of Teneriff, is peopled chiefly by the descendants of these ancient Guanches.

fields

fields of fugar-cane, vineyards, woods, and fhades for ever green (*a*). Thelifmar and Alphonfo knew not how to tear themfelves from the enchanting fpot; they paffed an entire day there, fometimes walking, fometimes fitting beneath the fhade of the plantain-tree, reading paffages from Ovid, or Camoen's Lufiad.

Alphonfo's imagination, full of the agreeable ideas of fable, wifhed, before he quitted that charming place, to carve four verfes he had juft written upon the bark of a tree: he, for this purpofe, went to one, much like the pine in appearance, drew his knife, began to cut, and faw the blood follow the wound (21); tempted to fuppofe he had wounded a nymph metamorphofed to a tree, he recoiled with terror, and the murderous weapon dropt from his hand. Thelifmar fmiled, and encouraged him, by protefting there was nothing miraculous, nothing wonderful, in this feeming prodigy.

Thelifmar paffed fome days at Laguna, a large and beautiful town, the houfes of which are moft of them embellifhed by parterres and terraces, interfected by immenfe walks of orange and lemon-trees; its fountains, gardens, and groves, its lake, and aqueduct, together with the cool

(*a*) See Abrégé de l'Hiftoire Générale des Voyages, par M. de la Harpe, Tom I.

winds

winds by which it is refreſhed, render it a delicious habitation.

Thelifmar paſſed through ſeveral other towns, till he came at laſt to one called Guimar, where are ſtill found many families, the deſcendants of the Guanches, the ancient inhabitants of theſe iſles. Theſe people, though they have renounced the idolatry of their ſavage anceſtors, have yet preſerved much of their wild ſuperſtition, and many of their old cuſtoms.

One day, as Alphonſo was walking alone by the environs of Guimar, he ſtrayed thoughtlefsly into an unfrequented wood, in which he was ſoon loſt. In ſearching his way out, he got entangled in a thicket, which he could ſcarcely make his way through, and which led to a kind of deſert, without trees, ſhrubs, or verdure, a dry plain covered with ſhells, and bounded by a mountain. As he beheld this diſmal place, he recollected that Thelifmar had, more than once, adviſed him never to walk in ſtrange places without a guide, but this recollection came too late.

Night drew on, and Alphonſo walked a little father; at laſt, overcome with fatigue, he ſtopt near a hill ſurrounded with briers, underwood, and huge ſtones, heaped confuſedly on each other. In ſitting down on one of theſe ſtones he deſtroyed the equilibrium of others, which began to roll

G 4

with.

with confiderable noife. Alphonfo fprang from his feat to avoid being hurt, and, turning round, he ob-ferved that the ftones, by being removed, had dif-covered a cavity large enough for a man to enter.

He again drew near, and, looking down the cavity, faw, with furprize, fteps like a ftair-cafe: incited by unconquerable curiofity, he entered the fubterranean grotto, and defcended by fteps ex-ceedingly fteep : when at the bottom, he looked upwards, but could no longer fee the light of day. He was inclined to re-afcend, had he not per-ceived a light very diftinctly at a confiderable dif-tance. The fight of this determined him to ac-complifh an enterprize which promifed fomething extraordinary, and he purfued his road. He pro-ceeded to a kind of obfcure alley, at the end of which he found a fpacious cavern, lighted by lamps fufpended from the roof. Alphonfo looked round, and faw himfelf in the midft of two hundred dead bodies, arranged, ftanding againft the walls of this dreary vault.

Into what place of death has my temerity brought me ? cried Alphonfo ; it feems to be the cave of Polyphemus, or, perhaps, a robber ftill more inhuman, and the dead, here, have, no doubt, been the victims of this monftrous cruelty. Well, if I have not the prudence of Ulyffes, at leaft, I have his valour.

Alphonfo

Alphonso drew his fword, and determined to fell his life dearly; he would not attempt to fly, left he fhould be affaulted in the obfcure narrow paffage; he thought he might more eafily defend himfelf in the cavern; befides that, he fuppofed it certain the affaffins had already clofed the mouth of the cave. A profound filence, however, reigned in the dreary vault, and Alphonfo had time to confider the difmal and furprifing object by which he was environed.

He remarked, that none of the bodies feemed to fuffer putrefaction, or fent forth the leaft fmell, but that they had all preferved their features. Alphonfo was loft in thefe reflections, when he thought he heard the trampling of feet; he liftened attentively, and foon diftinguifhed the voices of people fpeaking in an unknown tongue.

Alphonfo would not begin the combat, on a fuppofition that it might not be their intention to attack him, but placed his back againft the wall, hid his fword, and was filent; he foon faw twelve men appear, walking flowly two and two, and cloathed after a ftrange fafhion. Their peaceable and grave countenances did not announce any thing inimical; but no fooner did they fee Alphonfo, than, uttering fhrieks of horror, rage, and indignation, blazing in their countenances. They drew the long daggers which they carried at their

G 5   girdles,

girdles, and fell, inftantly, altogether on Alphonfo, who, brandifhing his fword, received them with intrepidity.

The combat was obftinate and bloody ; the addrefs and valour of Alphonfo triumphed over numbers, and, tho' alone, againft twelve enraged foes, he was the conqueror. He received two flight wounds, but his fword was mortal to fome of his adverfaries, and the reft fled, terrified, and howling.

Once more alone in the cavern, Alphonfo tore his handkerchief, applied it to, and bound it on his wounds with his garter ; then, cutting with his fword the thong by which one of the lamps was fufpended, he took that lamp, and returned without delay ; he again followed the dark alley, arrived at the ftair-cafe, haftily afcended, found the cavity, and leapt from this frightful gulph with tranfport.

He imagined himfelf leaving the gates of hell, and returning again to life, when he breathed the pure air, and once more beheld the ftarry heavens. Oh ! my father ! exclaimed he ; Oh ! Dalinda ! and you, dear Thelifmar, fhall I enjoy the happinefs of feeing you once again ; you alone make life dear to me. And ought I not to preferve it, fince with life I may perhaps attain what moft I love ?

It was the decline of day when Alphonfo entered the cavern, and near midnight when he left it ;

guided

guided by the brightnefs of the moon and ftars, Alphonfo fled this fatal cave, and, after wandering full three hours, ftopped, as day began to break, near a lake, adorned by the lemon-trèe and poplar : tormented by exceffive thirft, the fight of limpid water rekindled his power and courage ; he drank heartily, and eat of the wild fruits ; yet found himfelf afterwards fo feeble and exhaufted he could no longer continue his route, but laid down upon the-grafs, oppofite to a moun-- tain covered·with verdure, and here and there a tree.   He repofed about three quarters of an hour in this wild and folitary place, when the heavens became cloudy, the wind began to rife, and fome drops of rain to fall ; the rain foon ceafed, but the wind continued with redoubled fury.   Alphonfo rofe, looked towards the mountain, and faw a fight that filled him with aftonifhment.

On the fummit of the mountain he beheld an enormous pillar rife, the colour of which feemed gold towards the bafe, and at the top a beautifully deep violet.   This pillar defcended with impetuofity from the mountain, breaking and overturning the trees that ftood in it's way, attracting and engulphing leaves and branches, and tearing up fome by the roots ; at the bottom of the mountain it paffed over a ditch, which it filled with ftones and earth ; it's paffage was marked by deep

furrows,

furrows, and, during it's dreadful and rapid courfe, it made a noife like to the bellowing of bulls.

The formidable column directed it's way towards the Lake, pumping up the water, and leaving the vaft bafin dry ; then, turning towards the north, it was loft in a neighbouring foreft (22).

To this phænomenon fucceeded a deftructive hail, the ftones of which were enormoufly large; they feemed cut in the form of a ftar, and were accompanied with long fplinters of ice, like the fharp blades of poniards (23.) Alphonfo took refuge under a tree, and preferved himfelf, as well as poffible, with his hat, which he held at fome diftance from his head, though he received feveral wounds on his hands.

The tempeft, at length, ceafed, the fky became calm, and Alphonfo, full of amazement, wounded, bruifed, famifhed, and fatigued, once more purfued his forrowful way. In about a quarter of an hour, he perceived, with exceffive joy, a human habitation ; it belonged to a Spaniard, who received him with humanity. Alphonfo informed him he had been attacked by affaffins, and learnt, in return, he was not more than two leagues and a half from Guimar.

Not in a condition to continue his route on foot, he determined to repofe for a few days, and wrote a letter to Thelifmar, which the Spaniard
kindly

kindly undertook to send: After which, Alphonso, profiting by the humane offers of his compassionate host, accepted food, suffered him to dress his wounds, and was put into an excellent bed made up for his reception.

After sleeping three or four hours, he awoke, rose, and dressed himself; the first person he met, at leaving the chamber, was Thelismar; he ran to his arms, Thelismar received him with a tenderness as sincere as his heart could wish. He was going to begin the recital of his adventures, when Thelismar interrupted him, by telling him he would hear nothing, then, but must think only of his cure. A carriage waits for us, said he; come, let us take leave of the generous and hospitable Spaniard, and return to Guimar.

As he said this, the Spaniard returned, followed by the messenger, who had brought back Alphonso's letter to Thelismar; he gave it to Alphonso, telling him that Thelismar had just left Guimar as he got there. How, then, said Alphonso to Thelismar, did you know I was here, if you have not received my letter? Of that I will inform you another time, answered Thelismar, smiling; at present it is time we should depart.

Alphonso, turning now towards his host, testified the warmest gratitude; then mounted the carriage with Thelismar, and took the road to Guimar. Thelismar would not allow him to exhaust himself himfelf with fpeaking, but, as foon as they got home, put him to bed, where he flept twelve hours, and awoke in perfect health. Thelifmar then defired an account of what had happened to him. Alphonfo began his recital with informing Thelifmar the things he had to relate were fo extraordinary and miraculous he was afraid they might be thought fabulous; and yet Thelifmar heard the whole hiftory of the cavern without feeming to fhew the leaft furprize; which did not fail, however, greatly to excite the admiration of Alphonfo, and which he could not refrain from teftifying.

Dear Alphonfo, faid Thelifmar, had you a little more thought, and a little lefs vanity, you had not in the firft place ran the terrible rifk you fpeak of, and, in the next, it would ceafe to furprize you.

I can eafily imagine, anfwered Alphonfo, had I been more prudent I had followed your advice, and not have wandered in a ftrange country without a guide; but which way has my vanity contributed to my aftonifhment?

Were it not for that, I repeat, you would not have been in any danger. In every place you have come to, yet, I have feen you occupied by one fole idea, that of being very defirous to inform and aftonifh all the world by the recital of the wonderful things you have feen. We have met with many men of merit, Botanifts, Aftrono-

mers,

mers, Mathematicians, and Mechanics, to whom you have fpoken a great deal, and liftened very little. When you come to a ftrange country, if you find any perfon to whom you can make your-felf underftood, you are careful not to afk them a fingle queftion, but very anxious they fhould learn all you can teach them. This kind of folly gives no one an opinion of your great capacity, but deprives you of the fruits of all your travels. If, for example, fince you have been here, inftead of amufing yourfelf fo repeatedly, by telling what happened to you at the Azores, you had afked the people concerning the curious things in their own country, and it's ancient inhabitants, you would have known your cavern had nothing miraculous about it, and that to enter it muft be at the hazard of your life.

Which way, fir?

By being told the cavern is one of the fepulchral depofits of the Guanches. Thefe ancient caves are difperfed in the deferts, and are only known to the Guanches, who carefully conceal the entrance to them. They vifit them in fecret; and, if they find a ftranger there, they hold him facrilegious, a victim devoted to death; and, from motives of barbarous fuperftition, think it their duty to kill him (24).

Well, fir, faid Alphonfo, a little piqued, I owe, at leaft, to my ignorance and want of thought,
the

the advantage of having feen one of thefe curious caverns.

I have killed no man in my own defence, anfwered Thelifmar; I have fuffered neither hunger nor thirft; I have not lain in the inclement air, nor have I afflicted my friend by the moft cruel anxiety; and yet, I have, as well as you, been in a fepulchral cave of the Guanches.

Have you! How did you get admittance?

I knew thefe caverns exifted, had a ftrong defire to fee them, found an opportunity of effectually ferving a Guanch, and prevailed on him to fecretly conduct and fhew me one of them.

Alphonfo had nothing to anfwer, but held down his head, and was filent; recollecting himfelf a little after, he continued thus: I flatter myfelf, that what I fhall farther relate may yet incite your wonder. After quitting the cavern, I ran, at firft, where chance directed me: coming to the banks of a Lake——

You need fay no more, interrupted Thelifmar, I know the reft.

Know the reft! how can that be? I was alone, and I have told nobody?

After drinking the water of the Lake, you gathered fome wild fruits, laid down on the grafs, and a dreadful tempeft arofe ——

Good heavens! by what magic, what enchantment can you tell all this?

The

The column defcended from the mountain, the Lake was dried up, and——

What do I hear ! exclaimed Alphonfo ; conde-fcend, fir, to explain this new miracle ; who can have told you thefe things ?

No one ; I beheld them all.

Beheld them ! where were you ?

Here, at Guimar, upon my terrace.

That was three leagues diftant from me !

Very true ; and yet, I repeat it, I faw you all the while.

I can no longer doubt ! O Thelifmar ! you are fome fupernatural Being !

A man, my dear Alphonfo; and by no means one of the wifeft.

Explain then this ftrange enigma !

A day would not be fufficient ; I might eafily teach you terms and names, and fhew you certain effects, but this would be treating you like a child. If you wifh to know caufes, you muft gain more folid inftruction.

It is what I wifh ; inftructions fuch as your's which can make me comprehend your actions.

Well, I will lend you books : and when you have read them with attention, we will converfe together. I will then begin to unveil fome of thofe myfteries at which you are fo much fur-prifed.

Oh

Oh give me thofe precious books; fee with what ardour I will ftudy them; how utterly I will reject all other books.

I do not wifh you fo to do; but the contrary. You love poetry; cherifh that predilection; but read none but good poetry; leave novels, and read books that fhall teach you to know yourfelf; dedicate two hours a day to the books I fhall give you; think much, fpeak little, and be attentive to others; this is all I afk.

Thelifmar then took Alphonfo to his clofet, and gave him a few books; when you have read thofe, faid he, I will communicate a treafure to you which, will finifh the work of inftruction. Look at that cheft; it contains the treafure I talk of.

Ah! faid Alphonfo, fighing, muft I never hope for other reward!———He ftopt and blufhed, and the tears gufhed in his eyes.

Alphonfo, replied Thelifmar, I do not pretend to deny that I love you; but, to obtain the reward to which you afpire, you muft become worthy of my efteem.

Oh my father! cried Alphonfo, falling at the knees of Thelifmar; yes! my father! permit me the ufe of a word fo dear, and expect every thing from me; I will obtain that precious efteem, that efteem, without which I could not live. What muft I perform? Speak.

Correct

Correct yourself of a thousand defects, and especially of your ridiculous vanity; rid yourself of ignorance, and acquire useful knowledge.

Every thing will be easy to me.

Know, then, I have read your heart. I authorize your hopes; but I require you should never converse with me on that subject.

Never! Oh heaven!——Nor of the object of——

Never pronounce her name.

Dreadful sentence!

To which you must submit: and remember, if you would gain my esteem, you must begin by proving the empire you have over yourself.

Well; I submit with joy——but suppose *you* mention her name?

You then may answer; otherwise never utter a word which can be construed into the least reference.

I obey; happily you have not forbad me to think.

No; I permit you sometimes to think of her.

Sometimes! Ever; not a moment of my life, but——

What retracting already?

Which way?

Have not you promised me seriously to follow your studies?

Most certainly.

And

And how may that be, if you always think of Dalinda ?

Dalinda !. heaven be praifed ! I did not firft pronounce her dear name.

Is it thus, Alphonfo, you keep your engagement ? Is it thus you will drive Dalinda from your imagination, every time we read or fpeak together.

Not mention her ! nor think of her ! how is it poffible !

Every thing is poffible to reafon.

But the effort will be fo painful, fo cruel : however, I will endeavour ; my fubmiffion to you is unbounded, for there is nothing you have not the right to exact, and the power to obtain.

Here Madame de Clémire broke off, for the evening, and fent her children to reft, who dreamt all night of nothing but moving columns and enchanted caverns ; they fuppofed that Madame de Clémire had told, by this time, every thing fhe could collect that was marvellous and extraordinary ; but fhe affured them, what they had heard was little in comparifon to what fhe fhould relate, for fhe had referved for the denouëment incidents ftill more furprifing. This affurance redoubled the extreme curiofity of her little family, which Madame de Clémire fatisfied, in the evening, by thus continuing her tale :

Alphonfo,

Alphonfo, notwithftanding the laws prefcribed by Thelifmar, thought himfelf the happieft of mortals; his paffion was authorized by the father of Dalinda, he might reafonably entertain the fondeft hopes. Nothing was wanting to his felicity, but a letter, from Don Ramirez, containing a grant of the pardon he had implored.

Thelifmar did not leave the Canary Iflands, without firft vifiting the famous Peak of Teneriff (a); after which he embarked for the Cape de Verd Iflands. During the voyage, Alphonfo followed, with ardour, the plan Thelifmar had prefcribed for his ftudies; but he had great difficulty to fupprefs his continual inclination to fpeak of his paffion, he was prevented only by the fear of offending Thelifmar; and ftill he would occafionally hazard fome indirect allufions, the true fenfe of which Thelifmar would not underftand.

At laft, Alphonfo, unable longer to endure this conftraint, imagined a means to break filence, which appeared to him fublime. He preferved the fafh of Dalinda, as a thing the moft precious in his poffeffion; this, notwithftanding the great-

(a) This mountain rifes in the form of a fugar-loaf, in the middle of the ifland of Teneriff; its height is fo prodigious that the length of the road, which winds along the mountain to attain it's fummit, is faid to be 15 leagues; and yet, they fay, the mountain called Chimbo-Raco, one of the Cordilleras, in Peru, is much higher.

nefs

nefs of the facrifice, he determined to give back
to Thelifmar; the fuppofition that he fhould thus
enjoy the pleafure of fpeaking of this paffion, and
of Dalinda, the hope that Thelifmar would confider this act as proceeding from an eftimable de-
licacy, and the poffibility that he might therefore
refufe the fafh, were his inducements. Full of
thefe ideas, Alphonfo entered, one morning, with
a triumphant air, the apartment of Thelifmar. I
come, faid he, to make a confeffion, which muft be
followed by a painful facrifice.

Of what nature?

You muft firft give me your permiffion——to
fpeak of her——I only afk to accufe myfelf, to
repair my falut.

Well, well, let us hear; explain, explain;
though I dare engage the fault is not very im-
portant.

In my eyes it is; feelings the moft forcible, the
moft affectionate, on which the deftiny of my life
depend.

Come to the point? What have you to tell me?

You know to what excefs I love Dalinda.

Your preface difpleafes me, Alphonfo.

But it is neceffary; it leads to the confeffion of
my fault. The day on which I firft faw Dalinda,
on which I received a new exiftence, after
your cruel departure, overcome and loft in grief,
I wandered, like one diftracted, feeking in vain
fome

some traces of the celeſtial Being I had beheld ; conducted, at laſt, by ſome ſecret charm, I returned, approached the Fountain of Love, where chance, or rather the God of the Fountain, moved by my deſpair, gave into my hands a pledge the deareſt, the moſt precious.

Dalinda's ſaſh, you mean, interrupted Theliſmar. I recollect ſhe loſt it.

Behold it here, cried Alphonſo, with emphaſis, drawing it from his pocket ; behold that ſaſh, the ſole conſolation of an unfortunate lover : I poſſeſſed it without your knowledge ; it was wrong ; I have not the happy right to keep it ; a well founded de-licacy obliges me thus to ſurrender it:

Your ſcruples are very juſt, replied Theliſmar ; give it me, give it me, added he, taking the ſaſh ; and I promiſe to return it, Alphonſo, the very firſt proof I ſhall receive from you of real ſincerity and confidence.

How ! cried Alphonſo, thunderſtruck, do you doubt my ſincerity ?

I have great right ſo to do, at the very moment you employ artifice.

Artifice !

You bluſh, Alphonſo, and well you may ; but I dare hope, had you ſucceeded in deceiving me, your confuſion would have been ſtill greater. Had you ſeen me delighted with your candour, your de-licacy, your generoſity, tell me how you would

4   have

have looked, how you would have behaved, while hearing your own falſe praiſes ?

Alas ! ſaid Alphonſo, ſhedding the tear of re-pentance, you know my heart better than I do myſelf ; I own, I only ſought a pretext to ſpeak of Dalinda.

And you hoped I ſhould be your dupe ; hoped I ſhould return the ſaſh.

I was deceived ; convinced by falſe reaſoning.

No ; 'tis now you are deceived ; you never were *convinced* ; we connot hide from ourſelves what is in it's own nature blameable : in vain would ſpecious reaſons gloze over actions, and call them noble, delicate, refined : the heart and the conſcience give ſuch reaſonings the lie !

What have I done ! Oh Theliſmar ! has this fault, the whole extent of which I now per-ceive, has it deprived me of your eſteem without return ?

No; your ingenuous manner of acknowledging it, the ſincerity of your repentance, the neglected education you have received, and your conſequent want of reflection, all plead in your excuſe. Did I think cunning a part of your character, I ſhould then hold you paſt hope ; but, notwithſtanding the unworthy ſubterfuge you have juſt been guilty of, I read franknefs and candour in your boſom ; and I am certain, Alphonſo, you will yet vanquiſh your defects.

The

The concluding fentence gave a little fatisfaction to Alphonſo, who promiſed within himſelf to let no occaſion flip of demonſtrating his reformation to Thelifmar.

Our travellers landed firſt at the iſland of Goree, from thence they went to Rufiſco, and afterwards by land to Fort St. Louis, on the Senegal. They ſaw the Sereres, a Negro nation, whoſe hoſpitality, ſimplicity, and gentleneſs, they admired; theſe virtues are undoubtedly the effect of their love of labour and agriculture, which particularly diſtinguiſhes them from moſt other ſavages, who are generally indolent, and diſdain to cultivate the earth.

One night, as Thelifmar and Alphonſo, with their guides and companions, were rambling in a ſandy and deſert place, they ſaw a prodigious tree, the height of which did not exceed ſixty or ſeventy feet, while it's monſtrous trunk was above ninety in circumference; it's lower branches projected almoſt horizontally, and, as they were prodigiouſly large and long, their own weight bent them almoſt to the ground; inſomuch that they found, beneath this ſingle tree, a vaſt and extenſive kind of grove, which might eaſily give ſhelter to three or four hundred men (25).

After having admired this aſtoniſhing production of nature, our travellers continued their route. A few paces from the tree they beheld a lion, extended on the ground, and feemingly dead. Alphonfo was determined to examine the animal nearer, and Thelifmar followed. When they came up to him, they found he ftill breathed, but was without power and motion, and apparently expiring; his jaws were open, full of pifmires, and bloody.

Alphonfo pitied the creature, wiped away the infects that tormented him with his handkerchief, then taking a bottle of water from his pocket, poured it all down his throat, while Thelifmar held the end of a piftol to the entrance of that terrible jaw, in cafe of a too fudden recovery. The lion was greatly relieved by the water, and feemed with his languifhing eyes to thank with great expreffion and gratitude the compaffionate Alphonfo, who did not leave him till he had adminiftered every fuccour in his power.

Alphonfo and Thelifmar, rejoined their fmall company, and followed a path that led through fome exceffively high grafs. As Thelifmar was walking on before, at the end of the meadow, he fell into a kind of pit, and fuddenly difappeared. Alphonfo ran and faw him fitting in the pit. Thelifmar faid he had got a fprain, and that it was impoffible he fhould rife and walk without his affiftance. As Alphonfo was going to defcend and take him in his arms, he fuddenly heard a dreadful hiffing, and faw a monftrous ferpent, at

leaft

leaſt twenty feet long, in the pit, with head erect making towards Theliſmar, who, after an effort to riſe, fell helpleſs again among the graſs (26).

Alphonſo inſtantly leaped into the pit, placed himſelf between Theliſmar and the Serpent, drew his ſword, attacked the horrid Reptile, and, with a vigorous and firm ſtroke, ſevered his head from his body ; then turning to Theliſmar, he helped him up, and lifted him out of the pit.

Theliſmar embraced Alphonſo; you have ſaved my life, ſaid he, I could neither defend myſelf nor fly ; the Serpent was coming to attack me, and his bite is mortal. I promiſe you, Dalinda ſhall be informed of this. Alphonſo was too much agitated to anſwer, but preſſed Theliſmar with tranſport to his boſom. Gently, ſaid Theliſmar ſmiling, take care of my right arm, it is broken.

Broken ! cried Alphonſo ; good God !

Had it not, do you think I would not have defended myſelf ?

And you have not uttered the leaſt ſympton of complaint or pain !

You, dear Alphonſo, have no right at leaſt to be ſurprized at the fortitude of others.

Oh my father ! replied Alphonſo, I want the fortitude to ſee you ſuffer ; come, let us join our company. He then raiſed Theliſmar gently on his ſhoulders, and, in ſpite of all he could ſay,

carried

carried him, without ſtopping, to where their companions were waiting.

Theliſmar was obliged to remain in one of the
Negro huts, where he was humanely received.
He had a ſurgeon with him, who ſet his arm, and
in about eight or ten days he continued his route.

They came to the country of Foulis. The
king of theſe ſavages calls himſelf Siratick, and
ſome travellers give this name to his kingdom.
He entertained Theliſmar and his companions
with great hoſpitality, and propoſed they ſhould
accompany him to the chace of a lion, which,
within a few days, had committed great ravages in
his ſtates.

The king, young, courageous, and deſirous to
ſhew the company his valour and addreſs, ordered
his followers and the ſtrangers to ſtop ; and,
mounted on an excellent horſe, galloped to attack
the furious animal, which, perceiving him, leaped
to the combat. The Siratick let fly an arrow,
and the lion, wounded, advanced with a dreadful
bellow.

Alphonſo now forgot the orders of the king; he
darted like lightning, thinking him in danger,
and flew to his ſuccour: he had drawn his ſword,
and galloping with incredible ſwiftneſs, paſſed
near a tree, againſt which, by accident, his ſword
ſtruck and ſnapped ſhort in two. Alphonſo him-

ſelf,

felf, fhaken by the violence of the fhock, could
hardly keep his feat: his horfe fell, and the fame
inftant, the lion, feeing a new enemy coming
armed, had abandoned the Siratick, and rufhed
towards him; his dreadful claws were inftantly
buried in the fides of the horfe, and Alphonfo, dif-
armed, and without defence, thought his death inevitable. The Negroes, fearing to kill him, durft
not fhoot at the animal.

Thelifmar, the fame moment that Alphonfo
had gallopped to the combat, would fain have followed; but the Negroes, already irritated at the
young man's difobedience to the orders of their
king, angrily and violently held him, notwithftanding his crics, his fury, and defpair. What were
his feelings, when he faw the lion bounding to devour the overthrown Alphonfo? Oh! unhappy
young man! cried he.

But oh! what furprize! Oh! joy unhoped!

No fooner had the lion beheld the face of Alphonfo than all his rage was loft; he crouched to
him, and lifting up one of his bloody paws, wounded by an arrow, laid it gently on the hand of Alphonfo, and feemed to fhew him his hurt, and afk
his affiftance.

Alphonfo fhuddered, and remembering the adventure of the dying lion, cried, Oh noble animal!
I recollect thee; may thy example ever confound
ingratitude, and bring to fhame thofe who would

erafe

erafe from their memory the good which others have done them !———Yes, fince thou haft fo nobly granted me my life, I will fave thine in my turn, and defend thee, be the confequence what it will.

Alphonfo then ftaunched the blood of the wound, and tearing his handkerchief, made a bandage, which he faftened round the paw.

Thelifmar and the favages beheld the fpectacle with aftonifhment. His chirurgical operations ended, Alphonfo rofe : his horfe lay wounded and dying. The lion once more approached him, licked his feet, and careffed him a thoufand times. Alphonfo retreated gently : the lion ftopped, looked after him, then fuddenly turned about, directed his courfe toward a neighbouring foreft, and difappeared, leaving the fpectators of this ftrange adventure motionlefs with amazement (27.)

Thelifmar, after having preffed Alphonfo to his bofom, after having embraced him with the dear affection of a father, reproached him for his temerity and imprudence. Had you, faid he, afked the nature of this chace, or rather, had you liftened to the account which others gave of it, you would have known the Siratick was in no danger ; but that, ufed to thefe kind of combats, he waited for the lion to bury his jevelin in his throat; that he would have afterwards leaped off his horfe, and ended him with his fabre.

I promife,

I promife, my father, faid Alphonfo, I will be more attentive another time, and more prudent ; at prefent I have faved the life of my lion, of my generous and noble animal, and I am happy.

Yes, replied Thelifmar, but the Siratick is little pleafed with your difregard of his orders ; and though your motive was his prefervation, he will not pardon you, for having robbed him of the honour of the victory ; it will be therefore prudent not to ftay long in his territories *(a)*.

Accordingly, the next morning, Thelifmar, Alphonfo, and their followers, quitted Ghiorel, and continued their paffage up the Senegal, as far as the village of Embakana, near the frontiers of the kingdom of Galem ; they afterwards croffed the Gambia, traverfed the States of Farim *(b)*, and, after having travelled a great extent of country, arrived at Guinea.

Here Alphonfo met with an adventure which furprifed him exceedingly. As he was walking through a wood with Thelifmar, their converfation turned on the immortality of the foul. Would you believe, faid Thelifmar, that there are men fo deprived of fenfe as to maintain we have no other advantage, over inferior animals, than that of a more perfect conformation ; and

(a) See l'Abrégé de l'Hiftoire des Voyages, Tom. II.

(b) Or Saint Domingue.

who have faid, in exprefs terms, that if the horfe (that intelligent animal) had, inftead of a hoof, a hand like us, he would perform whatever we do *(a)*.

What! would he draw? would he defign?

What think you?

I do not think he could; he might, perhaps, trace fome unmeaning imitations.

The parrot, the pye, the jay, and various other birds, have the faculty of fpeech; that is, can learn a few words, but can neither comprehend their meaning, nor, confequently, apply them juftly: befides, there are many exifting animals, the conformation of which, both interior and exterior, is perfectly fimilar to that of man; they walk like him, have hands like his, and yet they neither build palaces nor huts; nay, they are even lefs induftrious than many other animals.

Monkies you mean; in fact, they are very adroit. And pray what fay thofe authors to this, who defire the horfe to have hands?

They acknowledge that the monkey might, from his conformation, be capable of doing the

(a) This ftrange reafoning is found in a work entitled De l'Efprit.

The Tranflator cannot forbear to enter his proteft here, againft the inconclufivenefs of the arguments he is obliged on this accafion to tranflate; without meaning to infinuate thereby any opinion of his own. T.

fame.

fame things as man, and that his natural petulance is an impediment; that he is always in motion; and could you deprive him of that reſtleſsneſs, that vivacity, he would be man's equal *(a)*.

And yet he does not ſpeak.

No; though in certain ſpecies the tongue and the organs of voice are the ſame as in man; and the brain is abſolutely of the ſame form and in the ſame proportion. *(b)*.

The brain in the ſame proportion! how can that be? The monkey is ſo ſmall!

Do you think yourſelf acquainted with all the ſpecies?

Why——Yes.

Thoſe you have ſeen were reſtleſs and turbulent.

Certainly; for wh'ch reaſon, the objection of the authors you mention ſeems juſt; in my opinion, beings which are perpetually in motion, however excellent their conformation, cannot learn, cannot become perfect.

But ſuppoſe the objection. you think ſo ſtriking ſhould originate only in a profound ignorance of things which are known to the whole world.

(a) All this is found exactly in the ſame work De l'Eſprit.

(b) See M. de Buffon on Quadrupeds, Tom. XVI. Edition in 12mo.

H 5

How!

How! People who write books ignorant of things known to all the world !——

Your doubt, dear Alphonſo, proves how little you have read.

Juſt as Theliſmar, ſaid this, Alphonſo gave a ſtart of ſurprize, and, jogging Theliſmar, cried ſoftly, Look, look——there——right before you; what ſtrange creature is that ſitting under the tree ?

Here let us break off, ſaid Madame de Clémire, interruping her narrative, I feel myſelf a little hoarſe this evening.

This was ſufficient to ſtop every entreaty to continue, though her young auditors were very deſirous to hear an explanation of what this *ſtrange creature* might be.

The next day, a quarter before nine, Madame de Clémire indulged the ardent curioſity of her children, by taking up her manuſcript and reading as follows :

Theliſmar looked firſt at the animal, and afterwards at Alphonſo. What do you think of that figure, ſaid he ?

It is a ſavage, replied Alphonſo, and exceedingly ugly. He riſes ! holds a ſtaff in his hand ! he avoids us !

And you take it for a man ?

Certainly I do.

It

It is a Monkey.

Monkey! what of that fize! he is higher than I am; he walks upright like us, and his legs have the form of ours.

Notwithftanding all which, it is a beaft *(a)*; " but an exceedingly fingular one, and which man " cannot fee without looking at, without knowing " himfelf, without being convinced, his body is " the leaft effential part of himfelf *(b)*."

How you aftonifh me! but is this monkey, who was fitting with fo much tranquillity at the foot of a tree, as reftlefs and precipitate in his motions as the fmall monkies?

No; " his walk is grave, his actions circum- " fpect, his temper gentle, and very different from " that of other monkies;" *(c)*——he has not the hoof of a horfe, he is higher than we are, formed as we are.——" The Creator would not form the " body of a man abfolutely different from all other " animals; but, at the fame time that he has given

---

(a) The Orang-Outang, fome of which are above fix feet high.

(b) M. de Buffon.

(c) In fpeaking of a monkey of another fpecies, called Gibbon, M. de Buffon fay, " this monkey feems to us to " have a natural tranquillity, and gentle manners; his mo- " tions are neither too fudden nor too reftlefs; he takes kindly " whatever is given him to eat, &c.

H 6 " him

" him a material body, a form fimilar to that of
" the monkey, he has breathed his divine fpirit
" into this body; he had done the fame favour,
" I do not fay to the monkey, but, to that fpecies
" of beaft which feems to us the moft ill orga-
" nized, fuch fpecies would. foon have become
" the rival of man ; quickened by his fpirit it had
" excelled others, had thought, had fpoken.
" Whatever refemblance there may be then be-
" tween the Hottentot and the monkey, the in-
" terval which divides them is immenfe ; fince the
" Hottentot within is diftinguifhed by thought, and
" without by fpeech *(d)*."

Alphonfo liftened to this difcourfe with admiration. At prefent, faid he, I am defirous to learn
how thofe authors, who pretend that it is our form
only which makes us fuperior to other animals, will
anfwer thefe arguments.

They do not know the animal that we have juft
feen, nor many other fpecies nearly like him, defcribed by all travellers ; yet their works are modern, and, as I have faid, thefe are facts known to
all the world.

Thelifmar here fat' down near a lake furrounded by rocks ; their giude propofed they fhould
wait for the reft of the company, whom they had

(d) M. de Buffon.

left

left at a confiderable diftance. He had feated himfelf under the fhade of fome trees, and taking two books from his pocket, gave one of them to Alphonfo, pointing out a chapter, which he de-fired him to read with great attention.

Alphonfo promifed he would ; adding, that he would go farther off and fit down, to be free from all difturbance.   This he accordingly did, and fat down, at about two hundred yards diftance, on the banks of the lake.

Inftead of reading he fell into a profound re-verie : the murmurs of the water, the frefh ver-dure, the rocks, all retraced a fcene which he had not the power to banifh from his mind : it recalled to memory the Fountain of Love; the form of Dalinda was prefent, he could think of nothing but her, and at laft could not refrain from repeat-ing a name fo dear.

Certain that Thelifmar could not hear him, he fang, in an under voice, a fong he had made to her memory.   As he finifhed the laft line of his fong, he heard footfteps, and turning his head, faw The-lifmar coming ; he took up his book and was filent, but the inftant he had done, a foft though fonorous voice feemed to iffue from the rocks, and again re-peated the couplet he had fung.

Thelifmar heard the name of Dalinda, as he ap-proached, and his aftonifhment was exceffive;

when

when he found it was not Alphonfo who was finging. As foon as the air was ended, he was going to queftion Thelifmar concerning this prodigy, when another voice began the fame couplet; fcarce had this fecond voice ceafed finging, but a third, from the oppofite fide, again repeated the fame words, and the fame founds: filence then fucceeded, and the concert ended (28).

What enchantment is this? cried Alphonfo.

We muft confefs, faid Thelifmar fmiling, the fawns and fylvans of thefe rocks are dangerous confidants; the nymphs of the Fountain of Love were more difcreet; but come, give me my book, and tell me if you are fatisfied with the chapter I defired you to read. Alphonfo blufhed, and anfwered only with a figh; and Thelifmar, changing the converfation, rejoined the reft of the company.

Thelifmar continued his route by the Gold Coaft, the kingdom of Juida, and the kingdom of Bennin: in this latter country he found the natives lefs favage, and more civilized than their neighbours. He next traverfed Congo, and here it was that Alphonfo had nearly loft his life, in confequence of his natural imprudence and impetuofity.

The fmall caravan of travellers being on their march, Alphonfo was walking about two or three hundred yards before the reft. They approached a
large

large pond furrounded by the huts of favages; and Alphonfo, looking forward, thought he faw, on the other fide of the pond, a long brick wall built upon the border : not conceiving what could be the ufe of this wall, he haftened forward to examine it ; but as he drew near, perceived this imaginary wall had motion.

He then thought that, inftead of a wall, he diftinguifhed warriors clothed in red, and ranged in order of battle : he prefently after obferved fentinels ftationed in advance, and foon faw he was difcovered ; for, the moment the fentinels perceived him, the alarm was given, and the air refounded with a noife much like the found of a trumpet.

Alphonfo ftopped, and while he was deliberating whether he fhould proceed or go back, he faw the army begin to move, rife from the earth, and at laft to fly away. Alphonfo then learned, with extreme furprize, that this formidable fquadron was nothing but enormous red birds, of fo bright a colour that, when they took flight, their wings abfolutely feemed inflamed.

Alphonfo had a gun, and being defirous of taking one of thefe extraordinary birds to Thelifmar, he fired at the flock and killed one. Several Negroes, on hearing the firing, immediately came out of their huts, which flood by the pond, haftily running. As foon as they faw Alphonfo dragging
away

away the bird he had killed, they fent forth the moft horrible cries, when inftantly all the other Negroes left their habitations, and came in crouds to attack Alphonfo, who faw himfelf affaulted on all fides by a fhower of ftones and darts.

Had it not been for the arrival of Thelifmar and the other travellers, Alphonfo could not have efcaped with life; but at fight of them the favages fled, and he came off with a few flight wounds, and a fevere reprimand from Thelifmar, who informed him, that the Negroes held the bird he had killed in fuch veneration, they would not fuffer any one to do it the leaft injury, but thought themfelves obliged in confcience to revenge the death of a creature which they held facred.

Alphonfo learnt, alfo, from Thelifmar, that the noife, which he had compared to the found of trumpets, was nothing but the cry of the birds, which is fo loud and fhrill that it is heard at more than a quarter of a league diftance (29).

Thelifmar continued his journey, only ftopping occafionally among various hordes of favages, whofe manners he wifhed to know. Of all the barbarous people of Africa, the nation which he thought moft interefting was that of the Hottentots: their virtues furpaffed their vices; they fulfilled, in their whole extent, the duties of friendfhip and hofpitality; and their love of juftice, their

courage,

courage, benevolence, and chaftity, rendered them far fuperior to other favages *(a)*.

It is remarkable that, among the Hottentots, the education of youth is committed to the mothers till the age of eighteen, after which the males are received to the rank of manhood; but, before that period, they have no communication with the men, not even with their own father *(b)*.

During their fojourn among the Hottentots, Thelifmar was walking one day with Alphonfo: their guide carried a wallet with provifions, it being their intention to dine during their walk. As they were croffing the ruftic bridge of a fmall river, the guide let the wallet fall, and, fearing probably the anger of the travellers, took to his heels and difappeared. This event was very difagreeable to Alphonfo, he being exceedingly hungry.

I am certain, faid Thelifmar, I can find my way; but before we walk any farther, let us reft a little under the fhade of thefe trees. They fat down on the grafs, and Alphonfo continued to complain of having a great way to go, and nothing to eat, when Thelifmar cried Silence, let us liften. Alphonfo prefently heard a very fhrill cry,

(a) See l'Abrégé de l'Hiftoire Générale des Voyages, Tom. III.

(b) See the fame work and the fame volume.

which,

which, to his great aftonifhment, Thelifmar anfwered in a graver tone: then, rifing, faid, Since
you are fo very hungry, Alphonfo, come with me,
and I'll give you a dinner.

Thelifmar then uttered feveral fucceffive cries;
and Alphonfo perceived a green and white bird,
which hovered round them. Let us follow this
new guide, faid Thelifmar, he will recompenfe
us for the carelefTnefs of the other who has run
away.

Alphonfo knew not what to think, but walked
filently, and looked attentively at the bird, which
in a few minutes went and refted itfelf upon a
large hollow tree: Stop, faid Thelifmar, the bird
will come and feek us, if he has any thing good
to difcover. As he faid, fo it happened, the bird,
feeing they did not approach, redoubled his cries,
came back to them, and then returned to his tree,
where he fluttered and perched.

Come, faid Thelifmar, he invites us to dinner
with fo good a grace we cannot refufe him. So
faying, he went to the tree, and, to the extreme
aftonifhment of Alphonfo, found a bee-hive in it,
full of honey.

While our travellers were eating the honey, the
bird, having fled to a neighbouring bufh, appeared
greatly interefted at all that paffed: It is but
juft, faid Thelifmar, to give him his fhare of the
booty: Alphonfo, therefore, left a fpoonful of honey
upon

upon a leaf, which, as foon as they were gone from the tree, the bird came and eat.   In the courfe of half an hour, the bird fhewed them two other hives; and Alphonfo, fatiated with honey, merrily continued his route (30).

· Thelifmar quitted the country of the Hottentots, and embarked for the ifland of Madagafcar; afterwards he journeyed through all the eaftern coaft of Africa; then quitted that part of the world, and, after a fhort ftay in the ifland of Socotora, landed in Arabia Felix.   He vifited Mecca (31), and Medina (32), traverfed a part of the Defert, entered Africa again by the Ifthmus of Suez, and came to Cairo (33); here he admired the famous Pyramids of Egypt (34) from thence he went to Alexandria, where he found a veffel ready to fet fail for the ifland of Thera (a).

Thelifmar, within the laft two months, had feveral times read over with Alphonfo tranflations of the Iliad and Odyffey.   Alphonfo, joyfully leaving the burning and barbarous climates of Africa, was delighted to find himfelf once more in Europe, beneath the azure fkies of Greece, in places where all the pleafant fictions of fable may be traced, and among people whofe manners Homer has defcribed.

(a) An ifland of the Archipelago, to the north of Candia; it is a part of the iflands called Santorin, or Santorini, from Saint Irene, the patron of them.

Before

Before they left Thera, Thelifmar and Alphonſo learnt that the Volcano, which is ſituated in that iſland, began to give great uneaſineſs to the inhabitants, by appearing to re-kindle, ſmoke, and caſt forth ſtones.

The next morning our travellers roſe with Aurora, and were conducted towards the Volcano; when they were at a league's diſtance, their guide ſtopt, telling them he thought he heard a very uncommon noiſe; our travellers liſtened, and heard a kind of bellowing, which ſeemed to ariſe out of the earth. They proceeded, however, about a quarter of a league farther; in proportion as they approached, the bellowing increaſed, and was ſoon accompanied with frightful hiſſings; at the ſame time they obſerved that the ſmoke of the Volcano grew thicker, and became of a deeper red.

Let us return, ſaid Thelifmar.

Scarcely had he ſpoken before a horrible noiſe was heard; and, as they turned their heads to look, while flying towards the ſea-coaſt, they ſaw the mountain all on fire, covered with flames, which roſe to the clouds, and caſting forth on all ſides volumes of red hot ſtones, and blazing matter. The terrified guide, loſing all recollection, led them aſtray, and took them a road which brought them back towards the Volcano.

As they now ſtood fronting this fearful mountain, they ſaw, with horror, torrents of fire running

ning

ning impetuously down its sides, and spreading over the plain: these destructive rivers burnt and overthrew every thing that opposed their passage: at their approach, the herbs and flowers withered, the leaves grew instantly yellow, and dropt from the trees; the brooks disappeared, the fountains were dried up, and the birds dropt breathless from the scorched branches.

At the same time, vast clouds of hot ashes and cinders, burnt white, obscured the air, and fell like rain upon the earth, breaking the branches, rooting up trees, and rolling with horrid din from the mountain to the plains, echoing far and near among the resounding rocks.

Thelismar and Alphonso fled from these desolate places, and, after long wandering in unknown paths, came at length to the sea-side; they judged, when at a distance, by the roaring of the waves, that the sea was violently agitated. They judged rightly; it was dreadfully tempestuous, though the air was entirely calm.

They were considering this phænomenon with an astonishment which was soon redoubled. Suddenly there appeared, in the middle of the waves, incredible volumes of flames, which, instantly spreading and dissipating in the air, were succeeded by an innumerable quantity of burning rocks, that were projected from the deep abyss of the ocean, and raised above the waters (35).

The

. The tempeſt after this decreaſed, the ſea was appeaſed, and ſome of the Iſlanders, who paſſed that way, informed Theliſmar that the Volcano no longer vomited flames. When the eruption was ended, Alphonſo and Theliſmar returned to their lodgings, and, two days after this memorable event, left that unhappy iſland.

From hence they went to the iſland of Poli-candro *(a)*, where they found a Swediſh traveller, a former friend of Theliſmar's, who offered to ac-company and guide them in their walks through the iſland. He brought them to his houſe, which he would partake with them ; and, after ſupper, addreſſing himſelf to Alphonſo, ſaid, My dwelling, you ſee, is ſimple, devoid of ornaments ; but, if you love magnificence, I have the means of gratifying your taſte. I am ſo happy to ſee my old friend, once more, that I have formed the project of giv-ing him an entertainment in a palace, the rich-neſs and brilliancy of which may well ſurprize you.

Frederic, for that was the name of Theliſmar's friend, then roſe, called his ſervants, who came with torches, and went forth with Alphonſo and Theliſmar.

. They came in about half an hour to an enor-mous maſs of rocks. Behold my palace, ſaid Fre-

(a) One of the Cyclades, to the ſouth of Paros and Anti-aror.

deric:

deric; the afpect, it's true, is a little wild, but we muft not always judge from appearances. Stop here, a moment, if you pleafe, and let the fervants enter firft.

The fervants then diftributed torches to about a dozen men who had followed them, each of whom lighted his flambeau, and proceeded forward. When Frederic faw them at a certain diftance, he and his company began to follow.

They had not gone above a hundred paces before they perceived an immenfe arcade, and their eyes were immediately dazzled by the fplendor of light. Come in, faid Frederic, this is the periftyle of my palace; what think you of it?

The queftion was addreffed to Alphonfo, but he was too bufy in confidering the brilliant fpectacle before him to reply. The walls of this vaft periftyle feemed covered with gold, rubies and diamonds; the ceiling decorated with waving garlands and pendant ornaments of cryftal; any, the very floor on which they trod, was paved with the fame rich materials (36).

Pardon me, my dear mamma, cried Caroline, for interrupting, but I can hold no longer. Were thefe pure diamonds?

No; they only feemed fuch; but the refemblance was fo perfect as to deceive the eye moft accuftomed to confider fuch objects.

well,

Well, that is very fingular; and is it true, dear mamma, that fuch a palace once exifted?

It exifts ftill.

O dear, ftill!

Yes; in the ifland of Policandro.

Oh the charming ifland! Will you fhew it us to morrow, mamma, in the map?

Yes; willingly.

Mamma, if you will permit me, my next geographical leffon fhall be to trace upon the maps all the travels of Alphonfo; for I can remember them all perfectly, and fo I can all the extraordinary things he has feen.

So be it; but, in the mean time, let us continue our tale.

Frederic fhewed Alphonfo how extenfive this fuperb palace was: and, after having paffed more than two hours in examining and contemplating the wonders before them, they once more returned to the houfe of their hoft. Alphonfo learnt, from Thelifmar, that the pretended palace of Frederic was all the work of nature; and the knowledge of this encreafed his admiration.

Thelifmar, having formerly made the tour of Italy, had no intention of returning thither; but his friend Frederic, who was going to Reggio, entreated his company; to which Thelifmar the more readily confented becaufe it was the only part of Italy he had not feen.

Frederic

Frederic, Alphonfo, and Thelifmar, left Poli-
candro, and failed for the Morea *(a)*. Here they
beheld the ruins of Epidaurus and Lacedæmon.
From the Morea they went to the ifland of Ce-
phalonia, whence, once more embarking, they
failed for Reggio *(b)*. The day after their arrival
in that city, our three travellers breakfafted in the
chamber of Thelifmar, the windows of which
looked towards the fea; their converfation was
interrupted by a thoufand fhouts of joy, heard
from every part. Alphonfo ran out, inftantly, to
know what was the reafon of fuch noify and ani-
mated acclamations: he afked feveral paffengers,
who all anfwered, ftill running as they fpoke, We
are going to the fea-fide to fee the *Caftles of the
Fairy Morgana.*

Alphonfo returned, and gave an account of this
ftrange anfwer; our travellers, therefore, opened
their windows, and beheld a fight the beauty and
fingularity of which furpaffed every thing they had
hitherto feen.

" The fea which bathes the coaft of Sicily
" began to fwell and rife by degrees; in a little
" while the huge waves formed a perfect reprefen-
" tation of an immenfe and dark chain of moun-

(*a*) The large peninfula of ancient Attica.
(*b*) Appertaining to the kingdom of Naples, in Calabria
Ulterior; there is another city of the fame name in Italy, in
Modena.

I " tains;

" tains ; while the furges which wafhed the coafts
" of Calabria remained with a tranquil and fmooth
" furface, like to a vaft and fhining mirror, gently
" inclining towards the walls of Reggio. This
" prodigious looking-glafs foon refleéted a moft
" miraculous picture ; millions of pilafters, of
" the moft elegant proportion, and ranged with
" the utmoft fymmetry, were diftinétly feen, re-
" fleéting all the bright and varied colours of the
" rainbow ; fcarcely did they retain this form a
" moment, before thefe fuperb pilafters were bent
" and changed into majeftic arcades, which like-
" wife foon vanifhed, and gave place to an innu-
" merable multitude of magnificent caftles, all
" perfeétly alike ; while thefe palaces were fuc-
" ceeded by towers, colonnades, and afterwards by
" trees and immenfe forefts of the cyprefs and
" palm (37)."

After this laft decoration, the magic picture
difappeared, the fea refumed its ordinary afpeét,
and the people, who ftood upon the ftrand, clapped
their hands in tranfport, a thoufand times repeating, with joyous fhouts, the name of the Fairy
Morgana.

And fo, mamma, interrupted Pulcheria, we are
at length come to our Fairy Tales again ?

Indeed we are not : this laft phænomenon, as well
as all the other, is taken from nature.

But

But there is a Fairy called Morgana, you know, mamma:

I have only told you what the people of Reggio fay; who are generally ignorant and credulous, are fond of fables, and eafily adopt them.

But thefe magic pictures?

Are produced by natural caufes.

I cannot conceive, at prefent, why every body do not pafs their lives in travelling, reading, and acquiring knowledge, in order to underftand and fee things fo curious and interefting; but, dear mamma, be pleafed to continue your recital.

Alphonfo began to think like you, the aftonifh-ment which fo many extraordinary events conti-nually raifed excited an ardent curiofity, and a ftrong defire of obtaining knowledge; his trifling amufements no longer pleafed; he became thought-ful, fpoke with referve, and liftened with attention; but, in proportion as his mind became enlight-ened, he difcovered faults in his paft conduct, every recollection of which made him bitterly repent.

He could not now comprehend how it was poffible he fhould have forfaken his father. The obftinate filence of Don Ramirez grievoufly afflict-ed him; he ardently defired to arrive at Conftan-tinople, where he expected to find letters from Portugal: and though he had a paffionate attach-ment to Thelifmar, though he had almoft a cer-

I 2   tainty

tainty of obtaining the hand of Dalinda, he yet determined to quit the former in Turkey, and return to Europe, there to facrifice his hopes and happinefs to filial duty, if he received no intelligence from his father.

This refolution plunged him into a ftate of melancholy, of which Thelifmar fearched in vain the caufe; which he even augmented, in wifhing to diffipate, by marks of the moft tender affection. He often fpoke to Frederic, in his prefence, of Dalinda, to drive away his dejection; while thefe converfations, far from foftening the fecret pangs of Alphonfo, but embittered them the more. Thelifmar at laft took leave of Frederic, quitted Reggio, and returned to Greece; and, travelling through it, came to Conftantinople towards the end of April.

Alphonfo found a letter at Conftantinople, from Portugal, which he received with inexpreffible anxiety: it was not from Don Ramirez, but informed Alphonfo his father had returned to Portugal, had paffed fome time at Lifbon, and had left that city, declaring he was going to undertake a voyage of eighteen months. The letter added, that nobody doubted Don Ramirez had had feveral private converfations with the King, and that the purpofe of his voyage was fome fecret negociations; that they were in great expectations of feeing him once more in office, becaufe his fucceffor and

enemy

enemy had been di'graced, eight days after his departure.

The gentleman, who wrote an account of all
this, ended his letter by faying, he had not feen
Don Ramirez, as Alphonfo had defired him to do,
becaufe, being on a tour to France, he had not
returned to Lifbon till three weeks after his departure.

From the date of this letter, Alphonfo calcu-
lated that his father could not be in Portugal in
lefs than fifteen or fixteen months, he therefore
abandoned his projeçt of returning thither immediately : in façt, having no money, he had no
means of fubfiftence in the abfence of Don Ramirez ; and he was pretty certain his travels would
be ended, and he fhould return to Europe in lefs
than a year. The filence of his father deeply afflicted him ; but the affurances, of his health and
fafety were great confolations, and he did not doubt
but time, and his future conduçt, might regain the
affeçtions of his father.

Alphonfo, now lefs forrowful, lefs abfent, converfed with Thelifmar as formerly ; who appeared
fo fatisfied with the change he had remarked in him
that Alphonfo thought he might venture to fpeak
of Dalinda. At firft, Thelifmar was fatisfied with
gently reminding him of his promife ; and Alphonfo, emboldened by this indulgence, feveral times
fell into the fame error; till, at laft, Thelifmar was

I 3   difpleafed,

difpleafed, and Alphonfo was obliged to be filent, though he ftill fought occafions to fpeak his fentiments indirectly, and to complain of the reftraint impofed upon him.

Frederic had given Thelifmar letters of recommendation to one of his friends, a Greek, who poffeffed a charming houfe on the canal of the Black Sea: this Greek, whofe name was Nicandor, was not then at Conftantinople. Alphonfo and Thelifmar, therefore, in about a fortnight, went to Buyuk-Dairai, a village eight miles from Conftantinople (a) where Nicandor and his family paft a part of the fummer.

It was the firft of May, and ten in the morning, when our two travellers arrived at Buyuk-Dairai. As they entered, they faw the ftreets full of young people, elegantly clothed, and crowned with garlands, finging and playing on various inftruments; every houfe was decorated with flowers, feftoons, and rofes, and adorned by a multitude of young Grecian beauties, furrounded by flaves magnificently clothed.

This fpectacle delighted Alphonfo; and Thelifmar, acquainted with the cuftoms of Greece, informed him, that it was thus they celebrated every firft of May; that on this folemn day, young lovers

(a) The fcite of this village is very pleafant. Ambaffadors and various others, have country-houfes there. *Voyage litteraire de la Grece*, par M. Guys, Tom. I.

fixed

fixed coronets of rofes over the doors where their miftreffes dwelt, and fang their praifes under their windows (38).

Alas! faid Alphonfo, they are happy, for they are heard. That favour, replied Thelifmar, is no proof of their happinefs.

But what happens when two rivals meet under the fame window, or at the fame door?

They faften their coronets on each fide, and fing alternately.

After our travellers had ftopt fome time in the firft ftreet, they continued their way; and Alphonfo, perceiving at a diftance, a houfe more ornamented with flowers than the reft, faid, certainly, that is the habitation of fome celebrated beauty; he was confirmed in this opinion when, coming nearer, he beheld two charming young virgins ftanding in a large balcony.

The guide informed them this was the houfe of Nicandor, and they entered; the mafter came immediately to receive them, and, after having read the letter of Frederic, embraced them both affectionately, and teftified the livelieft hopes that they would remain with him fome time. Nicandor and all his family fpoke French tolerably well: Thelifmar underftood that language perfectly, and Alphonfo knew fomething of it.

Nicandor called his flaves, who conducted the travellers into a fpacious hall, the walls of which

were

were Parian marble, where a bath was prepared (39).

After bathing, Nicandor came and conducted them into the apartment of his wife Glaphira; she was feated upon a fofa, with her two daughters, Glycera and Zoë, and an old and venerable woman, the nurfe of Nicandor, whom, according to the cuftom of the modern Greeks, the family called Paranama; a gentle epithet, expreffive of gratitude, and fignifying fecond mother (40).

The daughters were fuperbly dreffed, both had long floating robes, white veils bordered with gold fringe, and girdles richly embroidered, faftened with buckles of emeralds (41).

Glaphira and Nicandor queftioned Thelifmar concerning his travels, and prevailed on him to recount fome of his adventures. After which they fat down to table, and, their repaft being ended, Zoë brought her lyre, and accompanied feveral duets which fhe fang with her fifter (42).

This agreeable mufic being over, Nicandor propofed a walk to his guefts, which they readily accepted.

He led them into the meadows, in one of which they beheld a multitude of fhepherds and fhepherdefles, clothed in white, and adorned with garlands of flowers, almoft all holding in their hands branches of the green palm, the myrtle, and the orange-tree; fome danced to the found of the lyre, while

while others gathered flowers, and fang the praifes and the return of fpring.

Look, faid Nicandor, at that young virgin, crowned with rofes, and finer than her companions; fhe is the Queen; fhe reprefents the Goddefs of Flowers; and, while called by the charming name of Flora, receives the homages of all the village throng: but her reign is fhort; it is the empire of youth and beauty, and ends before the decline of day.

While Nicandor was fpeaking, the young Queen gave a fignal, and all the fhepherds affembled round her; one of her virgin companions then fang a hymn in honour of Flora and the fpring; at the end of each couplet of which the fhepherds repeated in chorus this burthen:

"Welcome fweet Nymph! bleft Goddefs of
"the May."

After this they continued their dances (43).

Having walked round the meadows feveral times, Nicandor re-conducted his guefts back to his houfe, where they found Glaphira and her daughters furrounded by their flaves, employed at embroidering, each in turn relating fhort ftories and moral fables (44). Though Alphonfo did not underftand Greek, he was charmed with the picture he beheld. The youthful Zoë was fpeaking, and Thelifmar conjured her to continue her recital: fhe accordingly began again, with a grace

I 5   which

which was augmented by the bloom of her cheeks, and her modeft diffidence.

Zoë related the hiftory of a young virgin on the eve of her marriage, quitting the paternal manfion. She told her tale with equal truth and feeling, and painted the interefting and deep grief of a tender and greatful daughter tearing herfelf from the arms of her beloved family. Glycera liftened to the detail with extreme emotion; involuntary tears then bathed her down-caft eyes, and watered the flowers fhe embroidered : her mother, who obferved her, called her, with a broken voice, and held out her arms. Glycera rofe, ran, and threw herfelf at her mother's knees melted in tendernefs.

The hiftory is interrupted; Nicandor approaches Glycera, kiffes her affectionately, clafps her to his bofom : the lovely Zoë quits her work, and flies to her fifter's arms : the flaves teftify their feelings at this touching fcene : and Nicandor, in a few moments, taking Alphonfo and Thelifmar into another apartment, explained the caufe of what they faw, by firft telling them the fubject of Zoë's fable, and then informing them that Glycera was herfelf on the eve of marriage.

The very fame evening the young man, chofen to be the fpoufe of Glycera, fent large bafkets magnificently embellifhed, containing ornaments and nuptial prefents for Glycera and the family.

The

The next day the young Greek came, attended by his parents and friends, to the houfe of Nicandor; the beauteous and affecting Glycera appeared; fhe had on a filver robe, embroidered with gold and pearls, and faftened with a girdle of diamonds; her treffes floated upon her fhoulders, and a Hymeneal crown adorned her head, while fhe wept, and hid herfelf in her mother's arms.

Glycera received the parental benediction, kneeling, which Nicandor pronounced with great tendernefs, but with a folemn and firm tone; while the feeling mother, incapable of articulating a word, raifed her fwimming eyes to heaven, and preffed between her trembling hands the hands of her daughter. After this moving ceremony, the two families, united, and, followed by all their flaves, walked to church; this fuperb train was preceded by a band of vocal and inftrumental mufic: after them came the young virgin, fupported by her father and mother; her pace was flow, timid, and trembling; her down-caft eyes were evidently bedewed with tears fhe vainly endeavoured to retain. According to the ancient ufage of Greece, the Torch of Hymen was carried before her, and her flaves, hufband, relations, and friends clofed the proceffion, in which order they arrived at church.

After the ceremony, the bride and bridegroom were re-conducted in pomp to their houfe, the

I 6

front of which was illuminated, and ornamented
with flowers and foliage; cups of wine were
given to all the guests, and the young people re-
ceiv d nosegays twined with threads of gold, the
person who presented them saying, *Go ye and
marry also.* These words roused the attention of
Alponso, who looked at Thelismar. A banquet
succeeded, and the dancing continued till midnight (45).

Alphonso left this feast in a sorrowful mood;
the remembrance of Dalinda, and the fear of never,
perhaps, tasting a happiness such as he had been
a spectator of, afflicted him deeply. This melancholy continued several days, but it was insensibly
dissipated by the new and agreeable objects which
surrounded him, and especially by the tenderness of
Thelismar.

Thelismar and Alphonso every day, after their
walk, went regularly to the embroidering room,
whither Glycera, and the young friends of Zoë,
always came; Nicandor explained, in a whisper,
to the strangers, the subjects of the tales related
by these young Greeks; and, when Zoë spoke,
Alphonso became particularly attentive: he often
would change places with Nicandor or Thelismar,
the better to see them embroider, and he remained
longest always at the frame of Zoë: he praised all
their performances, but he only looked at that of
Zoë; he once more undertook to design flowers,

s   and

and offered every day a new pattern to Zoë for
her embro dery ; at laft he began continually to
vaunt of the manners and cuftoms of Greece, and
thought Buyuk-Dairai the moft delightful place he
had ever feen.

One morning, when he was alone with Thelifmar, the latter praifed him highly for his conduct.
I am quite enchanted with you, continued he,
dear Alphonfo ; I fee you begin to acquire a command over yourfelf.

Do I ?

Yes ; and I cannot conceal my fatisfaction ; for
thefe three weeks paft you have learnt to hide
and overcome that melancholy at which I was fo
uneafy ; you are obliging, amiable, and attentive
in company ; and what muft have coft you more
than all the reft, you fpeak no longer of Dalinda ;
be affured I feel the value of this effort.

So faying, Thelifmar embraced Alphonfo, who
fuffered his embrace with a cold and mournful air,
without making any reply ; a moment's filence
fucceeded. Alphonfo walked thoughtfully about
his chamber, then, fuddenly turning, No, Thelifmar, faid he, I muft not deceive you ; I fhould be
unworthy of your kindnefs, were I to leave you in
an error——he ftopped and blufhed.

What would you fay ? anfwered Thelifmar.

Perhaps, exclaimed Alphonfo, I am going to
ruin myfelf.

Ruin

Ruin yourfelf! what, by being fincere! and to me, Alphonfo! Can you fuppofe it?

Know then, that though my heart is always the fame, though Dalinda alone has touched it, and though, were it not for the hope of becoming your fon, life would be a burthen——yet——if I have ceafed to fpeak of her, if I have feemed chearful, do not attribute this conduct to the efforts of reafon, but, on the contrary, to——

Come to my arms, interrupted Thelifmar, come, noble and dear Alphonfo, this proof of thy candour and confidence juftifies my affection for thee.

Oh, my father! Oh, my indulgent friend! cried Alphonfo.——

See, continued Thelifmar, how fleeting a fenfation love is, dear Alphonfo, when not confirmed by an affectionate and folid friendfhip: two large black eyes, an ingenuous countenance, a fweet fmile, and five or fix ftories which you did not underftand, have made you, in three weeks, forget the object of that paffion which you pretended was fo violent.

It is true, that the young Zoë amufed and interefted me; it is true, fhe banifhed my forrows from my mind, and that Dalinda was lefs frequently prefent to my imagination, but fhe was ever in my heart.

Do not deceive yourfelf, Alphonfo, you have

yet

yet no real attachment to Dalinda, becaufe, at prefent, you know nothing of her but her form.

.But that form proc'aims a foul fo pure, fo fuperior! Befides, I know Dalinda by her letters,
her acquirements, her tendernefs for you! In a
word, Dalinda is the daughter of Thelifmar, and
is not that enough to make her paffionately beloved?

All that is not a fufficient foundation for a deep
and durable attachment, which cannot exift without mutual confidence and friendfhip. But let me
afk you a queftion concerning Zoë: how has it
happened that you have not perceived the impreffion
fhe has made upon you?

- It muft certainly be a want of reflection.

Imagine then, for a moment, the confequence
of wanting fuch reflection. I have more than
once obferved that Nicandor and Glaphira do
not approve your exceffive refpect for Zoë; fo
many attentions, a preference fo marked, muft foon
injure the reputation of the young virgin to which
they are paid. You have rifqued troubling the repofe of, and bringing forrow into, a houfe, where
the treatment we meet demands all our gratitude.

Heavens! you make me fhudder—But hence-
forth I will think, I will each day feverally examine
my actions, my fenfations; and, what may be
more effectual, I will every day confult you.
Never more will I conceal my thoughts from you.
And

And now, faid Thelifmar, I muft quit myfelf of a promife which I have not forgotten. So faying, he opened a cafket, took out the fafh of Dalinda, and gave it Alphonfo. It belongs to you, faid he, you have a right to it, fince I promifed it to you on the very firft proof of your fincerity.——

Oh Thelifmar, faid Alphonfo, greatly affected, what a moment have you chofen! And am I permitted to receive a pledge fo dear in this houfe!

Yes; if it ftill continues dear to you; if you have ftill the fame fentiments.

Then I dare accept it——Alphonfo threw himfelf at Thelifmar's feet, received the fafh of Dalinda, kneeling, and kiffed with tranfport the hand that gave it.

Remember, Alphonfo, faid Thelifmar, this, from a father, is no light, no trifling gift; from this moment our engagement is mutually facred. I have adopted you as a fon; I promife you an amiable and virtuous companion for life; of whom you muft become worthy, not by a romantic paffion, but by a ftable and uniform virtue. Continue to infoim your mind, and improve your temper and underftanding; it is thus you muft prove your love for Dalinda, and fhew your gratitude for my affection.

Nicandor came and interrupted their converfation, and Alphonfo, too much moved to fupport

the

the prefence of a third perfon, retired : he wifhed for folitude, that he might indulge, without con-ftraint, the tranfports of his heart. It is needlefs to obferve that, from that day forward, he defigned no more patterns for Zoë, paid her no other atten-tions than fuch as good breeding demanded, and avoided going into the embroidering room.

The family of Nicandor, however, met an un-expected afflicion; one of their friends, lately returned from the Ifle of Çalki *(a)*, to which he had made a fhort voyage, fell ill, and died in four days time. Nicandor related many interefting par-ticulars of the friend he had loft; and told how he had renounced the riches and honours which he had a right to expect, that he might yield him-felf, without controul, to the delights of friendfhip and ftudy.

This fage, continued Nicandor, who had re-tired to a pleafant houfe (46) near mine, diftri-buted the greater part of his income to the un-fortunate; he confecrated the reft to the embel-lifhment of his habitation : his heart was virtuous, and his temper fimple; he cultivated his garden himfelf, watered his flowers, and bred birds, for

(a) It is the ninth of the Propontis Iflands, anciently called Dæmoneri, or the Ifles of the Genii. M. d'Anville miftakenly calls them *Les Ifles du Prince*, which name is given by the inhabitants only to the fourth. *This Note is by M. Guys.*

which

which he made an extensive aviary. Such were his innocent amusements. Beloved by his friends, adored by his slaves, he had a sister worthy of himself, who lived with him, went with him everywhere, and who never can forget his loss. Tomorrow, continued Nicandor, we shall perform the last duties of friendship; his sister will conduct the funeral rites.

But how will she have the fortitude, said Thelifmar?

You are a man, answered Nicandor, who wish to know our manners, to study nature, come and see this sorrowful ceremony; you will there behold the workings of despair. Grief among us is never repressed, it is seen in all it's energy. Among a people who are slaves to appearances and custom, sorrow is mournful and mute, but here it is eloquent and sublime.

This conversation excited the curiosity of Thelifmar, who did not fail, with Alphonso, to follow Nicandor to the funeral of his friend. They went first to the house of Euphrofine, the name of the sister above-mentioned, and entered a chamber hung with black, where the corpse, magnificently clothed, and with the face uncovered, was laid in a coffin; the slaves were kneeling round, and venting their grief by tears and groans. Among them Thelifmar distinguished an old man,

still

ſtill more profoundly afflicted than the reſt, to whom Nicandor went and ſpoke.

Thelifmar queſtioned Nicandor concerning this old man, who anſwered his name was Zaphiri. He was preſent at the birth of him we lament, ſaid Nicandor; he is almoſt paſt the uſe of his limbs, and the impoſſibility of following the burial adds to his grief: he has juſt told me, there is but one remaining pleaſure for him on earth, the feeding of the birds, and the culture of the flowers, which once were his dear maſter's delight.

Nicandor was ſpeaking, when Alphonſo and Thelifmar felt their blood run cold at the broken accents and dolorous cries they heard: it is the wretched Euphroſine, ſaid Nicandor. Immediately a woman appeared in long mourning garments, with diſordered hair, pale cheeks, and bathed in tears; ſhe was ſupported by two ſlaves, and ſeemed ſcarcely able to drag her ſlow ſteps along; the auguſt and affecting picture of a grief ſo profound, made her natural beauty more ſtriking, more majeſtic; and her ſhrieks, her lamentable groans, were uttered in an accent ſo penetrating, and ſo real, that it was impoſſible to hear them, and not at once feel aſtoniſhment, terror, and the moſt heart-rending pity.

The Patriarch and his attendants ſoon after arrived. The corpſe was taken up, and a funeral

dirge

dirge began. After paffing through the village, and proceeding lefs than a mile into the country, they came to a place over-fpread with cyprefs-trees, tombs, and fepulchral-columns.

Euphrofine fhrieked, and hid her face in her veil, as foon as fhe perceived at a diftance the fepulchre prepared for her brother. They came at laft to the grave, the proceffion ftopt, the Patriarch pronounced the burial-fervice, kiffed the dead, and retired.

Euprofine then, raifing up her veil, came fuddenly forward, and fell upon her knees by the fide of the coffin.

Oh, my brother! cried fhe, receive the laft farewell of thy unhappy fifter: Oh, my dear, my affectionate friend! Do I then look upon thee for the laft time?——My brother!——Is this my brother?——Alas! yes, here are his features ftill; but, oh, infupportable thought! while I bathe him with my tears, while I call him, while my heart is torn with defpair, his countenance ftill preferves the fame unalterable gloom, the fame mournful tranquillity——Oh dreadful filence!—— it is the filence of death——my brother is but a fhadow; it is his image only Euphrofine kiffes ——What then, have I for ever loft thee!—Shall I never fee thee more!——Never!——never!—— No——I cannot fubmit to this——this eternal ——this horrible feparation. No, I will not fuffer the

the hand of cruelty to tear thee from my arms, and plunge thee in the tomb——Stop Barbarian, ftop, forbear to dig his grave——pity my grief, or dread my defpair.

The Patriarch again advanced to take away the body. Euphrofine fent forth a dreadful fhriek; her flaves flew to her affiftance, and, in fpite of her ftruggles, held her at fome diftance form the grave, while fhe, quite befide herfelf, rent her garments, and tore up her hair by the roots to fcatter on the coffin.

Her tears then fuddenly ceafed: motionlefs, and ftupid, her eyes were fixed upon the coffin, as they were lowering it in the tomb. But when fhe faw them place the marble over it, by which it was to 'be for ever hid, fhe fhook fearfully, and fhrunk back. 'Oh God! cried fhe——Is it then done!

So faying, the colour left her lips, her eyes clofed, and fhe fell fenfelefs into the arms of her flaves. They bore her away from the tomb; and, as foon as fhe came to herfelf, her friends and relations, according to cuftom, conveyed her home.

To get to the houfe, it was neceffary fhe fhould crofs the garden; here, as foon as fhe entered, fhe met the old flave Zaphiri, holding in one hand a hoe, and in the other a watering-pot; fhe looked and fhuddered; it was the occupation of the deceafed;

deceafed; fhe ran towards the flave, What art thou doing, Zaphiri, cried fhe?

Alas! I am tending the flowers my mafter loved fo much.

Miferable old man, faid fhe, feizing the hoe, ţby mafter is no more; this place muft be ever-more the place of forrow, of defolation; let all that embellifhes it die; be it's pleafures annihilated; open the nets; give liberty to thofe birds, whofe warbling and mirth diftract my heart; and thefe flowers, nurtured by my brother's hand, let them perifh with him.

So faying, Euphrofine wildly and rapidly ran, cutting down, and trampling on, all the flowers in her path (47).

This affecting fcene made a ftrong impreffion on the heart of Alphonfo; tell me, faid he, to Thelifmar, when they were at home, how does it happen that ideas fo oppofite may be the refult of the fame feelings? Why does this old man de-light to cultivate the flowers of his mafter, while Euphrofine, on the contrary, finds a kind of confo-lation in their deftruction?

Which of thefe two actions do you prefer? afked Thelifmar in return.

That of the old man appeared moft natural, and yet the other moved me more.

Common feelings produce only common effects, while a deep fenfibility naturally begets extraordi-

nary

nary ideas and actions: thus, for example, if the woman, who has interested us so much, if Euphrosine had reason, taste, and discernment, as well as such strong passions, and if she were then to write, her works would certainly possess originality, energy, feeling and truth.

And is it not the possession of these qualities which constitutes genius ?

Undoubtedly ! If genius did not originate in the soul, would it be a gift so precious, so desirable, or could it so powerfully excite envy ?

Thelismar and Alphonso passed some few more days at Buyuk-Dairai ; after which they took leave of Nicandor and his amiable family, quitted Greece, and entered Asia by Natolia. They staid a little while at Bagdad (a) and Bassora (b), and stopped at the island of Bahrein, in the Persian Gulf, where they saw the famous pearl fishery (48). From thence they departed by sea for the kingdom of Visapour.

During this voyage, Thelismar and Alphonso were one evening walking the deck, and con-

(a) Bagdad is a great city, on the eastern borders of the Tigris ; it was taken by the Turks somewhere about 1638.

(b) Bassora is a fine city, below the confluence of the Tigris and the Euphrates ; the Turks have been masters of it ever since 1668 ; it is 100 leagues from Bagdad.

versing

4

verfing on the wonders of nature. 1 think at prefent, faid Alphonfo, I know them all.

Dear Alphonfo, fince you are fo learned, replied Thelifmar, explain the meaning of the phænomenon which at this moment appears; look this way on yonder waves.

Alphonfo went to Thelifmar, and, looking as directed, beheld the veffel encircled by fire, to which the total darknefs of the night gave an additional brilliancy ; the furface of the fea was entirely covered with fmall fparkling ftars, and every wave, as it broke, caft forth a fhining light.

The wake of the veffel was of a luminous filver white, interfperfed with dazzling azure fparks (49).

I confefs, faid Alphonfo, this is a glorious fight, and abfolutely new to me.

Come, let us go to bed, replied Thelifmar ; and fhould you happen to awake in the night, I am perfuaded you will make fome folitary reflections on that prefumption which is but too natural to you, and which perfuades you of the extent of your knowledge, when every day proves the contrary.

Alphonfo made no reply, but embraced Thelifmar, and went to bed.

Scarcely had he been afleep half an hour before there was a noife in his cabin that awakened him :

he

'he had put out his light, and was frightened
at opening his eyes, by perceiving fire on the
partition oppofite his bed; he rofe haftily, and
his furprize increafed at beholding, in large legible
letters of fire, thefe words witten upon the boards:

Learned Alphonfo, your terror is ill founded, this
fire burns not (50).

Afhamed and aftonifhed, Alphonfo put his hand
upon thefe fiery characters, and felt no heat: Oh
Thelifmar! cried he, what furprizes me the moft
is that you have the art to render the leffons
which wound felf-love agreeable. Thelifmar immediately appeared, with a light in his hand fmiling; and, after having explained to him the nature
of this feeming fire, retired, and Alphonfo once
more went to fleep.

. It is alfo time that we fhould go to fleep, interrupted the Baronnefs, for the evening has been much
longer than ufual.

The next evening Madame de Clémire again
continued her hiftory of Alphonfo.

Our travellers being arrived at Vifapour, vifited
the diamond mines (51), and afterwards went to
the Court of the great Mogul. Thelifmar, having
obtained an audience of the Emperor, was permitted with Alphonfo to fee the Palace. They
paffed through many apartments, and found, in
all of them, beautiful women, in magnificent habits, armed with lances, who formed the interior

guard of the palace. They came to a vaft and fplendid hall, hung with gold brocade, where the Monarch was fitting on a throne of mother-of-pearl, entirely covered with rubies and emeralds; four columns, all befpread with diamonds, fupported a canopy of filver, embroidered with fapphires, and ornamented with feftoons and pearls; a fuperb trophy, compofed of the Emperor's arms, his quiver, bow, and fabre, garnifhed with jewels, and connected by a chain of topazes and diamonds, was fufpended to one of the columns; the Emperor himfelf was clad in cloth of gold, and in the centre of his turban was a diamond of prodigious brightnefs, and fo large that it extended almoft over his whole front: various rows of fine pearl formed his bracelets and collar; and an infinity of precious ftones, of various colours, enriched his girdle and his bufkins: before him was a table of maffive gold, and all the great lords of his court, in moft fumptuous robes, were ftanding ranged round his throne.

Thelifmar prefented to him feveral mathematical inftruments, of which, by means of an interpreter, he explained the ufe. The Emperor feemed pleafed with the prefents and converfation of Thelifmar; told him, it was his birth-day; that the whole empire celebrated the feftival, and invited Alphonfo and Thelifmar to fpend the evening in his palace.

Evening

Evening came; wine was brought, in vafes of rock cryftal; every body was feated, fruits were ferved in plates of gold; the muficians entered, and the hall foon refounded with cymbals and trumpets. The Emperor filled a golbet of wine, and fent it to Thelifmar; the goblet was of gold, enriched with the turquoife, the emerald, and the ruby. When he had drank, the Emperor defired him to keep the cup as a mark of his friendfhip.

When the repaft was almoft ended, two large bafins of rubies were brought the Emperor, which he threw among the courtiers, who all fcrambled for them. Soon after two other bafins were brought full of gold and filver almonds, which were thrown, and fnatched with the fame avidity.

Thelifmar and Alphonfo, as you may well fup-pofe, fat ftill, afhamed of, and contemning the covetoufnefs and meannefs of the Mogul lords.

The Emperor alfo diftributed pieces of gold-ftuff and rich girdles to feveral of the muficians, and fome of the courtiers; after which the drink-ing began. Thelifmar and Alphonfo were the only people who remained fober; the Emperor, unable to fit upright, hung his head and fell afleep and then every body retired.

When Alphonfo and Thelifmar were alone, The-lifmar faid to the former, What do you think of this Court?

K 2

I think,

I think, replied Alphonſo, he is the richeſt and moſt magnificent ſovereign upon earth.

And the happieſt, and moſt reſpectable, likewiſe?

I know not if he be happy, for I know not if he be loved, if his reign be peaceable and glorious: but I confeſs there is nothing auguſt in his perſon; nothing which enforces reverence. There is not a ſingle Prince, in Europe, who has ſo little the air of majeſty.

And yet there is no European Sovereign who may be any way compared to him, for pomp and ſhew. Gold, pearls, diamonds, and all the Aſiatic oſtentation, do not therefore of themſelves impreſs any real reſpect. What muſt we think then of thoſe frivolous Europeans who affix ſo great and imaginary a value on theſe ſhining trifles? I wiſh the European women, who are richeſt in ſuch poſſeſſions, and who are ſometimes properly enough, by way of deriſion, called queens of diamonds, I wiſh they could be tranſported here for twenty-four hours. What would one of them ſay, at ſeeing herſelf totally ſurpaſſed in ſuch bright baubles, by the very ſlaves of the Emperor's wives?

For my part, anſwered Alphonſo, bluſhing a little, I ſhall no more mention the diamonds that my father loſt during the earthquake at Liſbon. But pray tell me how it happens that the great

Lords

Lords of this Court, who feem fo rich, are yet fo covetous? How meanly did they huftle one another for the gold and jewels the Emperor threw.

Their whole emulation is that of being more fuperbly dreft than others; they only feek to diftinguifh themfelves by filly outfide fhew; and you fee how much this kind of vanity, carried to excefs, can make men capable of the moft degrading acts. But to return to the Emperor: you fay you are ignorant if he be happy; can you fuppofe a monarch fo ignorant, fo debafed, happy.

If he be good, he may be beloved.

We do not love whom we defpife. Ought he not, for the good of his people, to be well informed, juft, and eftimable? Befides, this Monarch has no fubjects; they are only flaves and he is a defpot; he exercifes a tyrannical power outwardly, while he is inwardly tormented by all the fears and terrors which ever were the juft punifhments of tyrants. The homage paid him is forced; and, while adulation offers him incenfe, hatred is fecretly confpiring his deftruction; his life is paft in fufpicion, or the punifhment of traitors; he is in continual fear of all that approach him; and, to complete his mifery, his very children are fufpected.

The next day, Thelifmar and Alphonfo went early to the palace; the Mogul was then at war

with

with the Sovereign of Décan; and was going to visit the camp where his troops were assembled. His wives were mounted on elephants, that waited at their doors; Thelismar counted eighty of these animals, all pompously equipped; the little towers they carried were plated with gold, and embellished with mother-of-pearl; the same metal too formed the bars of their grated windows; a canopy of cloth of silver, with tassels hung with rubies, covered each tower.

The Emperor was carried in a palanquin of gold and mother-of-pearl, set with pearls and precious stones: many other palanquins followed that of the Emperor, and a vast number of trumpets, drums, and other instruments, mixed among a crowd of officers, richly clothed, who carried rich canopies and umbrellas of brocaded gold, hung with pearls, rubies, and diamonds, led the procession.

Our travellers after having admired the splendor of his camp, quitted the Court of the great Mogul (52), and went to the kingdom of Siam. Here they saw the famous white elephant, so much revered in India: his apartments is magnificent, he is served kneeling, and in vessels of gold (a). " These attentions," says an illustrious

(a) They have the same respect for white elephants at Laos, Pegu, &c.

philosopher,

philofopher, *(a)* " thefe refpeɛts, thefe offerings,
" flatter him, but do not corrupt; he has not
" then a human foul: and this fhould be fuffi-
" cient to demonſtrate it to the Indians." . .

There was now but one part of the world unknown to our travellers, America, for which they
embarked and came to California; from thence
they went to Mexico; and, as they were on their
route to the town of Ḻlaſcala, Thelifmar, looking
at his watch, ſtopt his carriage, and alighted;
telling his fervants to wait, and carefully look to
the horfes, for, added he, night will fuddenly
overtake us.

How! faid Alphonfo, laughing, night! Not
fo fuddenly, for it is only noon.

Thelifmar made no reply, but feeking the fhade,
turned towards fome trees at a little diſtance.
Alphonfo, as he followed, perceived an animal,
the extraordinary figure of which raifed his attention; it was nineteen or twenty inches long,
without reckoning the tail, which was at leaſt
twelve, and fcaly like a ferpent; its ears were like
thofe of the fmall owl, and its hair ereɛt

The animal ſtood ſtill, and Alphonfo wifhed to
examine it; he obferved it was waiting for its
young, which were running towards it; as they
came up, it put them one after another into a bag

(a) M. de Buffon.

er

or pouch beneath its belly, then ran towards the trees.

Defirous of obferving fo fingular an animal nearer, and finding that it could not run faft, Alphonfo purfued it; he had juft overtaken it when it came to the foot of a tree, up which it ran with furprizing agility, feized the end of one of its higheft branches with its tail, twifted it round, and there remained fufpended, apparently motionlefs (53).

Alphonfo was going to mount the tree, when he heard on every fide of him a loud crackling, which, redoubling, feemed like the difcharge of artillery; at the fame inftant he was covered with an innumerable multitude of fmall black grains, darted on him from all parts (54). He haftily drew back, and hid his eyes with his hands, which were confiderably hurt by the grains that had ftruck them.

The pain was fo great that he was obliged to keep them fhut for fome minutes; at laft he opened them, but no fooner had he done fo than he cried out, Oh heaven! I am blind! Oh Thelifmar! Oh Dalinda! I fhall never fee you more.——Thelifmar, Thelifmar, where are you?——Do not abandon the unhappy Alphonfo.

As he faid this, he heard pretty near him a burft of laughter, and knew it was the voice of Thelifmar. What then, continued he, does Thelifmar infult my mifery? No; it is not poffible.

He

He then recollected that The'ſmar, when he got out of his carriage, had told his ſervants that night approached; he began therefore to take courage, and doubt the truth of his blindneſs, notwithſtanding the midnight darkneſs that ſurrounded him; he followed the ſound of Thelifmar's voice, till he found and ſeized him in his arms.

I cannot at preſent, ſaid Thelifmar, ſerve you as a guide, Alphonſo, for I am as blind as you are.

Thanks be to heaven, replied Alphonſo, that I am acquitted for the fright only; I find, now, that the cauſe of my fear is nothing but an eclipſe of the ſun; but I did not think that eclipſes ever produced ſuch total darkneſs, nor can I conceive by what art you could foretell, with ſo much preciſion, the exact moment of this phænomenon.

While Alphonſo was ſpeaking, the ſun, once more beginning to appear, diſſipated the fearful obſcurity that had blackened every object; the profound ſilence, the midnight calm, ſoon ceaſed, and nature ſeemed to revive; the birds, with freſh animation, thinking they ſang the return of Aurora, gave notice, by their loud and lively warblings of the birth of day (55).

Thelifmar and Alphonſo now regained their carriage, and the eclipſe, the animal, and the ſtrange artillery, furniſhed our travellers with ſubjects for converſation, which were not exhauſted when they arrived at Tlaſcala.

K 5

Quitting

Quitting Mexico, Thelifmar and Alphonfo embarked for St. Domingo; here Alphonfo flattered
himfelf he fhould find a letter from his father; he
was miftaken, but he received news from Portugal,
though fuch as gave him great affliction.

He learnt that Don Ramirez had not returned
to Portugal; that the public opinion was totally
changed concerning his being again taken into
favour and fent on an embaffy; moft people even
fuppofed him exiled, but were totally ignorant to
what part of the world he was retired.

This intelligence overwhelmed Alphonfo with
grief; uncertain now of what might be his father's
fate, his remorfe became more keen than ever.

Thelifmar came to feek him, juft as he was in
the midft of thefe melancholy thoughts. I come
to tell you, faid Thelifmar, you will fee Dalinda
much fooner than you hoped; fhe is at Paris with
her mother; they will wait for us there: to-morrow
we will depart for Surinam, from thence we will
embark for France, whither we fhall go directly.
But in the mean time, added Thelifmar, before you
fee Dalinda, I will fhew you a prefent I have juft
received from her. Here, open this, do you recol-
rect that form?

Heavens! cried Alphonfo, it is the portrait of
Dalinda! What a wonderful picture! What a
ftriking likenefs! How perfect is the painter's art!

This

This picture will intereſt you ſtill more, when you know it is the work of Dalinda herſelf.

Dalinda! Has ſhe then every talent as well as every charm? Oh permit me once more to look on this, precious painting.——Yes; behold her angelic features; look, there is her enchanting ſmile. How happy, Theliſmar, are you in the poſſeſſion of ſuch a treaſure!

And yet I deſire another picture of her; I would have her paint herſelf once more, but with her huſband by her ſide; and, when, Alphonſo, ſhe ſhall give me that, I promiſe you ſhall have this.

Alphonſo only replied by tenderly preſſing the hands of Theliſmar, and watering them with his tears.

Far from feeling a joy pure and unmixed, he looked upon it as his indiſpenſable duty to return to Portugal, hoping there to find ſome ſort of information concerning his father: he was unalterably determined to declare his reſolution of going thither to Theliſmar; but this reſolution was too painful, not to cauſe the moſt violent agitations in his mind.

He had never had the courage to confeſs a fault for which he juſtly and bitterly reproached himſelf; he wanted the power to tell ſo dear a friend he had left Spain clandeſtinely, without his father's conſent; and this firſt diſſimulation had obliged him to diſguiſe the truth in a thouſand other in-

K6   ſtances:

ſtances: at laſt, however, he firmly purpoſed to expiate all his wrongs by his ſincerity, without reſerve, and, if neceſſary, by the moſt painful ſacrifices; and in this diſpoſition left Saint Domingo. They arrived at Surinam *(a)* about duſk, and were ſtruck by a moſt brilliant ſpectacle at their firſt entering that country. The coaſt ſeemed covered with an infinity of chandeliers, hung without order at unequal diſtances. Theliſmar and Alphonſo were admiring this agreeable illumination, when they perceived many of the lights were in motion, and advancing towards them.

A moment after, they plainly diſtinguiſhed eight or ten men who walked nimbly, though they ſeemed covered with ſmall lighted candles; ſome on their bonnets, ſome on their ſhoes, and ſome in their hands. This viſion greatly ſurprized Alphonſo, who wanted to come near theſe men; but they paſſed haſtily by, and, as Alphonſo did not underſtand the language of his guides, he could not ſatisfy his curioſity.

When they came to the houſe where they were to lodge, they were ſhewn into a pretty chamber, as clear as day; but, as Alphonſo remarked that the lights were placed in two ſmall glaſs lanterns, he wiſhed to ſee them nearer: he then diſcovered,

---

(a) Surinam is a Dutch colony, of about 30 leagues extent, along the river of Surinam, in Guiana.

with

with aftonifhment, they were nothing but green
flies, of a bright emerald colour, which gave all
this light.

We have now an explanation of the thing we
wanted, faid Thelifmar; the trees, being in a co-
nic form, are covered with thefe flies, and refemble, at a diftance, girandoles and chandeliers
hung in the air; the men, we met, had faftened
thefe fhining infects on their bonnets and feet, and
carried them in glafs tubes in their hands.

The very fame evening, Alphonfo learnt thefe
beautiful flies were more than one way ufeful.
When he was in bed, they were taken from their
little lanterns and let fly about the room, in which
he was informed they would kill the gnats, which
might otherwife difturb his reft (56).

Alphonfo, however, a prey to inward grief and
chagrin, could not clofe his eyes the whole night;
he rofe before day-break, determined no longer
to defer opening his heart to Thelifmar, but to inform him of all his faults and all his forrows.

He went to walk upon the fea-fhore till Thelifmar fhould rife, and, after ftraying a confiderable time, fat down at the foot of a tree, where
he fell into a vague and painful reverie; prefently
his eyes became heavy, he began to dofe, and in
a few moments was afleep. He was awakened by a
piercing and forrowful cry, and, opening his eyes,

saw

saw himself in the arms of Thelifmar, who was bearing him away.

Alphonfo endeavoured to speak, but could only utter some broken and plaintive sounds; pale and faint, he could not fupport himfelf, he wanted even the power of thought. Thelifmar laid him down on the grafs, ran towards the fea, filled his hat with falt-water, and made Alphonfo drink it; after which, with the help of fome fervants, he raifed, and took him home.

Alphonfo came to himfelf by degrees. Where am I, faid he, as he felt his ftrength returning?

Oh my fon, faid Thelifmar, have I not fpoken to you of this fatal tree? Have I not told you that to fleep beneath its perfidious fhade is to die (57)?

It is true, cried Alphonfo, with a languifhing voice, I recollect it now.

Providence be praifed, you are out of danger; but had not my fears for you brought me where you lay, the very inftant they did, I fhould have loft you, Alphonfo.

And do you weep for me, my father? For me! Oh moft affectionate of friends! beft of benefactors! Wherefore have you fnatched me from the arms of death? I had then been regretted by you. Thelifmar, while weeping for the miferable Alphonfo, would then have been ignorant of his worft errors.

What

What do you mean Alphonso?

I am overpowered by your favours, penetrated by your bounties; my affection for you is the reigning sentiment of my heart, and yet I am the most unfortunate of men.

Heavens! Which way? How?

A single word, Thelismar, may make you judge of my situation; I cannot follow you to France?

And why not?

Sacred duty dictates my return to Portugal: Oh! that by this painful sacrifice I could expiate my fault!

What fearful remorse is it that overwhelms you?——But——no——thou art incapable of wickedness or meanness; speak, be confident, open thy heart to thy friend.

Alphonso shed tears of gratitude and joy at hearing this, was silent a few moments, then, taking courage, owned, without reserve, how he had deceived Thelismar, when he assured him that Don Ramirez approved his travels; related the circumstances of his flight, and painted, in the most moving manner, his remorse, and uninterrupted inquietude concerning the fate of his father.

When he had finished his recital, Thelismar, with a softened heart, looked at him, and said, No, I will not abandon thee; I myself will conduct thee to Portugal.

These

These words infpired Alphonfo with gratitude fo ftrong, fo paffionate, he could only exprefs it by falling at the feet of his generous friend.

Yes, continued Thelifmar, we will find this unhappy father; I will enjoy the pleafure of giving thee again to his arms; for I dare affure him thou now wilt make him happy. We fhall arrive fomewhat later in France, but Dalinda will fee thee reconciled to heaven and thyfelf, and honoured with the paternal benediction. Don Ramirez will certainly confent without fcruple, to your union with Dalinda. My fortune is not immenfe, but it is more than fufficient; the ties which attached Don Ramirez to Portugal, are all broken; it will be no difficult thing to engage him to regard Sweden as his country and my houfe as his own.

This is too much, faid Alphonfo; Oh Thelifmar! let me breathe; my heart cannot exprefs its feeling towards a benefactor fuch as you; gratitude becomes a paffion; words are weak; I cannot tell you what I think.

This converfation delivered Alphonfo from one part of his troubles; the indulgence and tendernefs of Thelifmar affuaged the bitternefs of remorfe, and gave birth to the fweeteft hopes.

Before they quitted Surinam, Thelifmar and Alphonfo were invited on a fifhing party, and rofe

on

on the day appointed early in the morning. In their way to the sea-side, they crossed a marsh full of extraordinary trees; from their flexible branches, bundles of filaments hung down, lay upon the ground, took root, grew, and formed other trees, as beautiful as those to which they were united, and of which they were only shoots, which again multiplied after the same manner; insomuch that a single tree might become the parent stock of a whole forest.

But what most surprized Alphonso was that these trees were covered with shell-fish! A multitude of oysters were fixed to their branches ('58).

Thelismar was explaining the cause of these singular things, when they arrived on the strand; they went on board; the fishing began, the net was thrown and the haul was a good one.

Alphonso seeing an exceedingly large fish, very like an eel, went and touched it with a little switch that he had in his hand; no sooner had he done so than he felt so great a pain, in his arm and hand, that he gave a loud cry before he could recollect himself. The fishermen all began to laugh; and Alphonso, piqued and astonished, remained motionless awhile.

Recovering himself, he went again to the fish, and said I do not know how the touching this fish, can cause so violent a shock; but I will shew you,

at

at leaſt, that, though I may be ſurprized, I am not to be intimidated.

So ſaying, he ſtooped down and touched the fiſh with his hand. He did not cry out this time; but he received ſo terrible a ſhock that, if Theliſmar had not ſtepped forward, and catched him in his arms, he would have fallen; and was ſo ſtunned by the violence of the ſtroke that he almoſt loſt the uſe of his ſenſes.

As ſoon as he was perfectly recovered, I will ſhew you, ſaid Theliſmar, a ſtill more aſtoniſhing effect produced by this fiſh. We are fourteen people in all, let us form a circle, and each hold the other by the hand; I will ſtand firſt, and you laſt; I will touch the fiſh with a ſtick, and, although ſeparated from me by twelve people, you ſhall yet feel the ſame ſhock as I.

The experiment was made, and confirmed all that Theliſmar had predicted (59).

The day after this adventure, our travellers quitted Surinam and America, and embarked for Portugal. During the voyage, Theliſmar, in return for the confidence Alphonſo had placed in him, ſatisfied a curioſity he had long entertained. Alphonſo could not conceive how Theliſmar might reſolve to quit his country for four years, and tear himſelf from a family ſo dear to him, for ſo long a time.

Theliſmar

Thelifmar informed him that his Sovereign, being the protector of literature and learned men, had engaged him to make this facrifice: the benefactions of my King, continued he, my love of fcience, and the particular delight I take in natural hiftory, have determined me to undertake an enterprize the fatigues of which my friendfhip for you has madé me cheerfully fupport; the care of forming your heart, and enlightening your mind, together with the affection you have infpired me with, alone could foften the uneafinefs and chagrin I have often known, and which are infeparable from the feeling mind, abfent from its native home.

After a favourable voyage our travellers landed at Portugal, where all the information that Alphonfo could procure, relative to Don Ramirez, was very feeble and infufficient. They affured him that his father had not been feen there during the laft two years, and, after an infinity of refearches, Alphonfo was perfuaded Don Ramirez was either in England or in Ruffia. The interefts of his family required Thelifmar fhould go to England; this Alphonfo knew: therefore, on quitting Portugal, he had the confolation to think he fhould not ftay in France, but follow Thelifmar and Dalinda to a land in which he hoped to find his father.

NOTES,

N O T E S,

In VOL. II.

(1) A FAMOUS Florist, in Holland, told me he had given 6,800 livres (265l.) for a root? adding, that he had seen others far dearer. Many Amateurs will not allow there are more than six species of flowers worthy the care of cultivation : these are the Hyacinth, the Tulip, the Auricula, the Carnation, the Ranunculus, and the Anemony : the Hyacinth is one of the most beautiful, but least various in its colours; it is less common too than the other. The Ranunculus is said to have been brought from Syria, during the time of the Crusades; the Anemony was transported from America in the last century, by M. Bachelier; and they pretend that the Hyacinth is a native of the Cape of Good Hope; the most beautiful Hyacinth is the Ophyr; it is yellow, with purple spots on the inside.

(2) The earthquake which happened in Sicily 1692-3, the history of which is given by Mr. Hartop, Father Alessandro Burgos, and Vin Bonajutus, is one of the most terrible ones in all history: it shook the whole island; and not only that but Naples and Malta shared in the shock. It was of the second kind mentioned by Aristotle and Pliny, viz. a perpendicular pulsation or succession. It was impossible, said the noble Bonajutus, for any body in this country to keep on their legs on the dancing earth; nay,

those

thofe that lay on the ground were toffed from fide to fide as on a rolling billow, and high walls leaped from their foundations feveral paces, &c. *Phil. Tranf.* No. 207. The mifchief it did is amazing; almoft all the buildings, in the countries were thrown down; fifty-four cities and towns; befides an incredible number of villages, were either deftroyed or greatly damaged. We fhall only inftance the fate of Catania, one of the moft famous, ancient, and flourifhing cities in the kingdom, the refidence of feveral Monarchs, and a Univerfity. This once famous, now unhappy Cátania, to ufe the words of Fa. Burgos, had the greateft fhare in the tragedy. F. Anton. Serrovita, being, on his way thither, at the diftance of a few miles, obferved a black cloud, like night, hovering over the city; and there arofe from the mouth of Montgibello, great fpires of flames which fpread all around; the fea, all of a fudden, began to roar and rife in billows; and there was a noife, as if all the artillery in the world had been at once difcharged; the birds flew about aftonifhed; the cattle in the fields ran crying, &c. His and his companions horfes ftopped fhort, trembling, fo that they were forced to alight. They were no fooner off but they were lifted from the ground above two palms; when, cafting his eyes towards Catania, he, with amazement, faw nothing but a thick clowd of duft in the air. This was the fcene of the calamity; for of the magnificent Catania, there was not the leaft footftep to be feen. S. Bonajutus affures us that, of 18,914 inhabitants, 18,000 perifhed there. The fame author from a computation of the inhabitans, before and after the *earthquake*, in the feveral cities and towns, finds that near 60,000 perifhed, out of 254,900.

(3) The greateft part of Lifbon was, in fact, deftroyed by incendiaries; who, during this dreadful difafter, fet fire

to

to the houfes that they might pillage them with more impu-
nity. The unfortunate inhabitants, who were the victims
of this unheard of wickednefs, found relief in the humanity
of a generous nation. No fooner were the Englifh informed
of this terrible event than they haftened to fend them· every
fuccour of which they ftood in need. This benevolent act
coft the Englifh fix millions, but it gave them, new claims to
the efteem of all Europe.

(4) I find, in an Englifh work, as inftructive as enter-
taining, a fingular Anecdote, little known relative to Catalonia.

" From that period, the Emperors, Kings of France,
" governed Catalonia, by appointing Counts, or Vicegerents,
" removeable at pleafure, till the government was rendered
" hereditary in the family of Wilfred the Hairy : whether
" this happened by a conceffion of Charles the Bald, or by
" ufurpation, remains a doubt among the learned. It con-
" tinued in his pofterity for many generations. This Prince
" having been grievoufly wounded, in a battle againft the
" Normans, received a vifit from the Emperor, who, dipping
" his finger in the blood that trickled from the wound,
" drew four lines down the gilt fhield of Wilfred, faying,
" Earl, be thefe thy armorial Enfign. Four Pallets, Gules,
" on a Field, or; remained from that time the coat of
" Arms of Catalonia, and afterwards of Arragon ; when
" Raymund the fifth married Petronilla, only daughter and
" heirefs of Ramiro, the fecond King of Arragon."———
Travels through Spain, in the Years 1775 *and* 1776, *by Henry
Swinburn, Efq.*

(5) The following is what a French Traveller fays on the
fubject of the Cafcades I mention.

" One is aftonifhed, while travelfing thefe threatening
" rocks, to meet delicious valleys and fine verdure, and
" trees

" trees in the bosom of sterility; to see natural cascades pre-
" cipitate themselves from their rude pinnacles, and trouble
" the silence which reigns in that asylum, only to render it
" more interesting."

Essais sur l'Espagne, Tome I. Page 35.

And here follows what an English Traveller says on the same
subject:

" The greatest hardship here is a scarcity of good water.
" Except one spring at the parish and another at the con-
" vent, they have no other than cistern water, and that bad
" enough. This, in summer, is a terrible inconvenience,
" and gives the lie to the florid descriptions I have read of
" the purling streams, and beautiful cascades, tumbling
" down on every side, from the broken rocks. The want
" of water is so great that neither wolf, bear, or other wild
" beast, is ever seen on the mountain."—*Travels through
Spain, by Henry Swinburn, Esq; London, 4to—Page 50.*

This quotation is striking enough; and, were pains taken
to compare the accounts of travellers, I believe many such
like might be found. For my part, I have taken a liberty
which many historians have likewise taken, that of choosing
the most agreeable; however, I do not dissemble my motives
of preference, and readily confess that the name, reputation,
and works of the English Traveller, ought to inspire the greatest
confidence.

(6) Among the combats between the Spaniards and the
Moors, was one, in which the women of Tortosa gained
great renown. They exposed themselves on the ramparts
of the town, and performed such prodigious acts of valour
that Raymond Berenger, the last Count of Barcelona, insti-
tuted, in 1170, the Military Order of La Hacha, or the
Torch.

Torch. They obtained many other honourable privileges, which now no longer exift, except that of taking the right-hand of the men, be their rank what it will, in their marriage ceremonies.

The hiftory of Germany affords a fimilar anecdote. In the year 1015, the Poles befieged the town of Meiffin, which muft have been taken, had it not been for the heroifm of the women who partook all the labours of the fiege. The Emperor Henry II. to perpetuate the memory of the women of Meiffin, who had, on that occafion, fhewn greater courage than their hufbands, ordained an annerfary feftival for the deliverance of the town, and that the women alone fhould go in proceffion to the church, as a teftimony that Meiffin owed its fafety to them. This proceffion was continued with great pomp till the fixteenth century, when the Lutherans abolifhed the Romifh religion.

Hift. Gener. d'Allemagne, by M. Montigny, Tome IV.

During the war between John I. King of Caftile, and John I. King of Portugal, the Englifh having befieged Valencia, in the Kingdom of Leon, which was then without men, and the nobility having all followed the Prince to the field, the ladies defended the town, repelled the affault of the enemy, haraffed them by fallies, and obliged them to retire. John, in recompenfe of their valour, permitted them to wear a fcarf of gold, and granted them all the privileges of the Knights of the Scarf. The date of this order is uncertain, but is faid to be between 1383 and 1390.——*Encyclopédie, at the word* ECHARPE.

(7) The town-houfe of Toledo, near the Archbifhop's Palace, is ftill admired; the colonadeal architecture is very beautiful. On one of the walls of the ftair-cafe are Spanifh verfes, of which the following is a tranflation :

" Noble

" Noble and judicious men of Toledo, leave your paſſion on
" this ſtair-caſe; here leave love, fear, and covetouſneſs;
" forget private for public good; and, ſince God has made you
" the pillars of this auguſt palace, remain always firm, up-
" right, and unſhaken."

Eſſais ſur l'Eſpagne, Tom. I.

(8) Theſe mountains, abſolutely deſert, ſerved, many ages,
as an aſylum to robbers and wolves. In vain had ſome
patriots propoſed to grub and clear them. M. Olavides,
however, after having peopled the deſerts of Andaluſia,
covered the Sierra Morena with coloniſts and labourers. Government favoured the eſtabliſhment, and it proſpered; but,
notwithſtanding the attentions, benefactions, and repeated
exemptions of government, there are many diſcontented ſpirits
among theſe people; their complaints, generally ill-founded,
are the conſequence of man's natural inquietude, who wiſhes
for eaſe and independence without making uſe of the means by
which they are procured.

Eſſais ſur l'Eſpagne, Tom. I.

The chief place in the colony is called Carolina; both
the French and Engliſh travellers have given charming de-
ſcriptions of this eſtabliſhment. Thoſe of the latter are
delightful.

(9) In the days of the Muſſelmen this Moſque was a
ſquare building, with a flat roof, upon arches. It wanted
proportion, for it was only thirty-five feet high, while its
breadth was four hundred and twenty, and its length five hundred and ten. The roof was ſupported by near a thouſand
columns according to ſome accounts and by ſeven hundred
and ſeventy-eight according to others. The Moſque had
24 gates, and 4700 lamps were lighted in it every night, which
annually conſumed near 20,000 pounds of oil.

At prefent a part of the Mofque only exifts, which is turned into a church which has feventeen gates, and is 510 feet long, and 240 broad (*a*) ; and in one part of it ftand a vaft number of columns, marble, but of various fpecies, forming a vaft quincunx.——*Travels through Spain, by Henry Swinburn, Efq. page* 297.

(10) Grenada is fituated at the foot of Sierra Nevada, or Mountain of Snow, and is built on two hills on each fide of the Darro. The Xenil bathes its walls, and thefe two rivers are formed from the melting of the fnows, with which the Sierra is always covered.——*Effais fur l'Efpagne,* Tom. I.

(11) The moft remarkable monument of Granada is the Caftle of the Alhambra, an ancient Moorifh palace, in the centre of which is feen one more modern, built by Charles V. which yet is in ruins, with only the walls remaining. Its extent was not great, the better to preferve the Moorifh palace, which was deftined to be a fummer habitation. In the Alhambra, are found the remains of prodigious magnificence, colonnades of marble, fountains, baffo relievos, a prodigious number of infcriptions, &c. among others the fuperb court, called the Court of the Lions, is greatly admired: the Generaliph is another Moorifh palace, which communicates with the Alhambra. It is built on a great elevation, and watered from every part. The gardens are in the form of an Amphitheatre; the fituation is charming, and preferable to that of the Alhambra.

Effais fur l'Efpagne, Tom. I.

(12) In the days of Boabdil or Abouadoulah, the laft King of Granada, the Alabeces, Abencérages, Zegris, and Gomeles, were the moft powerful families in that city ; they filled

(*a*), The French traveller fays, 600 long, and 250 broad. *Effais fur l'Efpagne,* Tom. I. *page* 285.

filled moſt of the great employments about court, and
ſcarcely a brilliant atchievement in war was heard of that
was not performed by the arm of ſome knight of theſe 'four
houſes.   High above the reſt towered the Abencerages,
unequalled in gallantry, magnificence, and chivalry.   Note
among the Abencerages was more accompliſhed, more diſtinguiſhed, than Albin Hamet, who, for his great wiſdom and
valour, ſtood deſervedly foremoſt in the liſt of the King's
favourites.   His power roſe to ſuch a pitch, that it excited
the moſt violent envy in the breaſt of the Zegris and Gomeles, who determined to pull him down from this poſt of
ſuperior eminence.   After concerting many ſchemes for his
deſtruction, none appeared to them more effectual than one
propoſed by a conſummate villain of the Zegri family.
He ſeized an opportunity of being alone with the King,
whoſe character was, as yet, frank, and unſuſpicious; aſſum-
ing an air of extreme anguiſh of mind, he obſerved to the
Prince how very weak his conduct appeared to all wiſe men,
by repoſing ſuch unbounded confidence in, and truſting his
perſon with, ſuch traitors as the Abencerages, who were
well known to be laying a ſcheme for a general revolt;
thereby to deprive Abouabdoulah of his life and crown.
Nay more, he, and three men of honour, had ſeen the
Queen in wanton dalliance with Albin Hamet Abencerage,
behind the lofty cypreſſes in the gardens of the Generaliph,
from whence Hamet had returned inſolently crowned with
a garland of roſes.   Theſe calumnies rouzed all the furies
of jealouſy in the breaſt of the credulous Monarch, and the
deſtruction of the whole lineage of Abencerage was planned
by the bloody junto.   The principal men of the devoted
family were, under ſome pretence or other, ſummoned one
by one to attend the King in the Court of Lions.   No
ſooner was each unhappy victim admitted within the walls
than he was ſeized by the Zegris, led to a large alabaſter

bafon in one' of the adjoining halls, and there beheaded.
Thirty-fix of the nobleft of the race had already perifhed
before the treachery was difcovered. A Page, belonging
to one of thofe noblemen having found means to follow
his mafter in, and to get out again unfeen, divulged the fecret
of this bloody tranfaction. The treafon once known,
all Granada was in an inftant up in arms, and many def-
perate combats enfued, which, by the great havock made
amongft the moft valliant of its chieftains, brought the ftate
to the very biink of ruin. Thefe tumults being appeafed
by the wifdom of Mufa, a baftard brother of the King, a
grand council was held, in which Abouabdoulah declared
his reafons for the punifhment inflicted on the Abencerages,
viz. their confpiracy, and the adultery of the Queen. He
then folemnly pronounced her fentence, which was, to be
burnt alive, if, within thirty days, fhe did not produce four
knights to defend her caufe againft the four accufers. The
Queen's relations were upon the point of drawing their
fcimitars in the audience chamber, and refcuing her from
the danger that threatened her; but their fury was checked
by the eloquence of Mufa, who obferved to them, they
might by violence fave the life of the Sultana, but by no
means clear her reputation in the eyes of the world, which
would certainly look upon that caufe as unjuft which refufed to fubmit to the cuftomary trial. The Queen was
immediately fhut up in the tower of Comares. Many
Granadine warriors were ambitious of having the honour of
expofing their lives in her quarrel, but none were fo happy
as to prove the object of her choice. She had conceived fo
high an idea of the chriftians, from the valour fhe had
feen them difplay in a great tournament lately held at
Granada, and the treachery of the Zegris filled her with fo
defpicable an opinion of Moorifh honour, that fhe was de-

6   termined

termined to reſt her defence upon the gallantry of the Spaniſh Knights. In hopes of rouſing their noble ſpirits to action, ſhe diſpatched a truſty meſſenger with a letter to Don Juan de Chacon, Lord of Carthagena, entreating him to eſpouſe her cauſe; and like a true Knight, bring with him three brave warriors to ſtand her friends on the day appointed. Chacon returned for anſwer that he ſet too high a price upon that honour not to be punctual to the hour of trial. The fatal day arrived and all Granada was buried in the deepeſt affliction to find that their beloved Queen had been ſo remiſs as not to have named one of her defenders. Muſa, Azarque, and Almoradi, the judges of the combat, preſſed her, in vain, to accept of their ſwords, or thoſe of ſeveral other warriors willing to aſſert the juſtneſs of her cauſe. The Sultana, relying on the Spaniſh faith, perſiſted in her refuſal; upon which the judges conducted her down from the Alhambra to a ſcaffold in the great ſquare, hung with black, where they ſeated themſelves on one ſide. At the ſight of this beauty in diſtreſs, the whole place reſounded with loud cries and lamentations; and it was with difficulty that the ſpectators could be reſtrained from attacking her enemies, and reſcuing her by main force. Scarce were the judges ſeated, when twenty trumpets announced the approach of the four accuſers, who advanced, armed cap-à-pie, mounted on the fineſt courſers of Andaluſia. Over their armour they wore looſe veſts, with plumes and ſaſhes of a tawny colour. On their ſhields were painted two bloody ſwords, and theſe words: *For the truth we draw them.*——All their kinſmen and adherents accompanied them to their poſts within the liſts. In vain did the crowd caſt a longing eye towards the gate, through which the champions of injured innocence were to enter; none appeared, from eight in the morning to two in the afternoon. The Sul-

tana's

tana's courage began to fail her; and when four valiant
Moors prefented themfelves to fue for the honour of drawing their fwords to vindicate her innocence, fhe promifed
to truft her life in their hands, if, within two hours, the
perfons fhe expected fhould not appear. At that inftant a
great noife was heard, and four Turkifh horfeman came
prancing into the fquare. One of them addreffed the judges,
requefting the favour of fpeaking to the Queen; which being
granted, he knelt down, and told her aloud, that he and his
companions were Turks, come to Spain with the defign of
trying their ftrength againft the heroes of Ferdinand's army;
but that, hearing of this folemn trial, they had changed their
refolution, and were now arrived at Granada to devote their
firft effay of arms in Spain to her fervice, and hoped fhe
would approve of them for her champions. As he fpoke,
he let drop into her lap the letter fhe had written to Don
Juan; by the fight of which, fhe difcovered this feigned Turk
to be no other than the Lord of Carthagena, who had
brought with him, as companions in this dangerous conflict,
the Duke of Arcos, Don Alonzo de Aguilar, and Don
Ferdinand de Cordova. The Queen accepted of their pro-
pofal; and the judges having folemnly declared her choice,
gave orders for the charge to found. The onfet was fierce,
and the fight long doubtful. At length, Don Juan overthrew Mahandin Gomel, and the Duke flew Alihamet Zegri;
Mahandon Gomel fell by the fword of Aguilar; and,
laft of all, the arch traitor, Mahomed Zegri, difabled by repeated wounds, and fainting with the lofs of blood, funk at the
feet of Don Ferdinand; who, fetting his knee on the Infi-
del's breaft, and holding his dagger to his throat, fummoned
him to confefs the truth, or die that inftant. " Thou needeft
" not add another wound," faid Mahomed, " for the laft
" will prove fufficient to rid the world of fuch a monfter.
" Know

" Know then, that, to revenge myself of the Abencerages,
" I invented the lye that caused their destruction, and the
" persecution of the Sultana; whom I here declare free
" from all stain or reproach whatsoever, and with my dying
" breath implore her forgiveness."   The judges came down
to receive this deposition of the expiring Zegri, and it
was afterwards announced to the people, who expressed
their joy by the loudest acclamations.   The day ended in
festivity and rejoicing.   The Queen was escorted back in
triumph to the Palace, where the penitent Abouabdoulah
fell at her feet, and, with floods of tears, endeavoured to
atone for his crime, but to no purpose : for the Queen remained inflexible, and, retiring to the house of her nearest
of kin, refused to have any farther intercourse with him.
The four Knights left Granada, without discovering themselves to any other person; and, soon after, the numerous
friends and adherents of the Abencerages abandoned the
city, and, by their secession into Castile or Africa, left
Abouabdoulah destitute of able officers, and entirely at the
mercy of his enemies, who, in the course of a few months,
deprived him of his kingdom.

(13) This globe of fire was a meteor, and similar appearances have been observed in the remotest ages.   It was
this kind of meteor which formerly spread terror in Rome,
which Aristotle, Seneca and Pliny have described.   It was
anciently called, and is so still by the vulgar, flaming sword,
and fiery dragon.   I have not invented any circumstances
relative to this phænomenon in my tale, as may be seen by the
following account :

" The Globe of fire which was the subject of the *Memoire*
" of M. le Roy was observed the 17th July, 1771, about
" half past ten in the evening.——There suddenly appeared,
" in the north-west, a fire like to a great falling star, which,

" augmenting

" augmenting as it approached, foon took the form of a
" globe, that afterwards had a tail.   This globe, having
" traverfed a part of the heavens, became flower in its
" motion, and took the form of the Prince Rupert's drop
" when it fhed a moft powerful light; its head appeared
" enveloped in fparks of fire, and its tail edged with red
" exhibited all the colours of the rain-bow.   At length it
" burft, fhedding a vaft number of luminous particles like
" the *Brilliants* in fire-works.

" The 12th of November, 1761, M. le Baron des Adretz,
" one league from Ville Franche, in Beaujolois, faw a bright
" globe of fire, which feemed fwiftly falling and increafing
" in fize as it fell.   A train of fire marked its route; after
" it had traverfed nearly an eighth of the horizon, it feemed
" as large as an exceeding large tun, cut horizontally in
" half.——It turned upfide down, and out of it came a pro-
" digious quantity of flaming fparks, like the largeft of thofe
" feen in fire-works.

" In the town of Beaune, this meteor gave a light equal to
" that of noon-day.

" The 3d of November, 1777, at half paft nine in the
" evening, a very extraordinary meteor was feen at Sarlat (a)
" The heavens became fo light, that day feemed again go-
" ing to break.   A moft luminous globe of fire appeared,
" from which came large fparks, like artificial ftars, and the
" circle by which it was furrounded, was formed of different
" coloured rays. ——When this enormous globe was about
" fix fathoms high, two fpecies of volcano came from it,
" which took the form of two large rainbows, one of which
" loft itfelf toward the North, and the other toward the
" South."

Dictionaire des Merveilles de la Nature,   Tome II.

(14)   It

(a) A fmall town of Perigord, 120 leagues from Paris.

(14) It muſt be remembered that Alphonſo's ſhoes were nailed, and that his ſtaff had an iron ferrule.

" The Ancients, ſays M. de Bomare, knew the load-
" ſtone would attract iron; and if Pliny may be believed,
" it was found out by a ſhepherd, who felt that the nails of
" his ſhoes, and the ferrule of his ſtaff, ſtuck to a rock of
" load-ſtone over which he paſſed; but, they knew not its
" polar direction.

Alphonſo, full of ignorance and remorſe, and already terrified at the meteor he had ſeen, feeling himſelf fixed to the rock, believed it proceeded from the wrath of heaven, as a puniſhment for his flight. This idea redoubled his terror, rendered him motionleſs, and aided the effects of nature.

" The load-ſtone is ferruginous, and is found in iron-
" mines; its colour varies with the country where it is
" found; it has five remarkable properties: 1. That of
" attracting iron, called *Attraction*. 2. That of tranſmitting
" its virtue——*Communication*. 3. That of turning towards
" the poles of the earth——*Direction* 4. Its variation,
" called *Declination*. 5. Its dipping as it approaches either
" pole——*Inclination*. All theſe ſingular properties, the
" effects of the nature of the load-ſtone, are produced by
" ſome general property hitherto unknown. It is ſuppoſed
" there is a kind of atmoſphere round the load-ſtone, which
" forms an active vortex, and is ſenſibly diſcovered by its
" contrary effects, the one of attracting, the other of re-
" pelling iron. The attracting force of the load-ſtone, juſt
" taken from the mine, is not great, for which reaſon it is
" obliged to be armed to augment its power. It may he
" remarked that the ruſt of iron has ſometimes the effect of
" the load-ſtone.

" Among

" Among the curiosities of the English Royal Society, is a
" load-stone, weighing sixty pounds, which does not lift
" weight in proportion to its size, but which attracts a needle
" nine feet distance. *L'Histoire de l'Academie des Sciences* speaks
" of a load-stone, which weighed eleven ounces, and raised
" twenty-eight pounds of iron; that is to say, more than
" forty times its weight." *Dict. d'Hist. Nat. par M. de Bomare.*
Magnetism is the general name for the different qualities of
the load-stone. I have placed the adventures of the Load-
stone Rock in Spain, because it would have the most effect
in the first moments of Alphonso's flight; and there is
sufficient probability for a tale like this, in so doing, since,
in fact, the environs of Loxe are full of rocks, and Spain
contains many mines.

(15) " The pretended rain of blood happens only during
" a storm, and more especially in summer. It is not astonish-
" ing that the most part of insects which feed on trees, are
" swept off by winds and torn in pieces, so that in falling
" they seem bloody, and it rains the blood of insects."——
Dict. d'Hist. Nat. par M. de Bomare, au mot Pluie.

. I confess this explanation does not satisfy me; for were
it only necessary, to produce this phænomenon, to have a
high wind or rain in the months of July or August, every
period must have seen it rain blood more than once, which they
certainly have not seen.

" The waters of the Lake of Zurich, in 1703, says M.
" de Bomare, suddenly became red like blood; and, on
" examination, it was found to proceed from currents of
" bituminous waters, full of red ochre, which currents fell
" into the lake.

" There is also what they call sulphur rain, which is so
" named from yellow grains that seem to fall from the

" clouds,

" clouds, mingled with the water. This is nothing but the
" yellow duft from various fpecies of plants in bloom, and
" which is the caufe of this pretended fulphur-rain that fo
" frequently falls in the neighbourhood of mountains. This
" phænomenon often happens at Bourdeaux in the month of
" April, when the pine is in flower."

Diél. d'Hiſt. Nat. par M. de Bomare.

(16) Quitting Loxe, travellers crofs Mount Orefpeda;
and in the neighbourhood of Archidona, a city built in the
very midft of rocks, on the frontiers of Andalufia, is feen *la
Tena de Los Enamorados*, (the Lover's Rock) a rock which
this tragic adventure has rendered famous. A young French
Knight was made prifoner by the Moors, when they were
in poffeffion of Granada. The Moorifh King gave him his
liberty, heaped favours upon him, and retained him at
his Court. In return, the Frenchman feduced the King's
daughter, and prevailed on her to fly fecretly from her father's palace. They made their efcape in the night; but
heaven purfued an ungrateful and vile ravifher, and a criminal and unnatural daughter. At day-break, they faw a
company of Moors chafing them, and they clambered up a
prodigioufly high rock. They were foon furrounded, and,
torn by remorfe, reduced to defpair, they flung themfelves
from the fummit of the precipice, which ftill bears the name
of the Lover's Rock.

Effais fur l'Efpagne, Tom. I. page 225.

(17) A poifon known to fome hordes of Savages, Moun-
taineers of Peru, was brought to Europe in 1746, by M. de
la Condamine, which was moft fubtil and mortal. Its effect
is fo prompt, that monkies or parrots pricked to the quick by
fmall arrows, which the Savages fhoot from Sarba canes,
immediately drop. M. de Reaumur had a bear of two years
old, which, becoming mifchievous, he determined to kill.

The

The effect of the poison was tried on this animal; the point of a dart, proper to shoot from a Sarba cane, was steeped in it, and the bear received the first dart above the shoulder, but without being apparently wounded; a second was shot and the animal made a bound, was convulsed, trembled, foamed, and fell dead in about a minute and a half. It must be remarked that the monkies and parrots killed by this poison, which are eaten in Peru, without any precaution, contract no pernicious quality. Sugar is the most certain antidote to this powerful venom, and given to dogs and cats, a quarter of an hour before they have been wounded, has prevented all its effects.

This note was given the Author by a person who was a witness of the above experiments.

(18) Every body knows this experiment in electricity was first made by Doctor Franklin.

(19) The key was electrified.

(20) " In the year 1755, when Lisbon suffered so much, " the Azore Islands were wonderfully agitated. In the island " of St. George, twelve leagues from Angra, the earth shook " so violently, that most of the inhabitants were buried in " the ruins of their houses. Their terror was next morning " redoubled, when from the same parts were seen eighteen " islands newly risen from the sea. On the other side a shock " was felt which threw portions of earth into the sea. On " one of these was a house, surrounded by trees, the inhabi- " tants of which did not, till the next morning, perceive the " change of place."——*Diff. d'Hist. Nat. par. M. de Bomare, au mot Tremblement de Terre.*

(21) " This is vulgarly called the dragon-tree, and, by " botanists, is divided into four species. That of the Canary " islands resembles the pine, at a distance. Its fruit is " sound.

" round, as large as fine peas, yellow, and a little acid.
" Its trunk, which is rugged, opens in many places, and
" sheds, during the dog-days, a liquor like blood, which
" condenses to a red-drop, soft at first, but afterwards dry,
" and capable of being reduced to powder. This is the
" dragon's-blood of the shops. When an incision is made
" in the trunk of one of those trees the liquor begins to
" run."

M. de Bomare, au mot sang de Dragon.

(22) " This pillar, or water-spout, is only a thick cloud,
" compressed and reduced to a small space by contrary and
" opposing winds, which, meeting, give the cloud the form
" of a cylindrical whirlwind, and thus occasion the water
" to fall all at once under this cylindrical form. The
" quantity of water is so great, and the fall so sudden, that
" if it happen on a ship at sea it sinks it instantly. In
" the month of July, 1755, a stroke of thunder beat down
" a cloud, in Bavaria, which directed itself perpendicularly,
" and formed a kind of a marine water-spout. Passing over
" a pond, it drew up all the water, raised it a prodigious
" height, and, afterwards, dispersed it with such force, that
" it resembled a thick smoke. The cloud overturned in its
" passage several houses and trees.

" Another singular phænomenon happened, near the Baltic,
" on the 17th of August, 1750. This was a column of
" water, attached to a thick cloud, which the wind carried
" along the earth. It attracted every thing it met with,
" corn, bushes, and branches of trees, raised them about
" thirty feet high, intwined them, and let them fall in small
" parcels.——Some pretend that firing of cannon will break
" and dissipate these water-spouts.

" There is yet another species, called typhon, which does
" not descend from the clouds, but raises water from the sea
" to

" to the fky. Thefe typhons are caufed by fubterranean fires;
" for the fea is feen to boil on fuch occafions, and the air is
" full of fulphureous exhalations."

M. de Bomare, au mot Vents.

In the *Memoirs de l'Academie de Stockholm*, we read that, on
the 17th of Auguft, 1746, one of thefe columns was feen near
yftad, which attracted ftubble and wheat-fheafs, and tore up
fmall bufhes by the roots.

There was another more fingular in 1727, at Beziers of fomething like a violet colour, which took up a quantity of young
olive fhoots, tore up trees, tranfported a large walnut-tree
forty or fifty paces, and marked its route by a well beaten
track, on which three coaches might pafs a-breaft; it was
accompanied by a thick fmoke, and made a noife like the
roaring of a troubled fea.

Another appeared, in the fame year, in la Brie, which paffing over a ditch, filled it with earth and ftones, and marked
its paffage by fuch kind of furrows as a harrow might
make.

A column of a confiderable height, was feen at Carcaffona,
in the year 1776. It feemed to defcend from a neighbouring
mountain, was of a deep marigold colour, from the bottom
half way, while the reft appeared inflamed. The noife of
this meteor refembled the bellowing of a herd of oxen. It
threw itfelf into the river Aude, which it dried up for a confiderable fpace,

Dict. des Merv. de la Nat. Tom. II. mot Trombe.

(23) In 1740, hail-ftones fell at Rome as large as eggs. In
Thuringia, a province of Germany, there fell hail-ftones in
1738, as large as geefe eggs.

Vallade

Vallade affures us, in his defcription of the Orcade iflands, that in the month of June, 1680, there fell pieces of ice a foot thick, during a ftorm. Morton obfervcd at Northampton, in 1693, blades of ice, which fell in a ftorm, that were two inches long, and one inch thick. Befides which, he obferved fpherical grains, an inch in diameter, in which were feen five different coloured rays, which formed a kind of ftar.

In 1720, hail fell at Crembs, fome of the ftones of which weighed fix pounds.

Dict. des Merv. de la Nat. Tome I. mot Grêle.

" Hail is a kind of rain condenfed and chryftallized by the " cold, as it paffes through the middle region of the air, " before it reaches the earth.————Nicephorus-Califtus re- " ports, after the taking of Rome by Alaric, hail-ftones fell " in many places of eight pounds weight. In 8:4, there fell, " near Autun, in Burgundy, among the hail, pieces of ice, " fixteen feet long, feven wide, and two feet thick.————In " 1723, there were hail-ftones fell at Leicefter of five inches.———— " In the famous ftorm that happened in Picardy, Auguft, " 1722, the leaft hail that fell, accompanied with thunder and " lightning, weighed a pound, and the largeft eight.————Many " of the ftones were forked and pointed, &c."————*M. de Bomare, au mot Grêle.*

(24) " Edens, an Englifh traveller, relates, that having " as a phyfician, rendered confiderable fervices to the inhabi- " tants of the Canary iflands, he obtained of them the liberty " to vifit the Sepulchral Caverns; a favour they grant to no " one, and which cannot be obtained, againft their will, " without life being expofed to the greateft danger.

" They have an extreme veneration for the bodies of their " anceftors, and the curiofity of ftrangers is to them profa- " nation.

" nation.——Thefe caves are places anciently dug out of the
" rocks, or formed by nature.——The corpfe is fewed in goats-
" fkins, with thongs of the fame, and the feams are fo equal
" and clofe, as to become very admirable; but what aftonifhes
" moft, is, that the bodies are almuft all entire; and in both
" fexes are equally found the eyes, (clofed) the hair, ears,
" nofe, lips, teeth, and beard.——

" One day, when the author of this account was taking
" rabbits by a ferret, this little animal, which had a bell round
" it's neck, was loft in a burrow, and difappeared, without
" their being able to know how. One of the hunters, to
" whom he belonged, feeking for him in the midft of rocks
" and brambles, difcovered the entrance to a fepulchral cave
" of the Gaunches, he defcended, &c.

" If the account of the oldeft of the Gaunches may be
" believed, there was a particular tribe among their ancef-
" tors, who knew the art of embalming, and preferved it as
" a facred myftery.——This tribe compofed the prieft-hood,
" and did not intermarry with the others; but, after the
" conqueft of the ifland, moft of them were deftroyed, and
" their fecret perifhed with them. Tradition has only taught
" us a part of the ingredients neceffary to that operation."

Abrég. de l'Hift. Gen. des Voy. Tome I. par M. de la Harpe.

Among the ancients, the Egyptians, more than any others,
practifed embalming; and bodies have been preferved above
two thoufand years. In the breaft of one of thefe corpfe,
a branch of rofemary was found, fcarcely dried. This art
has only been known in Europe during thefe latter ages;
formerly they made deep incifions in the corpfe, falted it,
and enclofed it in a tanned ox's hide.——*Encyclopedie.*

(5) Tha

(25) The French call this tree calebaffier, and it's fruit baboon's-bread. It grows in Senegal, and the natives call it gooee, and it's fruit booee; it's real name is boabab. It's firft branches, which project almoft horizontally, are commonly fixty feet long, and it's trunk about feventy feet round; though many travellers have feen them larger. Ray fays that, between the Niger and the Gambia, fome have béen meafured fo monftrous that feventeen men, with extended arms, fcarcely could embrace them. According to which, thefe trees muft be about eighty-five feet in circumference. The boabab, adds M. de Bomare, is probably the largeft of known vegetables; though there are accounts, in the works of different naturalifts, of well known trees fo prodigious as to be reckoned vegetable monfters. Ray cites the account of travellers who have feen a tree, in Brazil, 120 feet round; and there are ftill trees more marvellous, mentioned in late hiftories of China; one of which is in the province of Suchu, near the town of Kian; it is called Sieunich, that is to fay, the tree of a thoufand years; and is fo vaft that one of it's branches only will afford fhelter to 200 fheep. Another tree, in the province of Chekianga, is nearly 400 feet in circumference.

(26) There is a ferpent, called the Serpent of Damel, which is very common in the wefterly province of Africa. The Negroes, when bitten, put powder on the wound, and apply fire; and if this operation is but a little while deferred, the poifon gains ground, and death foon follows.———The Sereres, a Negro nation, catch and eat them. Some of them are fifteen, fome twenty feet long, and fix inches in diameter. There are fome green, others black, fpotted, and ftriped with beauteous colours.

On the Slave coaft, in the kingdoms of Juida and Benin, all the Savages adore a kind of ferpent, which they call the Fetiche.

Fetiche. Thefe ferpents are very gentle, not venomous, and extremely familiar. It is death to kill them. The Negroes look upon them as benevolent deities, and have particular rites for them; though they deftroy, with great care, thofe ferpents which are poifonous.

(27) " The French of Fort St. Louis had a lionefs, which
" they kept chained. The animal had a difeafe in the jaw,
" that reduced it to extremity; and the people of the fort,
" taking off the chains, threw the body into a neighbour-
" ing field. In this ftate it was found by M. Compagnon,
" Author of the Voyage of Bambuck, as he returned from
" the chafe. The eyes were clofed, the jaw open, and,
" already, fwarming with ants. Compagnon took pity on
" the poor animal, wafhed the gullet with water, and
" poured fome milk down the throat. The effects of this
" fimple remedy were wonderful. The lionefs was brought
" back to the fort, recovered by degrees, but, far from
" forgetting the fervice done her, took fuch an affection
" for her benefactor that fhe would receive food only from
" him; and, when cured, followed him about the ifland,
" with a cord about her neck, like the moft familiar
" dog.

" A lion, having efcaped from the menagerie of the Great
" Duke of Tufcany, entered the city of Florence, every
" where fpreading terror. Among the fugitives was a
" woman with a child in her arms, which fhe let fall. The
" lion feized, and feemed ready to devour it, when the
" mother, tranfported by the tender affections of nature,
" ran back, threw herfelf before the lion, and by her geftures
" demanded her child. The lion looked at her fteadfaftly;
" her cries and tears feemed to affect him, till, at laft,
" he laid the child down without doing it the leaft in-
" jury.

" jury.——Mifery and defpair, then, have expreffions intel-
" ligible to the moft favage monfters; but what is yet more to
" be admired, is the refiftlefs and fublime emotion which can
" make a mother offer herfelf a prey to a ferocious animal, be-
" fore which all fly: that lofs of reafon, fo fuperior to rea-
" fon's felf, which can impel a defpairing woman to recur
" to the pity of a beaft breathing only death and carnage.
" This is the inftinct of fupreme grief, which always would
" perfuade itfelf it is not poffible to remain inflexible to it's
" feelings."

Abrégé, &c. par M. de la Harpe, Tom. II.

" It is very certain fays M. de Buffon, that the lion, when
" taken young, and brought up among domeftic animals, may
" eafily be brought to live, and even play harmlefs among
" them; that he is gentle to his mafters, careffes them, efpe-
" cially in the former part of life, and that though his natural
" ferocity may fometimes break forth, it feldom is turned
" againft thofe who do him good.-

" I might cite a number of particular facts, in which, I
" own, I have found fome exaggeration; but which are fuf-
" ficiently eftablifhed to prove, at leaft by their union, that
" his anger is noble, his courage magnanimous, and his
" heart feeling.. Often has he been feen to difdain weak
" enemies, defpife their infults, and pardon their offenfive
" liberties.   When reduced to captivity, though weary,
" he is not peevifh; but on the contrary, becomes habi-
" tually gentle, obeys his mafter, flatters the hand that
" feeds him; fometimes grants life to animals given him as
" prey, and as if attached to them by this generous act,
" continues afterwards the fame protection; lives peaceably
" with them, gives them part of his fubfiftence, lets them

" fometimes

" sometimes take it all, and would rather suffer hunger than
" lose the fruit of his first benefit."

The circumstances relative to the chase of the lion are
taken from *l' Histoire des Voyages.*

(28) There is a remarkable echo near Rosneath, a fine country seat in Scotland, situated to the west of a salt-water lake
that runs into the Clyde, 17 miles below Glasgow. The lake
is surrounded by hills, some of which are barren rocks, others
are covered with trees. A good trumpeter, standing on a
point of land that gives an opening to the water towards the
north, has played an air and stopped: the echo repeated the air
faithfully and distinctly, but not so loud, this echo having
ceased, another has done the same, and a third, as exactly as
the two former, with no difference but that of becoming more
feeble. The same experiment, several times repeated, had still
the same success.

There was formerly, in the Chateau de Simonette, a windowed wall, whence what was said was forty times repeated.
Addison and others, who have travelled in Italy, mention an
echo which would repeat the report of a pistol fifty-six times,
even when the air was foggy.

In the Memoires of the academy of Sciences at Paris, for
the year 1692, mention is made of the echo at Genetay,
two leagues from Rouen, which has this peculiarity, that
the person who sings does not hear the echo, but his voice
only; and, on the contrary, those who listen do not hear
the voice, but the echo, but with surprizing variations; for
the echo seems sometimes to approach, and sometimes to retire: sometimes the voice is heard distinctly, at others not
at all; some hear only a single voice, others several; one
hears to the right, another to the left, &c.——This echo still
exists,

exifts, but is not what it was, becaufe the environs have been
planted with trees, which have greatly hurt the effect.

(29) This bird is called flamingo, or phœnicopterus, or
becharu. The fecond name among the Greeks, fignified the
bird of flaming wing, becaufe, when it flies againft the fun,
it appears like a firebrand. The plumage, when young, is
rofe coloured, and at ten months old the colour of fire. " It's
" beak, fays M. de Buffon, is of a very extraordinary form,
" its legs exceffively high, its neck long and dented; its
" body ftands higher, though it is lefs, than the ftork's; and
" its form, fomewhat odd, makes it diftinguifhable from that
" of every other fifhing bird.

" This bird is found on the old Continent, from the coafts
" of the Mediterranean, to the moft fouthern part of Africa.
" Flamingos are plentiful in the weft of Africa, at Angola
" and Congo; where, out of fuperftitious refpect, the Negroes
" will not fuffer one of them to be killed."

The flamingo is certainly a bird of paffage, and numerous
at St. Domingo and the Antilles; they fly in fociety, and
naturally form themfelves into a line, fo that at a certain diftance they refemble a brick-wall, and, fomewhat nearer,
foldiers arranged in rank and file. They place fentinels,
which give the alarm by a very fhrill cry, like the found
of a trumpet, at which they all take flight. Their flefh is
much admired as food, and ancient Epicures were very fond
of their tongues.

(30) " This bird, called *Cucullus Indicator*, fays M. de
" Buffon, is found in the interior parts of Africa, at fome
" diftance from the Cape of Good Hope, and is famous
" for indicating where wild bee-hives may be found; twice
" a day its fhrill cry is heard founding *cherr cherr*; which
" feems to call the honey-hunters, who anfwer by a foft
" whiftle,

" whiftle, ftill approaching. When it is feen, it flies and
" hovers over a hollow tree, that contains a hive; and if
" the hunters do not come, it redoubles its cries, flies back,
" returns to the tree, and points out the prey in the moft
" marking manner; forgetting nothing to excite them to
" profit by the treafure it has difcovered, and which pro-
" bably it could not enjoy without the aid of man; either
" becaufe the entrance to the hive is too fmall, or from
" other circumftances which the relater has not told us.
" While the honey is procuring, it flies to fome diftance,
" intereftingly obferving all that paffes, and waiting for its
" part of the fpoil; which the hunters never forget to
" leave, though not enough to fatiate the bird, confequently
" not to deftroy his ardour for this kind of chafe. ·

" This is not the tale of a traveller, but the obfervations
" of an enlightened man, who himfelf affifted at the de-
" ftruction of many bee-hives, betrayed by this little fpy, to
" the Royal Society of London. He procured two of thefe
" birds that had been killed, to the great fcandal of the
" Hottentots, for in all countries the exiftence of a ufeful
" being is precious."

M. de Buffon adds, in a note, that the honey-hunter is
fometimes devoured by wild beafts; whence it has been faid,
that they and the bird underftand each other, and that it allures
their prey.

Hift. Nat. des Oifeaux, Tom. XII. Edit. in 12mo.

(31) Mecca is a town of Arabia Felix, about as large as
Marfeilles. The magnificence of its mofque, draws a prodigious concourfe of all the Mahometan fects, who go thither
on pilgrimages. It is the birth place of Mahomet.

(32) Medina is a city of Arabia Felix, the name of which
fignifies, in Arabic, a city in general; and here *the city,* by

way

way of excellence; for here it was that Mahomet fixed the
feat of the empire of the Muffulmans, and here he died. It was
before time called Lotreb. In the midft of Medina is the famous mofque, to which the Mahometans go in pilgrimage; and
in this mofque are the tombs of Mahomet, Abubecker, and
Omar. Medina is governed by a Scherif, who fays he is of the
race of Mahomet, and who is an independend fovereign.——
Encyclopedie.

(33) Cairo is the capital of Egypt; Sultan Selim took it from
the Mamaluks, in 1517; fince which time it has been fubject to
the Turks. Old Cairo is three quarters of a league diftant
from it, on the borders of the Nile; the Cophtes have a magnificent church there (a).

(34) The pyramids of Egypt were built to ferve as tombs
for their conftructors. The Egyptians of lower rank, inftead
of building pyramids, dug caves, in which every day mum-
mies are difcovered. Each pyramid has an opening into a
long low alley, which led to a chamber, where the ancient
Egyptians depofited the bodies for which the pyramids were
built. Their conftruction is very regular : each of the three
remaining large ones is placed at the head of others, fmaller
and difficult to diftinguifh, they are fo much covered with
fand. All are built on one fole rock, hid under white
fand.

In all the pyramids there are deep pits, cut fquare in the
rock; on the walls of fome are hieroglyphics, cut alfo in
the rock. The three principal pyramids known to travellers
are about nine miles from Cairo; and the moft fuperb of
them is upon a rock, in a fandy defert of Africa, a quarter of
a league diftant, towards the weft, from the plains of Egypt.
This rock rifes about 100 feet above the level of the plains,

(a) A Chriftian fet of Jacobines, or Monophyfites.

but

but with an eafy afcent and contributes much to the majefty of the building.

The pyramid contains chambers, galleries, &c. and thofe who afcend on the outfide reft occafionally to take breath. There is a fquare chamber, about half way up, which ferves only for a refting-place. When arrived at the top, a platform is found, whence a moft agreeable landfcape is feen. This platform is fixteen or feventeen feet fquare, yet the pyramid feems to end in a point; the defcent, which is on the outfide, muft be very dangerous.

(35) " The ifland of Thera, in the Archipelago, which
" is twelve great French leagues in circumference, was
" thrown from the bottom of the fea by the violence of a
" volcano, which has fince produced fix other iflands.
" This volcano is not yet extinguifhed, for in 1707 it
" broke out , with redoubled fury, and fent forth a new
" ifland, fix miles in circumference. The fea, at that
" time, appeared greatly agitated, and covered with flames,
" and from it rofe, with dreadful noife, feveral burning
" rocks. The earth has been fo rent and torn in thefe
" latitudes, that veffels can no longer find anchorage
" there.

" One of the moft violent'eruptions of Vefuvius, (the twenty
" fecond) happened on the 20th of May, 1737; the moun-
" tain vomited, from feveral mouths, huge torrents of burn-
" ing, melted, metallic matter, which overfpread the country,
" and took its courfe towards the fea. M. de Montealégre,
" who communicated the account to the Academy at Paris,
" obferved, with horror, one of thefe rivers of fire. Its courfe
" was fix or feven miles before it reached the fea ; its breadth
" was fifty or fixty paces; its depth twenty-five or thirty
" French palms; and, in certain bottoms or vallies, 120, &c."
——M. de Bomare.

" The

" The eruptions of volcanoes are ufually announced by
" fubterranean noifes like thunder ; by dreadful hiflings, and
" interrior ftrife.   Hiftory inform us, that during two erup-
" tions of Vefuvius, the volcano caft up fo great a quantity
" of afhes that they flew as far as Egypt, Lybia, and Syria.
" In 1600, at Aréquina, in Peru, was an eruption of a
" volcano, which covered all the neighbouring lands for
" 30 or 40 leagues round, with calcined fand and afhes,
" which lay in fome places two yards deep.   The lava vo-
" mited by Mount Ætna, has fometimes formed ftreams that
" ran 18,000 paces.

   " Volcanoes often have been known to caft from their en-
" trails boiling water, fifh, fhells, and other marine bodies.
" In 1631, during an eruption of Vefuvius, the fea in part
" became dry ; it feemed abforded by the volcano, which foon
" after overflowed the country with falt water.———Vol-
" canoes are found in hot as well as cold countries."———
Encyclopedie.

   (36) The entrance to the Cavern of Policandro (or Poli-
cando) is grand, the bottom is covered with congelations,
formed from drops of water, which diftil from the fummit,
but of a ferruginous nature, pointed, and hard enough to
wound the feet.   The ceiling affords various and great beauties.   Thefe congelations, though exceedingly elegant,
are not the only ornaments the grotto has received from
nature, for here is plentifully found a fpecies of iron ore,
in the form of ftars, and fhining like polifhed fteel.   The
pieces, in fome places, have a red caft, and are as brilliant as
diamonds.

   In another part of the vault are feen large maffes of round
bodies, pendent like grapes, fome red, others of a deep
black, but perfectly bright and fhining.   The greateft ornament of the ceiling confifts in the fame fpecies of conge-

lation in the form of cryftals ; feveral are brought to a point, as if purpofely fo laboured ; and what is more remarkable, fome of them are naturally gilded, in as regular a manner as if they had juft come from the hands of an able artift.——— *Merv: de la Nat. Tom. I.*

(37) Mr. Swinburne, an excellent author already cited, has written another very interefting work, entitled *Travels through the two Sicilies,* where I have found a defcription of the phænomenon, called by the country people *La Fata Morgana ;* which name, Mr. Swinburne fays, is derived from an opinion, eftablifhed, among the vulgar, that this fpectacle is produced by a fairy, or a magician.   The populace are enchanted at the fight of the phænomenon, and run through the ftreets to be behold and invite others to behold it, with fhouts and acclamations of joy.   It feldom appears at Reggio : Mr. Swinburne did not fee it, but fays, its caufes are learnedly explained by Kircher, Minazi, and other authors.   Mr. Swinburne gives an exact defcription of it, taken from the account of Father Angelucci, who was an eyewitnefs of the phænomenon ; and it is from this fame defcription, by Father Angelucci, cited by Mr. Swinburne, that I have made a literal tranflation, without embellifhment, for my tale.

This phænomenon is mentioned, but very fuperficially, in a French work, entitled *Tableau de l'Univers.*

(38) " Lovers, fays Athenæus, an ancient Greek author,
" decorate with flowers the doors of their miftreffes, like
" as they ornament the gates of a temple ; whence, no
" doubt, the prefent cuftom of the Greeks to adorn their
" doors, and thofe of the perfons they love, on the firft of
" May, is derived.   They fing and walk before the houfes
" of their fair miftreffes, to draw them to their windows ;
" and fuch were the gallantries they practifed in the days
" of

" of Horace.—The young maidens dreffed their heads with
" natural flowers, with which they made themfelves garlands ;
" and the young men, who wifhed to be thought gallant, did
" the fame."

Voy. de la Grèce, 3me Edit. Tom. I. par M. Guys.

(39) " There was anciently a feaft inftituted in honour of
" Hecate, who had hofpitably entertained Thefeus, and who
" had likewife offered up victims and vows for his victory and
" fafe return ; hence fhe obtained her rank among the God-
" deffes."

" In ancient Greece, when a ftranger arrived, the mafter
" of the houfe took him by the hand, in token of confi-
" dence, and his firft duty was to lead him to the bath, and
" prefent a change of raiment.——Among the moderns,
" when a ftranger arrives, the mafter of the houfe meets and
" embraces him, then conducts him to his moft commodious
" apartment, and interrogates him concerning his travels,
" while the flaves prepare the bath ; where he finds linen and
" clothes to change, and thofe he has left off are taken by the
" flaves, wafhed, and repaired while he ftays."

M. Guys, Tom. I.

(40) " Now, as anciently, the nurfe of the mafter or
" miftrefs, in all refpectable Grecian houfes, is confidered
" as one of the family. Of old, a woman who had nurfed
" a child, never quitted it, not even after marriage : and
" among the moderns, as well as the ancients, the nurfe is
" generally a flave, purchafed when the time of delivery
" draws near."

" The attachment of nurfes to the children they have
" fuckled is fo ftrongly interwoven with their manners,
" that the modern name for nurfe is *Paramana*, a moft kind
" word, and even more expreffive than the ancient appella-
" tion, fince it fignifies *fecond mother*. The nurfe is always

" lodged

" lodged in the houfe, when fhe has fuckled a child, and,
" from that moment, is in a manner incorporated in the
" family."

" Female flaves, now, as well as anciently, are treated with
" much kindnefs and humanity by the Greeks, and, after a cer-
" tain time, are freed; fome are adopted while young, and thefe
" are called *Daughters of their fouls.*"

" The maids and flaves work, as formerly, at embroidering
" with their miftreffes, and do all houfehold duties. When
" their miftreffes go abroad, they follow as they did of old.
" ——The Legiflator, Zaleucus, to reprefs the vanity and
" luxury of his time, ordained that no free woman fhould go
" abroad attended by more than one maid, *at leaft, unlefs fhe
" was drunk.*"—*M. Guys, Tom. I.*

(41) " The Grecian ladies have always delighted to adorn
" themfelves with jewels; they enrich their girdles, necklaces,
" and bracelets, with them; and, while their heads are deck-
" ed with the moft beautiful flowers of the fpring, the dia-
" mond is feen fparkling befide the jaffamine and rofe: they
" drefs themfelves thus when going abroad, or without an in-
" tention of being feen."

" Thefe ornaments are only facrificed to fome ftrong
" caufe for grief.—Almoft all the Grecian women forbear
" to wear them in the abfence of their hufbands.—At pre-
" fent, when they go any diftance, unwilling to walk through
" the ftreets with their jewels, they have them carried, put
" them on before they enter the houfe they are going to, and
" take them off when they return: this likewife is a very
" ancient cuftom."

" The ufe of the veil is very old; and now, as formerly,
" is an effential part of drefs, by which rank is diftinguifhed.
" The veil of the miftrefs and the maid, the free woman
" and the flave, all are different.——The origin of the
" veil

" veil is attributed by the Greeks to modesty and bashfulness,
" equally timid."

" The veil of the Grecian ladies of modern times is muslin ·
" fringed with gold."——*M. Guys, Tom. I.*

(42) " The repast of the Greeks, however little ani-
" mated, finished always by songs. The modern lyre of the
" Greeks resembles that of Orpheus, according to the de-
" scription of Virgil, and is sometimes nipped with fingers,
" and sometimes touched with a bow (*a*).——The guittar and
" the lyre are the principal instruments in use among the
" modern Greeks. The shepherd plays, indifferently, the
" musette, the flute, or the lyre."——*M. Guys, Tom. I.*

(43) The modern Greeks, have preserved dances in honour of Flora ; the wives and maidens of the village ga-
ther and scatter flowers, and bedeck themselves from
head to foot. She who leads the dance, more ornamented
than the others, represents Flora and the Spring, which the
hymn they sing announces the return of ; and one of them
sings,

" Welcome sweet nymph, Goddess of the month of May."

In the Grecian villages, and among the Bulgarians, they still
observe the feast of Ceres. When harvest is almost ripe, they
go dancing to the sound of the lyre, and visit the fields, whence
they return with their heads ornamented with wheat ears interwoven with the hair.

(44) " Embroidering is the occupation of the Grecian
" women ; to the Greeks we owe the art, which is exceed-
" ingly ancient among them, and has been carried to the
" highest degree of perfection.——Enter the chamber of a
" Grecian girl, and you will see blinds at the windows,

(*a*). I cannot conceive how they can play the lyre with a bow.

M 3   " and

" and no other furniture than a fofa, and a cheft inlaid with
" ivory, in which are kept filks, needles, and their embroi-
" dery.

" Apologues, Tales, Romances, owe their origin to Greece.
" The mordern Greeks love tales and fables, and have re-
" ceived them from the Orientals and Arabs, with as much
" eagernefs as they formerly adopted them from the Egyp-
" tians.——The old women love always to relate, and the
" young pique themfelves on repeating thofe they have learnt,
" or can make, from fuch incidents as happen within their
" knowledge."

M. Guys, Tom. I.

(45) " The Greeks, at prefent, have not a fixed time for
" the celebration of marriages, like the ancients, among whom
" the ceremony was performed in the month of January.
" Formerly the bride was bought by real fervices done the fa-
" ther. This was afterwards reduced to prefents, and, to
" this time, that cuftom is continued, tho' the prefents are ar-
" bitrary. The man is not obliged to purchafe the woman he
" marries, but, on the contrary, receives a portion with her
" equal to her condition.

" It was on the famous fhield of Achilles, that Homer has
" defcribed a marriage proceffion :

" Here facred pomp, and genial feaft, delight,
" And folemn dance, and hymeneal rite.
" Along the ftreets the new-made brides are led,
" With torches flaming to the nuptial bed :
" The youthful dancers in a circle bound,
" To the foft flute and cittern's filver found.
" Through the fair ftreets the matrons in a row,
" Stand in their porches and enjoy the fhow."

POPE.

" The

" The fame pomp, proceſſion, and muſic, are ſtill· in uſe.
" Dancers, muſicians, and ſingers who chant the Epithalamium,
" go before ; the bride, loaded with ornaments, her eyes down-
" caſt, and herſelf ſuſtained by women, or two near relations,
" walks extremely ſlow, &c.——Formerly the bride wore a
" red or yellow veil ; the Armenians do ſo ſtill. This was
" to hide the bluſh of modeſty, the embarraſſment and tears
" of the young virgin.

" The bright torch of Hymen is not forgotten among
" the, modern Greeks ; it is carried before the new married
" couple into the nuptial chamber, where it burns till it is
" conſumed ; and it would be an ill omen, were it, by
" any accident, extinguiſhed ; wherefore it is watched with
" as much care as was of old the ſacred fire of the veſ-
" tals.

" Arrived at the church the bride and bridegroom each wear
" a crown, which, during the ceremony, the prieſt changes,
" by giving the crown of the bridegroom to the bride, and
" that of the bride to the bridegroom ; which cuſtom alſo
" is derived from the ancients.——I muſt not forget an eſ-
" ſential ceremony which the Greeks have preſerved, which
" is the cup of wine given to the bridegroom, in token of
" adoption ; it was the ſymbol of contract and alliance ; the
" bride drank from the ſame cup, which afterwards paſſed round
" to the relations and gueſts.

" They dance and ſing, ſtill, all night, but the companions
" of the bride are excluded ; they feaſt among themſelves,
" in ſeparate apartments, far from the tumult of the nuptials.
" The modern Greeks, like the ancient, on the nuptial day,
" decorate their doors with green branches· and garlands of
" flowers."

M. Guys, Tom. I.

M 4   M. Guys,

M. Guys, the eldeft fon of him already cited, gives an
interefting account of a Grecian marriage, at which he was
prefent.

" The young bride, richly dreffed, wearing long treffes of
" threads of gold, interwoven with her beautiful hair, after
" the manner of the Greeks, defcended from her apart-
" ment ; fhe eagerly advanced to kifs her father and mother,
" who waited to receive her, at the head of ten children.
" —Who, among us, could behold with dry eyes, a tender
" and refpectable mother, unable to detach herfelf from a
" daughter, whom fhe preffed in her arms, and whom fhe
" bedewed with tears, which an excefs of joy and affec-
" tion caufed abundantly to flow on her maternal bofom ?
" ——The father wept alfo, but, with eyes raifed to heaven,
" pronounced, with a firm tone, a paternal benediction on
" his daughter, and vows for the happinefs of her and her
" hufband.——At their return, nofegays, woven with threads
" of gold, were given to the young men, faying, Go you and
" marry alfo."

M. Guys terminates the recital by faying, the bride's mother conducted her daughter into an apartment fuperbly fur-
nifhed ; the tapeftry and bed of which, embroidered on a
ground of white, adorned with beautiful flowers, were the
work of this good mother. " She had laboured at them, pri-
" vately, adds M. Guys, for ten years, without the knowledge
" of any one." M. Guys, Tom. II.

(46) " The Grecian houfes are divided into two parts, by
" a great hall which takes up the centre and whole width.
" In this hall they give feafts, and perform all ceremonies that
" require room, &c."

M. Guys, Tom. I.

(47) " A Grecian woman weeps for the death of her
" hufband, her fon, &c. with her female friends, for feve-
" ral

" ral days, who fing their praifes and regrets.—Their man-
" ner of fhewing grief is now, as formerly, by plucking up
" their hair, and tearing their garments.   Fathers and mo-
" thers follow their children, when carried to the grave;
" and the body is now, as of old, wafhed before it is buried.
" If it is the corpfe of a young virgin, they clothe it in its
" fineft robes, crown it with flowers, and the women throw
" rofes and fcented water from their windows upon the cof-
" fin as it paffes.   The ancients adorned the dead with
" crowns of flowers, to indicate they had at length over-
" come the miferies and vexations of life.——The funeral
" repaft is not neglected by the modern Greeks; the neareft
" relation undertakes the charge, and with this the cere-
" mony ends.——Fathers and mothers, in Greece, wear
" mourning for their children (a), and this mourning is
" very long; which is alfo an ancient Grecian cuftom.——
" The Greeks have preferved the ufage of dreffing the
" dead in their beft habits, and of carrying them to the grave
" with their faces uncovered."   (b)

In this fame work, by M. Guys, is a letter from Madame
Chéniér to the author, (c) which firft gave me the idea of
the Epifode of Euphrofyne.   I fhall only cite fuch paffages
from this letter as I have profited by, the reft having no relation to my Epifode.

" A Grecian lady, equally diftinguifhed by her rank and
" the beauties of her mind, and who to the charms of her
" fex added thofe of a good education, lived with a youn-
" ger brother, who, from excefs of virtue, had renounced
" honours and emoluments, to which his alliances and rank:

(a) They do the fame in Italy.
(b) The fame cuftom is obferved in Italy.
(c) Tom. I. page 283.

" might

" might naturally have taught him to afpire. For his fifter
" he had all the affection of a brother, and all the friend-
" fhip of a congenial mind. This dear brother was attacked
" by a malignant fever, and died.—His fifter, according
" to the cuftom of the country, accompanied the proceffion,
" preceded and followed by part of the Grecian nobility.
" Every thing announced the dejection of an affectionate
" heart; the diforder of her veil and drefs, the negligence
" of her hair, added new traits to the grief vifible in her
" countenance.——After the cuftomary prayers, they per-
" formed the ceremony which the Greeks have preferved,
" which they call the laft farewell. When the Patriarch
" has embraced the corpfe, the relations, and thofe who walk
" in the proceffion, do the fame. This fcene, which the
" idea of an eternal adieu rendered but too affecting, be-
" came more fo, when the fifter, with ftreaming eyes, at-
" tending only to her caufe of grief, rent her garments,
" and tore her hair up by the root, to ftrew over the coffin
" of a brother, whom fhe was foon no more to fee. Efforts
" were ufed to fhorten this gloomy fcene, and bring back
" the afflicted fifter to her houfe; fhe then became lefs agitated,
" and her grief more calm."

After this detail, Madame Cheniér fufpends her narration, in
order to defcribe the garden of the deceafed.

" The fea was feen from this garden, which was orna-
" mented by beautiful flowers, fruit trees, and an area full
" of birds; there was likewife a refervoir of water, recruited
" by the fea, in which all forts of fifh were kept. This
" garden, thefe birds and fifh, were the amufement of
" the fage, who juft had been torn from his fifter and
" friends.—*Where is my brother?* faid this defpairing fifter,
" as her eyes wandered over the garden.—*He is gone——*
" *has*

" has paſſed away like a ſhadow——Ye flowers which he culti-
" vated with ſo much pleaſure! ye have already loſt the freſhneſs
" his hand beſtowed!——Periſh with him!——Droop and wither
" even to the root!——Ye fiſh, ſince ye have no longer a maſ-
" ter nor a friend, to watch over your preſervation——return
" ye to the great waters!——Return and ſeek uncertain life!
" ——And ye little birds! if ye may ſurvive your grief!
" accompany my ſighs with your plaintive ſongs——Thou
" peaceful ocean, whoſe ſurface begins to be diſturbed, art thou
" alſo ſenſible to my ſorrows (a)?——Then, turning towards
" her ſlaves, ſhe ſaid, Weep, my children, weep! Ye have loſt
" one who was kinder than a father to you!——My brother
" is no more!——Cruel death has dragged him from us!
" ——He has diſappeared like a ſhadow, and we ſhall ſee him no
" more! Theſe haunts, which his preſence rendered ſo de-
" lightful, muſt now become the reſidence of gloom and af-
" fliction."

" The tombs of the Greeks, like thoſe of the Turks,
" and other Eaſtern people, are ſituated near the highway;
" and though without incloſure are not the leſs ſacred. The
" Greeks and Armenians plant elm trees round them;
" which tree the ancients choſe becauſe it bears no fruit, and
" therefore is a proper repreſentative of the dead. They like-
" wiſe uſe the cypreſs.——Beſides the ſtones which cover the
" tomb, there are little ſepulchral columns, which, as former-
" ly, bear the name of the interred; and this cuſtom is adopt-
" ed by the Turks.

" The Grecians come, occaſionally, and weep over the
" tombs——At Eaſter, which the Greeks celebrate with

(a) The ſea in the channel is ſmooth, evening and morning, and only begins to be agitated about ten o'clock, and till
ſun-ſet. The time of the day muſt juſtify the allegory.——
M. Guys.

" great

"'great rejoicings, feaſts, and public dances, there is one
" day on which they go in multitudes to viſit the tombs,
" where they weep for their relations, their friends, and, per-
" haps, the loſs of their liberty.——At preſent, the Grecian
" women are ſatisfied with tearing up their hair, though they
" formerly cut off their long treſſes, and ſtrewed them over
" the tombs of thoſe they lamented."

M. Guys, Tom. I.

Of all the people on earth, none are more magnificent
in their funerals than the Chineſe.

" The idea of death ceaſes not to torment them ; it ap-
" pears, however, leſs cruel, if they can purchaſe a coffin,
" and erect a tomb on the ſide of à hill, in an agreeable
" ſituation. They expend exceſſive ſums on their funerals,
" which are ſometimes performed ſix years after death, with
" unexampled magnificence. They hire men, and dreſs
" them in white, for mourning, to weep in the proceſſion
" for ſeveral ſucceſſive days ; they carry the deceaſed by
" water to the ſound of inſtruments, while the boat which
" bears the body, and thoſe which accompany it, are ſo
" illuminated, that the different coloured lights form de-
" ſigns even to the maſt-head.——<i>Voyages aux Indes Ori-
" entales & à la Chine fait par ordre du Roi, par M. Sonnerat,
" Tome II.

" (48) There are two ſeaſons of pearl fiſhing in the year ;
the firſt in March and April, the ſecond in Auguſt and
September : the more rain there falls in the year, the more
plentiful are the fiſheries. In the opening of the ſeaſon,
there appear ſometimes 250 barks on the banks. In the
larger barks are two divers, in the ſmaller, one. Each bark
puts off from ſhore, before ſun-riſe, by a land-breeze, which
never fails, and returns again by a ſea-breeze, that ſucceeds
it at noon.

As

As foon as the barks are arrived where the fifh lie, and have caft anchor, each diver binds a ftone, fix inches thick, and a foot long, under his body, which is to ferve him as ballaft, prevent his being driven away by the motion of the water, and enable him to walk more fteadily among the waves.

Befides this, they tie another very heavy ftone to one foot, whereby they are foon funk to the bottom of the fea; and, as the oyfters are ufually ftrongly faftened to the rocks, they arm their fingers with leathern mittens, to prevent them from being wounded, in fcraping them violently off; and fome even carry an iron rake for the purpofe.

Laftly, Each diver carries down with him a large net, in manner of a fack, tied to his neck by a long cord, the end whereof is faftened to the fide of the bark. The fack is intended for the reception of the oyfters gathered from the rock, and the cord is to pull up the diver, when his bag is full, or when he wants air. In this equipage, he precipitates himfelf above 60 feet under water. As he has no time to lofe there, he is no fooner arrived at the bottom, than he begins to run from fide to fide, fometims on fand, fometimes on a clay earth, and fometimes among the points of rocks, tearing off the oyfters he meets with, and cramming them into his budget.

At whatever depth the divers be, the light is fo great that they eafily behold what paffes in the fea, with the fame clearnefs as on land; and, to their confternation, they fometimes fee monftrous fifhes, from which all their addrefs in mudding the water, &c. will not always fave them, but they become their prey; and of all the perils of fifhery, this is one of the greateft and moft ufual.

The

The beſt divers will keep under water half an hour, the reſt do not ſtay leſs than a quarter ; during which time they hold their breath, without the uſe of oils, or any other liquors, only acquiring the habit by long practice. When they find chemſelves ſtraightened, they pull the rope by which the bag is faſtened, and hold faſt by it with both hands ; the people in the bark take the ſignal, and heave them up into the air, and unload them of their fiſh, which is ſometimes 500 oyſters, and ſometimes not above 50.

Some of the divers need a moment's reſpite, to recover their breath, others jump in again inſtantly, continuing this violent exerciſe, without intermiſſion for many hours. They unload their barks on ſhore, and lay their oyſters in an infinite number of little pits, dug four or five feet ſquare ; then raiſe heaps of ſand over them, to the height of a man, which, at a diſtance, looks like an army ranged in battle. In this condition they are left, till the rain, wind, and ſun obliges them to open, which ſoon kills them ; upon this the fleſh rots and dries, and the pearls, thus diſengaged, tumble into the pit, upon taking the oyſters out.

After clearing the pits of the groſſer filth, they ſift the ſand ſeveral times to ſeparate the pearls ; but what care ſoever they take herein, they always loſe a great many. When the pearls are cleaned and dried, the ſmalleſt are ſold as ſeed pearls, the reſt by auction to the higheſt bidder.

Pearls of unuſual figures, that is neither round nor in the form of a pear, are called *Baroguas*, and ours *Scotch Pearls* ; thoſe of unuſual ſizes are called *Parargons.* Such was that of Cleopatra, valued by Pliny at centies H. S. or 80,000l. ſterling ; that brought in 1574, to Philip II. of the ſize of a pigeon's egg, valued at 14,400 ducats ; that of the Emperor Rudolph, mentioned by Boetius, called *la Pereguina,*

Pereguina, or *the Incomparable,* of the shape of a muscade pear, and weighing 30 carats; and that mentioned by Tavernier, in the hands of the Emperor of Persia, in 1633, bought of an Arab for 32,000 tomans, which, at 30l. 9s. the toman, amounts to 110,400 sterling.—*Cyclopædia.*

(49) The shining of the sea-water is a common phænomenon in some seas. The prow of the vessel, plowing the waves, seems, during the darkness of the night, to set them on fire; the ship rides in a circle of light, and the wake leaves a long luminous track. This happens often on the coast of Malabar, and the Maldivia islands, where Mr. Godeheu observed the following appearances:

The sea seemed covered with small stars, the wake of the vessel was a lively bright white, strewed with brilliant and azure points. He learned that the sea, where most luminous, was full of small living animalcula, which not only shone but gave an oily liquor, which swam on the surface, and afforded that lively azure light. The animalcula could not be seen without a good microscope, and the liquor they shed remained on the strainer through which the sea-water passed, which, by this filtration, was deprived of it's luminous quality.—*M. de Bomare.*

(50) Natural Phosphori, are matters which become luminous at certain times, without the assistance of art or preparation. Such are the glow-worms, in our cold countries; and, in hot, lantern-flies, and other shining insects; rotten wood, the eyes, blood, scales, flesh, sweat, feathers, &c. of several animals; diamonds, when rubbed after a certain manner, or after having been exposed to the sun or light; sugar and sulphur, when pounded in a dark place; sea-water, and some mineral waters, when briskly agitated; a cat's or horse's back, duly rubbed with the hand, &c. in the dark; nay, Dr. Croon, tells, that, upon rubbing his own body,
. briskly,

briskly with a well warmed shirt, he has frequently made both to shine: and Dr. Sloane adds, that he knew a gentleman of Bristol, and his son, both whose stockings would shine much, after walking.—All natural phosphori have this in common, that they do not shine always, and that they never give any heat.—*Cyclopædia.*

(51) Diamond, in *Natural History*, by the ancients called *Adamant*, a precious stone, the first in rank, value, hardness, and lustre, of all gems.

Diamonds are found in the East-Indies, principally in the kingdoms of Golconda, Visapour, Bengal, and the island of Borneo. There are four mines, or rather two mines and two rivers, whence diamonds are drawn. The mines are, 1. That of Raolconda, in the province of Carnatica, five leagues from Golconda, and eight or nine from Visapour. It has been discovered about 250 years. 2. That of Gani, or Coulour, seven days journey from Golconda, eastwardly. It was discovered, about 170 years ago, by a peasant; who, digging in the ground, found a natural fragment of twenty-five carats. 3. That of Soumelpour, a large town in the kingdom of Bengal, near the diamond-mine: this is the most ancient of them all. It should rather be called that of Goual, which is the name of the river in the sand whereof these stones are found. Lastly, The fourth mine, or rather the second river, is that of Suecudan, in the island of Borneo.

The most remarkable *diamonds*, for size, now known, are, that known in France under the name of *Grand Sancy* by corruption of *cent six*, which is one of the crown jewels, weighing 106 carats; Governor Pitt's *diamond*, purchased by the late Duke of Orleans for Louis XV. King of France, weighing 136.3-4ths carats, and said to be bought for 125,000l. the *diamond* of the Great Duke of Tuscany, which weighs

139 1-half carats; that of the Great Mogul, weighing 279 9-16ths carats; and one mentioned by Mr. Jefferies, in a merchant's hands, weighing 242 1-16th carats.

According to Mr. Jefferies's rule, that the value of *diamonds* is in-duplicate ratio of their weights, and that a manufactured *diamond* of one carat is worth at a medium 8l. the Great Mogul's *diamond* must be valued at above 624.962l. this being the value of a *diamond* of 279 1-half carats.

(52) This account of the magnificence of the Great Mogul is found in many travellers.

(53) Opossum, or Possum, the name of a very remarkable American animal; the DIDELPHIS *marsupialis* of Linnæus. It's tail is round, and a foot long, and is of great service to it, as it uses it to twist round the branches of trees, hanging itself to them by that means; the tail is hairy, near the insertion, but naked all the other part, covered with small scales, and is partly black, partly of a brownish white; it's hinder feet are considerably longer than the fore ones, and each have five toes; they much resemble hands, and the nails are white and crooked, the hinder one being, as in the monkey kind, the longest.

What distinguishes this creature from all the other animals of the world is, that it has a bag or pouch into which it receives it's young as soon as delivered; this is a sort of open uterus, and is placed under the belly, near the hinder legs; in this the young are sheltered till they are able to shift for themselves; and, when they begin to be strong enough, they frequently run out and return in again. The creature is of a stinking smell, like our fox or martin. It feeds on sugar-canes and some other-vegetables; but not wholly on these, for it frequently preys on birds, which it catches on the trees, and often plays the fox's trick of stealing poultry.

The

The male *opoſſum* as well as the female, has this kind of pouch under it's belly, and takes upon himſelf, at times, the care of carrying and preſerving the young, in caſe of any impending danger.

The fleſh of the old animals is very good, like that of a ſucking pig; the hair is died by the Indian women, and wove into garters and girdles, and the ſkin is very fœtid.

Cyclopædia.

(54) " There is a tree, called the Devil Tree, which grows " in America; it's fruit, in a ſtate of maturity, is elaſtic; " and, when dried by the heat of the ſun, noiſily ſplits " and burſts, and darts forth it's grains. To this ſport of " nature the tree owe it's name, for at the moment of burſt- " ing, the effect of ſmall artillery is produced, the noiſe of " which ſucceeds rapidly, and is heard tolerably far off. " If this fruit be tranſported, before it be ripe, to a dry place, " or expoſed, on a chimney-piece, to a gentle heat, it will " have the ſame effect, and produce the ſame phænomenon."— " *M. de Bomare.*

(55) " Livy relates, how Sulpicius Gallus, lieutenant of " Paulus Æmilius, in the war againſt Perſia, predicted an " eclipſe of the moon to the ſoldiers, which ſhould happen " the next evening; and thus prevented the terror it would " otherwiſe have cauſed.

" A total eclipſe of the ſun is a ſingular ſpectacle. Cla- " vius, who ſaw that which happened on the 21ſt of Auguſt, " 1560, at Coimbre, tells us that the obſcurity was, as he " might ſay, greater, or at leaſt more ſtriking, than the dark- " neſs of night; people could not ſee where to ſet a foot, and " the birds fell with terror to the earth.—*Encyclopædia.*

The Acudia is a flying and luminous inſect, found in America; and ſuſpected to be the ſame with the cucuju or cocojus.

" It

" It is of the clafs of Scarabeus of the bignefs of the
" little finger, two inches long, and fo luminous that,
" when it flies by night, it fpreads great light. Some fay
" that if you rub the face with the humidity which iffues,
" in fhining fpots or ftars, from this little living phofphorus,
" it will appear refplendent.   Before the arrival of the
" Spaniards, the Indians made no ufe of candles, but
" of thefe infects, to light their houfes ; by one of which
" a perfon may read or write as eafily as by a lighted
" candle.

" When the Indians walked in the night, they fixed one
" of them to each great toe and others to the hand.
" When taken, thefe infects do not live above three weeks
" at moft; while they are in good health they are very lu-
" minous, but their light decreafes with their powers, and
" after they are dead they fhine no more.   They are doubly
" ufeful, for they fly about the houfes and devour the
" gnats."

" It is uncertain whether the acudia is not the fame in-
" fect as the lantern-fly ; fo named becaufe the fore-part
" of the head, whence the light iffues, has been called a
" lantern.——Mademoifelle Merian (a) who obferved
" this

(a) Maria Sybilla Merian, daughter of Matthew Merian, a
famous engraver and geographer, was born in Germany, in 1647 ;
and learnt, from Abraham Minion, to paint flowers, fruits,
plants, and infects, in which fhe excelled.   She underftood Latin, perfectly, and made natural hiftory her particular ftudy.
She paffed two years at Surinam, painting the infects of the
country ; and compofed a work, in German, called, *A Hiftory of*
the Infects of Europe, with Defigns after Nature ; and an Account
of

" this fort of infect at Surinam, fays, their light is fo ftrong
" that one alone was fufficient, at each fitting, to paint the
" figure of the infects of the country, which are engraved in
" her work

" There are fhining flies, found in Italy, or rather a fpe-
" cies of fcarabeus, about the fize of a bee, the belly of which
" is fo luminous, that three of them, inclofed in a tube of
" white glafs, will light a chamber.   M. l'Abbé Nollet has
" proved that the light of the infect extends over the place
" where it has been cruflied (a).

M. de Bomare.

    The moft fingular fcarabeus is that defcribed by M. Ro-
lander.   " The firft time M. Rolander picked up this in-
" fect, which is phofphoric, there came a noife from it's
" body, like that of fire arms, and a clear blue fmoke. An-
" other time he pricked the infect with a pin, and it went
" off as many as twenty times fucceffively.——M. Rolander
" opened the infect, and found a vacant bladder in it's
" body, but could not difcover whether this was it's refer-
" voir for air, or fome inteftine. This infect may be called
" the Bombardier (a).

Dict. de Merv. de la. Nat. Tom. II.

of the different Metamorphofes of Infects, and of the Plants on which
they feed.   She died at Amfterdam, aged 70, leaving two daughters, whom fhe had taught to paint. One of them, efpecially,
named Dorothea, was eminent for her knowledge and abilities.

Vie de Peintres, Tom. II.

    (a) The ditches of Mantua are full of thefe infects, and the
grafs and trees are covered with them, which, by night, produces a moft agreeable effect.

(56) Man-

(56) Manchineel *Hippomane*, in botany, a genus of the *Monoecia Adelphia* class.

" The wood of this tree is much esteemed for cabinet-work,
" being very durable, taking a fine polish, and, as is said, not
" being eaten by worms; but the tree abounding with a
" milky caustic juice, before it is felled, they make fires
" round the trunk, to burn out the juice, otherwise those
" who fell it would be in danger of losing their sight by this
" juice flying into their eyes. Wherever the juice touches
" the skin it raises blisters; and if it falls on linen, it turns
" it black, and it washes into holes. The like danger to the
" eyes is to be apprehended from the saw dust: the work-
" men, therefore, generally cover their faces with fine
" lawn.

" The tree produces fruit, somewhat like a golden pippin,
" which, if ignorantly eaten, inflames the mouth and throat
" to a great degree, and is very dangerous to the stomach, un-
" less timely medicines are applied. Dr. Peyssonel, in his
" observations on this fruit, informs us, that the savages use
" the juice of it to poison their arms, the wounds of which
" are thereby rendered mortal; that the rain which washes
" off the leaves causes blisters to rise like boiling oil; and
" that even the shade of the tree is fatal to those who sit un-
" der it. Timely evacuations, however, by purges and emetics,
" have prevented their ill effects."

Cyclopædia.

" The Cassada, or Cassava, is also a remarkable American
" shrub, from the root of which bread is made, though the
" juice expressed from the root, to prepare it for bread, will
" kill any animal that drinks it crude; as will the root eat-
" en with it's juice. Yet this juice may be boiled over the
" fire till a great part is evaporated; and the remainder, if
" it

" it be far evaporated, will be fweet, and ferve in the place of
" honey. If lefs evaporated, and fet by to ferment, it will
" make a very good and wholefome vinegar.

Cyclopædia.

(57) The Mangle, or Manglier, is a tree that grows in the
Weft-Indies, and chiefly in the Antilles, towards the mouths
of rivers.

" Bunches of filaments part from it's flexible branches,
" and hang to the earth, where they take root, and grow
" into new trees, as large as thofe to which they originally
" belonged, which again multiply in the fame manner; fo
" that a fingle tree may become a foreft. In the ifle of
" Cayenne, the marfhes are covered with them; and oyfters
" attach themfelves to the foot and pendant branches, by de-
" pofiting their fpawn on them, which adheres, grows, and
" as the tide ebbs and flows, is fometimes in water and fome-
" times in air."

" There is another very fingular tree, called the *Fromager,*
" or *Saamona*, which grows, in the Antilles, as high as the
" pine. The top and bottom of the trunk are of the thick-
" nefs of common trees, while the middle is more than
" twice as thick. The roots, which are very thick, fhoot
" out of the earth feven or eight feet high, and form a kind
" of buttreffes round the trunk. It is called Fromager, be-
" caufe it's wood greatly refembles cheefe : it's fruit, when
" ripe, contains feed of a dark red colour, as large as fmall
" peas, and garnifhed with a kind of pearl-grey-cotton, ex-
" tremely fine, fhining, and filky to the touch; but the
" filaments are fo fhort it is very difficult to fpin. The Indians
" ufe it as we do down, for their ears and feet :

5

M. de Bomare.

(58) The

(58) The Gymnotus, or Electrical Eel, a kind of Torpedo, is a fish well known at Surinam. The common size is from three to four feet in length, and from ten to fourteen inches in circumference. Some, however, it is said, have been seen in the river Surinam, upwards of twenty feet long; and the stroke, or shock, of which, was instant death.

END OF THE SECOND VOLUME.